WHEN PUSH COMES TO SHOOT

RENA KOONTZ

When Push Comes to Shoot

Copyright © 2021 Rena Koontz

Book Design by J R Burns Consultancy

Cover Art: 123rf.com

Editor: Tamara Eaton

Published in the United States of America by

Rena Koontz

1181 S. Sumter Blvd. #143

North Port, FL. 34287

renakoontz.com

❀ Created with Vellum

WHEN PUSH COMES TO SHOOT

By
Rena Koontz

For my family

ACKNOWLEDGMENTS

My husband, Jed, for his never-ending support
My friend and colleague, Jackie Floyd

1

————

B lood was everywhere, pooling on the faded Persian rug, splattered against the peeling wallpaper as if an oscillating fan had spread it, coagulated on the pale blue sofa in a spot sunken by years of weight dropped into it.

Emma stared at the sight, her stomach threatening to return her morning coffee even though the asshole deserved this.

For a brief moment, her mind drove her back to happier times in this room. Christmases. Birthday parties. Summer barbecues when the breeze from the trees bordering the property fluttered the curtains. The memories were hazy snippets recalled from some deep recess in her brain she'd almost lost. How long had it been since she stepped foot in this house? Too many years to count.

The place was eerily quiet. Like when the dead are present. Even the birds outside sensed it and stayed silent.

Her brother slouched in front of the TV. His feet were propped on a pile of newspapers, his tea mug leaving yet another ring on the coffee table. Only the TV wasn't on. And he was dead.

Not much had changed in this room since the days when

she was welcome here except the piles of paper, amount of mail, unread magazines and boxes lining both sides of the hallway had tripled. The passage from the living room to the family room was merely a precarious tunnel between the stacks. She shivered.

From his high school picture perched in the right-hand corner of the mantle, her brother stared back at her under a thin film of dust. His eyes were defiant even back then, some twenty-five years ago. Demeaning. Angry.

The sweet odor of blood stung her nostrils and she gulped. Homicide scenes were not her bag. Her eyes watered from the smell. There were twelve years between them, enough of a gap for him to resent a pesky little sister. Nevertheless, she'd worshipped him as her older brother, not comprehending that his disdain for her spread even then, like a slow-growing cancer. Disdain that would mutate into contempt. An attitude she refused to accept once she was older.

She reached for the picture but stopped her hand in mid-air. She wouldn't touch him if he stood alive in front of her. Why should she touch him now that he was dead?

"Lieutenant?"

She whirled around, the intrusion of the officer's voice startling her, and shoved her hands in her pockets like a guilty child.

"Ma'am, I'm afraid you can't be here. The sergeant asked me to secure the premises from everyone until forensics arrives. The scene hasn't been processed yet."

"That's all right, Officer..." His name gleamed from the polished nametag. "Petrus. I assure you I haven't touched anything. I just wanted to see..." she cleared her throat, "you're right, of course. I'll leave. Do you know where my sister-in-law is?"

"Ma'am?"

"My sister-in-law. The victim is my brother."

The young patrolman snapped to attention. "My condolences, Lieutenant."

"At ease, Officer Petrus. Thank you but it's not necessary. I'm concerned about his wife. D'you know where she is? Was she here when it happened?"

"I don't know, ma'am. You should speak to Sergeant Taylor. I believe he's on the grounds. I'm only assigned to the perimeter."

With one final glance at the couch, Emma walked to the kitchen door, noting the dirty dishes piled in the sink, the opened cereal box on the table and the puddled butter in the container on the counter. The hinges squealed when she stepped outside and inhaled deeply. The door needed oil. Odd. Her brother usually kept up with the house maintenance. Or at least he used to.

The back door had always served as the main entrance because the driveway that crawled up the hill circled the house to this point before descending again. It seemed natural to stop the car here and go inside.

Sergeant Taylor waved her over. "Lieutenant Hunter? What brings you here? Did the chief send you?"

She'd heard the rumors about Taylor's missteps on his last few cases and some off-duty shenanigans that the department frowned upon. The boss certainly wouldn't assign this homicide investigation to him, would he?

"Relax, Sergeant. I'm not here in an official capacity. The victim is my brother. As soon as I heard the radio call, I came over."

His shoulders visibly relaxed. "My sympathies, Emma. But you know you can't be involved in this investigation. It's a blatant conflict of interest."

"I understand. Are you handling the case?"

"And it means you can't ask any questions. Not without getting my ass in a sling and I've had enough of that recently."

His thumb jabbed the air in the direction of the navy blue four-door making its way up the drive behind the forensics van. "Here comes homicide now." She shaded her eyes and recognized the unmarked detectives' vehicle.

"Is my sister-in-law still here?"

"She's in the squad car." He pointed to the opposite end of the house. That's when she noticed the blue tarp on the roof, over the second-floor office if her memory was correct. Did the roof leak? Her brother had always bragged about his ability to fix anything. Too bad he hadn't climbed up there and fallen off. An accidental death would have been so much easier.

"Has anyone talked to her?"

"She hasn't said a word since she dialed 9-1-1. I would advise you not to interfere, Emma. You know how territorial homicide gets."

She smiled as she backed away from him. "I told you, I'm not here officially. I just want to check on her."

A young officer she didn't recognize stood sentry beside the rear passenger door of the running vehicle. "Officer, I'd like a minute with her please." Eyeing her lieutenant's bars, he stepped aside.

She opened the door and was smacked in the face with a blast of frigid air. Mary sat in the backseat shivering, kneading rosary beads between her fingers. Emma jumped back and barked at the patrolman.

"Turn this AC down immediately! What the hell are you trying to do, freeze a confession out of her? Shut it off now! And open the damn windows."

She slipped into the seat next to her sister-in-law and reached for her clasped hands. She might as well have dipped them into an ice bucket.

"Are you all right?"

Mary turned vacant eyes on her. No makeup and hair that begged to be brushed. When she was younger, her long blond hair softly fell to her shoulders. Emma supposed the chemo drugs had robbed it of its body and luster. Her face and clothes were clean. Not a drop of blood. Emma leaned forward to see her tennis-shoe clad feet. Not a speck.

"Don't say anything to anyone. They'll take you to the police station. I'll call a lawyer that I know. He's good. Don't speak to anyone until you talk to him. I'll meet you there."

She squeezed Mary's hands reassuringly. "It'll be fine, you'll see."

The urge to lean over and place a kiss on Mary's cheek surprised her. Mary had married her brother twenty-four or twenty-five ago. She didn't remember the exact year, but she'd already graduated from the Academy and secured a job with the Pittsburgh police. No matter. The two women were never close. How long had it been since they'd spoken?

Her brother was a tyrant and Mary a saint for having endured life with him. She assumed Mary's faith had a lot to do with that. She epitomized the word 'sweet.' She wouldn't say shit if it gagged her. She certainly wouldn't violate the sixth commandment. She wasn't a killer. But how could Emma prove that?

2

J ared Jones checked his notes before switching off the ignition. This read like a routine domestic violence case gone too far.

Rocky marriage. Ugly argument. Wife kills husband. Six years as a homicide detective had jaded him against any possible mitigating circumstances. No situation in the world merited murder as its resolution.

Surveying the grounds as he stepped out of the car, his heart jerked. What was Em doing here? Climbing into the rear of a cruiser?

"Jonesy!" Taylor moved into his line of vision, obscuring his view of Emma. Taylor grinned. "We gotta stop meeting like this." It was the same line he used at every crime scene with every detective on the squad. The guy needed new material.

Jared extended his hand while he looked around. "How ya doin', Taylor? Is our vic the homeowner? He didn't take much pride in his property, did he?" The place looked like a junkyard. Three cars in various stages of wreckage sat behind the house in weeds so overgrown, they practically served as a shield. A half-collapsed shed partially revealed rusted tools, a filthy lawn tractor that had prevented its complete collapse, and the bumper of what might be another wreck. The landscaping around the house was dead or dying, part of the gutter was missing, and a tarp covered a portion of the roof.

Taylor hiked up his pants, but they slid back beneath his beer belly the minute he let go. "I don't know. He was a businessman. Maybe he was too busy to take care of things at home."

Jared mentally noted to check out the victim's business dealings. "What's this look like inside?" He already knew the basic details, but he'd learned years ago to placate the uniforms whenever possible. In the long run, it made his life easier.

Taylor puffed out his chest.

"Looks like the little woman had enough of him. Found him sprawled on the sofa, his head shot to hell. No one home but her. She called it in. Said," he paused to check scribbles on a pad, "I think my husband's dead. Like she couldn't tell. His noggin was all over the room."

His description irritated Jared. Even if the guy was a bastard, the dead deserved some respect.

"Did you recover the weapon? What'd she use?"

He shrugged. "None found in the vicinity of the body. I waited for you to authorize a whole-house search. Got my tit in the wringer the last time I showed initiative. I have a couple guys searching the outside grounds but look at this place. There's crap everywhere. She coulda easily hid it out here."

"Who was first on scene?"

"Petrus. He found her standing outside holding onto her vehicle. Pale as a sheet, he said." He flipped a few more notebook pages. "Described her as calm. Possibly in shock. He thought she was going to pass out."

Jared jotted "weapon" with two question marks on his notepad. If it was missing, that indicated a plan, not an accidental discharge.

"She give any statements?"

"Nope, quiet as a mime."

"What about a burglary gone bad?" An armed burglar would take his weapon with him, although the run-of-the-mill burglar wouldn't haul it to the house to begin with. But he wasn't ruling out anything yet. "Any signs of a break-in? Did she say if anything is missing?"

"Not a peep."

He squinted in the morning sun to study the house. A surveillance camera appeared to be tucked under the eaves above the back door. "If it was a break-in, maybe we'll get lucky."

"There's another camera tucked above the front door, one strapped to that shed and, if my eyes don't deceive me, it looks like a couple positioned in the trees." Jared's focus followed where Taylor pointed. "The guy mighta been paranoid about trespassers. Either that or he didn't trust the wife, which, given his present condition, coulda been justified." Taylor laughed at his own humor.

"Wonder what he was so protective of. Or afraid of."

A car door slammed and he looked past Taylor to see Emma marching toward them. When their paths crossed in the line of duty, professionalism was foremost. Why was she here?

"Detective?" Her chest heaved. Something angered her. "The woman in that car is not a murderer." When she pointed toward the cruiser, her hand shook. "She should not even be considered a suspect. Nevertheless, until you decide that for yourself, I want her treated with kid gloves. Do you understand me? If she even burps, I want you to offer her an antacid. And instruct your goons to do the same." She leveled a stink eye on Taylor.

Emma didn't agree with his methods of dealing with the beat cops. But as a woman, she'd had to take a lot more bullshit than he had coming up in the ranks. She was a better shot than him or any of his fellow detectives and her prowess for physical defense was unparalleled by most of the men in the department. She deserved a gold shield as much as anyone but so far, it had eluded her. She pivoted and stormed toward her car.

Taylor exhaled. "You don't want to be in her path when she's mad. She's smart as a whip, that one. She can cut you down like one too."

"What was she doing here? This isn't her district."

Taylor's radio crackled and he spoke as he turned away. "The vic is her brother."

Jared searched his brain. Emma had never mentioned any siblings. Then again, they'd been in a relationship for less than a year. He could name a hundred things he hadn't told her yet. Luckily no one knew they were dating, or he'd be pulled off the case. Solving it for Emma just became more important.

Taylor lifted his radio. "Forensics needs more time inside."

"That's fine." He preferred to view a murder scene last, when possible. It kept premature conclusions out of his mind.

JARED REMOVED a fresh bottle of water from his car and approached the parked squad car, clearing his mind of Emma and the homicide details he already knew. Killers came in all shapes, sizes, and colors. They could be young or old, healthy or ailing. Some he'd interviewed had been accomplished liars while others fell apart at the sight of his badge. The initial interview with a subject was crucial. That's when answers weren't rehearsed, body language wasn't considered, and facial expressions weren't masked. What would Em's sister-in-law be like? Had Emma tipped her off on how to conduct herself? He doubted that. Emma was as by-the-book as they come.

"Mrs. Malvado?" He opened the back door and slid inside, showing his badge. "I'm Detective Jones. Would you like some water?" She looked like a frightened child. No blood spatter on her outfit. A denim dress with thick straps and a dull white T-shirt underneath. It didn't look like an appropriate dress for an adult woman. Had she showered before calling the police? Her blond hair didn't look clean.

She declined the water with a shake of her head and returned her attention to the rosary beads between her fingers. "Ma'am, please accept my condolences. I understand this is a difficult time but I have to ask you about this morning. Can you tell me what happened?"

She shrugged then slowly began to rock back and forth. From nerves or guilt?

"Were you here when it happened?"

She shook her head.

"But you found your husband?"

She nodded.

"Where were you this morning?"

She leveled clear blue eyes on him. Killer's eyes?

"At church."

"On a Wednesday?"

Her stare returned to the dashboard and she began rocking again. "Every morning."

"What time did you return home?"

She shrugged again. She wasn't very cooperative. If she was guilty, she'd be talking a mile a minute, explaining her where-abouts, detailing how she came home and was shocked to find her husband dead. Then again, if she was innocent, she'd be anxious to let him know that. Declaring her love for the man. Restraining her grief. This woman was none of that. Was she sedated? The coldest fish he'd ever encountered? Or had Emma schooled her?

"Was there anyone else here at the house?"

Her shoulders lifted and dropped again. Her eyes were a beautiful shade of blue but they looked hollow. It was possible she was deliberately being coy and uncooperative. Or, giving her the benefit of the doubt, stunned into silence. Whichever it was, questioning her in the car wasn't working. Sitting beside her was too friendly a position. Like they were equals. Or friends.

"Mrs. Malvado, I understand this has been a shock, but you could help us a great deal if you shared whatever information you can. It might be easier away from here. I'm going to ask you to come down to the station and discuss this further. Would you mind doing that?"

She stared at him as if not comprehending his question. "Ma'am, may I have an officer escort you to the police station?"

The rocking stopped. "I have to lock the door."

This was an active crime scene. Forensics would be here for hours and with the guy being shot in the living room, it would take a professional service to clean up that room once Jared released it, which could be days. Plus, there was the matter of the missing murder weapon. He wanted a look around before he instructed the uniforms to turn the place inside out to find it. In the meantime, a police unit would be assigned to preserve the location. Would Emma give her sister-in-law a place to stay? In her two-bedroom townhouse?

"I'm going to have a police officer guard the property while you're gone, Mrs. Malvado. Your belongings will be safe. Please come with me now."

He stepped out of the back seat and reached for her elbow once she was out. She was bony beneath her oversized, stretched-out sweater. Almost frail. Her steps were measured, as if it was painful to walk in her well-worn tennis shoes. Were these her church shoes? They were filthy. Or had she changed out of bloodied footwear?

"Would you prefer a change of shoes?" She shook her head, the beads moving methodically through her fingers. He signaled to his partner. Jeff could transport her and stay with her until he returned to the station and they were ready to interview her. It wouldn't hurt for her to sit in a room for a while and contemplate what she'd done.

He'd come across all kinds of killers during his career. His first case as a patrolman had been a murder suicide. The nicest old man, everyone said, married to his wife for more than fifty years. No one could believe he was capable of murder. But time on this job taught Jared differently. If the right buttons are pushed, any human being is capable of killing. That included Mary Malvado. All he had to do was figure out what pressed her buttons to this point?

3

Mary tightened her sweater around her core. The police station was as icy as the car had been. She wiggled her toes to feel them. Why did cops keep everything so cold? The room itself was barren, just like she'd seen in a hundred TV crime shows. The ones Don loved to watch over and over.

Only a poster on one wall warning to say no to drugs. The starkness of the room created an unnerving sensation. Nothing in here but a table and three metal chairs. A ring rose up near the middle of the table. Probably for someone in handcuffs. Thank God they hadn't locked her up like that.

Since seeing Emma in the police car, she'd been treated with respect. Like a visitor on a PR tour. How much weight did Emma throw around here? Either Don didn't know or never said. He wasn't much for talking about his sister unless it was to mock her. The fact that she'd become a cop and he'd failed to become one ate at him every day. Hate was a sin, but Don hated Emma.

She should've said something to Emma in the car when they sat side by side. At least expressed her condolences that her brother was dead. Instead, all she could do was pray for mercy on his soul. Mercy he didn't deserve.

She jumped when the door opened. Emma stood out in the hall, half hidden by a large man carrying a briefcase, who entered and shut the door. His lion-sized paw extended toward her.

"Mrs. Malvado? I'm Terrence O'Hare. I'm a friend of Emma's. She's retained me on your behalf." Her hand slid in and out of his as if buttered. "May I call you Mary? Would you like a hot cup of coffee? It's chilly in here."

The chair scraped on the floor when he drew it back and creaked when he settled his bulk on it.

"Would it be possible to ask for a hot cup of tea with lemon?" Not so much to drink as to wrap her hands around.

Mr. O'Hare bolted up. "Of course. Let me find someone."

He opened the door and she caught a brief glance of Emma again, leaning against the far wall, chewing her thumb. She still did that?

Mr. O'Hare plopped back onto the seat. "It will just be a minute." He folded his thick hands in front of him. "In a short while, when I think you're ready, the police are going to come in here and ask you questions."

She knew it was coming but she drew in a startled breath. Her heart raced.

"No need to fret. I'll be right here with you." He reached across the table and patted her folded hands. Her gaze lowered to the gesture meant to convey assurance. Her knuckles were white.

"Don't answer anything you can't. Don't try to satisfy them with an answer if you aren't absolutely sure of your response. They may ask you the same question more than once only phrased differently. They aren't trying to trick you, but it can be confusing. Especially since you've been through a devastating trauma and it's still quite fresh."

He couldn't begin to know what she'd been through. Years of Don berating her for any little perceived wrong, exploding at the slightest mistake she made like burning his toast or serving soup that he deemed too hot to eat. Yesterday he blamed her because the newspaper was missing. Years of emotional and psychological abuse. Was it over now?

Mr. O'Hare removed a pen and legal pad from his case. "Let's go over this so you're comfortable with the questions. Were you the one who found your husband?"

"Yes."

"And what was the first thing you did?"

The memory straightened her shoulders. Her throat closed. So much blood. More blood than she'd ever seen in her life. The top half of his head was gone, brain matter dripping from the walls and the curtains. How would she ever clean it up? Barely anything was left of his face. In spite of that, his lips were in that familiar sneer, that gap in his lower teeth all she needed to know it was him.

"I called the police."

A soft knock and the door opened. She expected it to be Emma who'd fetched her tea. But the young man who handed it in to Mr. O'Hare was a stranger. No sign of her in the hall.

Mr. O'Hare waited while she leaned back and cupped the mug. Heat seeped through her hands, up her arms and warmed her chest. She raised her gaze to her attorney.

"All right. Did you call the emergency number?"

She nodded again.

"And prior to that discovery, where were you?"

He used the word as if she'd mined for gold and hit a main vein. Discovery hardly described finding your husband bleeding to death on the living room couch. Tears rimmed her eyes at the vision. It was such a mess. "I was at church."

He looked surprised.

"I attend church every morning."

Her memory jogged by her words, she dropped her hand into the pocket of her sweater. Her rosary beads were still there. "I go to seven o'clock Mass every morning. I never miss." Her voice sounded odd to her ears, as if she were speaking through a tin can.

"Can the police corroborate that if they check?"

"Yes. Father Greg greets me every morning." She could use a bear hug from Father Greg right now. And his words to keep the faith, God had a plan. It seemed he was right.

Mr. O'Hare scrawled on the blue lines. Like him, his handwriting was large. "What did you do when you returned home?"

She didn't want to relive it. "I walked through the kitchen straight into the living room and found him. He was dead."

"Are you sure he was dead?"

It would be inappropriate to laugh in this man's face, but his question was ridiculous. Don had no brains left. The top of his head was gone. "Yes, I'm sure."

"What did you say when you called the police?"

She didn't remember her exact words. Why did it matter? "I believe I said I thought my husband was dead."

"You *thought* he was dead or he *was* dead?"

She pressed her fingers to her temple. "I thought so."

"Yet you told me you saw he was dead. How do you account for that discrepancy?"

"I-I had hope that he wasn't."

"Wasn't what?"

The word choked her. "Dead."

It gagged her because she knew immediately that he was dead, and she was finally free. She'd thanked God out loud. There were no tears of remorse, no cries of grief. She was rid of him. For good. No one would ever know that though, certainly not their children. She could play the grieving widow for as long as it was appropriate, but she wouldn't be grieving the loss of Don Malvado's life. She mourned for all the years she lost with him.

"Mary, did you touch the body? Feel for a pulse or lay your hand on his chest to detect a heartbeat?"

Dear Lord, no. She stopped dead in her tracks the second she rounded the corner from the kitchen. Her hands flew to her mouth to stifle a scream that never came. Then she'd backed out of the room slowly, unable to tear her eyes away from the gore. "No, I didn't touch him."

Hadn't for years.

"Can you describe the nature of your relationship with your husband, Mary?"

The teacup had lost its warmth. She lowered it to the table and folded her hands in her lap. "It was good once. We were happy. And then we weren't."

"Was it bad enough to leave him? Did you ever consider divorce?"

Her hand dropped into her pocket again and she pressed the rosary beads for strength. Even her own son had asked why she stayed. Why she endured the angry rampages, the endless belittling, the weeks of silence when Don refused to speak to her as if she didn't exist at all.

"I took a vow, Mr. O'Hare, for better or worse. Til death do us part. Leaving was never an option."

He cleared his throat. "Was murder?"

"No sir. Exodus, chapter twenty, verse thirteen. Look it up if you don't believe me. The Bible says you shall not murder."

4

Jared tied the strings on his paper booties and tugged on his nitrile gloves. He strode from the galley kitchen through the dining room to the living room silently repeating, "brace for impact." Like most bodies he viewed, the sight would stay with him for a while. Murder was never pretty.

Don Malvado was out of shape for a forty-four-year-old. Overweight. No visible muscle tone in his arms, exposed beneath a food-stained T-shirt. Hands calloused. Fingernails dirty. Dead but still looking comfortable in his own home. Jared would bet he spent hours nestled in that sofa staring at the television. The cushions no longer offered support.

The police photographer moved stealthily about the room, capturing every possible angle of the scene.

Jared tapped the coroner on the shoulder, knowing it was much too early for answers but asking anyway.

"What's it look like, Sam?"

Sam flipped up his protective eyeglasses and lowered his mask. "The impact is broad, resulting in the extensive damage. Had to be point blank range or close to it. My preliminary guess would be a shotgun. One shot would do it. Did you find any spent shells?"

Jared shook his head. "No murder weapon either." He lifted his gaze to the wall behind the body. A shotgun shell might be embedded in there. He made a note to check. "Any guess on the time of death?"

"I'm just seeing signs of rigor now."

That meant Don Malvado died within the last two hours. He checked his watch. The timeline fit with the story Mary told. She said she came home after seven o'clock Mass and called the police immediately. The dispatcher logged the call at eight-thirty-seven.

"I'll have an official TOD after I autopsy him. I'll be outta your way in about ten minutes, Jared. Then the room is all yours."

"Thanks. Do what you need to do, don't worry about me. I'll check out the rest of the house. What's your backlog look like? Can I expect your report in twenty-four hours?"

"Closer to forty-eight at the earliest. Sorry. The team was called out shortly after midnight and around four this morning. At least this guy gave me time for a cup of coffee."

"It's not a problem. Text Jeff when it's Malvado's turn on the table. He'll observe."

Sam raised his gloved hand and they knocked fists, then Jared stepped out of his way to explore the house.

Mary's housekeeping skills weren't the best. Piles of stuff were everywhere. Papers. Mail. Clothes. A laundry basket of jeans. Clean or dirty? At least he hadn't seen any bugs. The house was decorated with mounds of shit. These two appeared to be borderline hoarders. A second living area down a crowded hall was full of two sets of furniture, a china cupboard, and boxes stacked on boxes. The room wasn't usable as a living space.

Upstairs wasn't much neater. The bed in the master was

unmade and men's clothes lay over the chair, at the end of the bed and on the floor. The closet door stood ajar, exposing more clothes smashed into the space than it was designed to hold. A thick layer of dust coated the nightstand except where a cell phone and car keys lay. There was a clear swath there, as if he swiped everything into his hand each day.

A second bedroom was more orderly, but the lack of a closet required clothes to hang from two portable racks. Women's clothes. These two no longer shared a bedroom. Mary's bed was neatly made, fur-lined moccasin slippers tucked under the side. Three framed photos sat atop the dresser, one of Mary and two young kids, a girl and boy, both blond, presumably her children, and a family photo of the four of them, each displaying wide smiles. Whatever the occasion, they were happy. Malvado had a detectable gap in his lower teeth and the boy had braces, probably to avoid the gap. A miniature shrine was off to one side with a statue of the Madonna behind a half-melted votive candle.

A third room appeared to once have been a boy's room. Sports banners still hung on the wall, but this room now was used for sewing and ironing. More clothes. Frilly pink curtains still hung in the last room, but it was jammed with cartons and plastic bins. A pathway led to the desk and a laptop sitting open. He tapped the spacebar, but the screen required a password. This might be the device that monitored the security cameras. The tech team would have a crack at it. Water damage was evident in the far corner of the room, beneath a tarp that flapped occasionally.

Every room he entered had a television.

Taking the steps down to the first floor he opened first a coat closet and then the door to the basement. The steps were plain wood to the cement floor. A musty odor bit at his nose as he descended. Holy hell. Mounds of clothes, containers, bags and who knows what were piled from floor to ceiling. He spotted car tires and oil cans, children's toys and what appeared to be a small freezer, unreachable with all the junk blocking it. A treacherous path led from the bottom step to the washer and dryer, just wide enough for a body to walk through. It could take days to search this area for a weapon. The evidence response team might need hazmat suits.

Disheartened over the daunting task, he returned to the living room and stared at the now vacant sofa. Two ways to enter this room, one from the kitchen through a corner of the dining room and one from the hallway, connecting the over-crowded family room to this one. The front door was in that hall but, with so much crap in front of it including a loaded card table, it was obvious they never opened it.

Which entry had Mary used? She'd come from church and her car was parked outside the kitchen. He went there, turned around and strode into the living room.

Based on Malvado's posture, he hadn't had time to react so the shooter surprised him. He raised his hand, his thumb upright and his first two fingers extended in the shape of a pistol. "Bang!"

He'd stopped in the middle of the room. A handgun wouldn't have caused the extensive damage he'd seen to Malvado's head. Had to be a rifle or shotgun. Maybe Malvado was a hunter.

Mary would have needed time to hoist the gun to shoulder level, rack it and fire. Did she do that in the kitchen and enter this room ready to fire? Surely Malvado would have heard the shell sliding into the barrel. Unless the TV muffled the sound. But the TV wasn't on.

Did she do it outside before entering? She'd need time to aim and shoot. She'd been nervous sitting in the squad car talking to him. Surely she'd be anxious when she was about to commit murder, nervous and moving as she walked in the room. Not so easy to hit a target.

Jared yanked on his tie to loosen it at his Adam's apple. None of this added up.

Just walk in and shoot? No words exchanged? Nothing like I've had enough you son of a bitch or this is your fault? No second thoughts? Unless Malvado was asleep, he would have had time to jump up or veer right or left. Mary's aim was dead center. It had happened fast.

He returned to the kitchen, rushed back into the living room and fired his imaginary weapon again. "Bang!"

No. The adrenaline rush she'd experience would affect her. Her arms would be unsteady. The shot rushed. The recoil would alter the path of the shell. The human head wasn't a large target.

Jared planted his feet beneath him in the middle of the room and raised both arms as if he were shooting a bow and arrow. Or a rifle. "Hi honey, I'm home. Bang!" Had she walked into the room with a shotgun, raised and fired without his reacting? Maybe he *was* asleep.

He slipped out of his booties and peeled off his gloves outside the kitchen door. The evidence response team waited for his okay to enter and begin collecting anything and everything that might be important. If there was a weapon, upstairs or downstairs, they'd find it. He doubted they'd be successful. Mary Malvado had a plan that included stashing the gun. He knew it in his bones.

"Look for bloody clothing and shoes, boys. Any signs of blood. There's a laptop upstairs and some ledgers. I want everything out of that office area. Collect the cell phone on the nightstand in the master bedroom. Probably our vic's. Take anything in that room that belonged to Malvado and could be incriminating. Hell, bag anything in this house that raises an eyebrow."

Taylor's patrolmen waited with him outside. "I want your men here until ERT is finished. Then I want twenty-four-seven security."

He looked at the neighboring properties. Homes in this neighborhood came with property and a thick stand of trees surrounded this lot. The driveway was at least a football field to the road and the home across from this one sat back at least that far. From the kitchen side of the house, one home was visible through the brush. He motioned for Petrus to follow and strode in that direction, scanning the ground as he walked. He didn't stumble across a weapon as he made his way to the neighbor.

No one responded to his knocks. He pivoted and stared through the trees at the Malvado home. He wouldn't want to live next door to them. The place looked like a residential junkyard compared to the pristine property of this neighbor. Maybe the neighbor finally got fed up and shot Malvado. It was plausible.

At the moment, the obvious suspect was Mary Malvado. Minutes ago, acting out his charade, he assumed she'd had enough. This wasn't a crime of passion or a spontaneous discharge in a moment of anger. Mary Malvado had thought this through.

5

J ared drove to the police station dictating notes to his phone.

Item: Check Malvado's business contacts.

Item: Interview relatives. Interview friends.

Item: Contact immediate neighbor on east side of house. No one home today.

Item: Delve into Malvado's finances. Was there a hefty life insurance policy?

Money is always a good motivator to commit a crime. So was infidelity. Were the Malvados on the brink of monetary disaster? Based on what he'd seen at the house, it didn't scream financial success. Was Mr. Malvado involved with another woman? Another man?

Item: Interview Mary Malvado's priest and her friends. Did she have a motive?

Item: Inspect her shoulder for a bruise. The kickback from a shotgun can be brutal if you don't know how to shoot one or aren't prepared for it.

Item: GSR test to see if Mary had gunshot residue on her

hands. That one would be iffy and a good lawyer could easily discount the results by arguing cross-contamination. If she didn't voluntarily submit to the examination and GSR swab, he'd need a warrant. In a murder case, that was easily obtained. Item: Fingerprint Mary Malvado for exclusionary purposes. He doubted she ever received a traffic ticket. The chances of her prints being on record were nil.

He hesitated before adding his last point.

Item: Talk to Em.

AT THE STATION, he wasn't surprised to find Terrence O'Hare already listed as counsel of record for Mary Malvado. He and Em often joked that he was the worst attorney for prosecutors and the best for criminals. They cringed when they saw him in action but agreed he'd be the man to call if they were ever in trouble. Em had wasted no time protecting her sister-in-law.

His heart jerked again when he saw her in the hallway consulting with O'Hare. He was falling for her a lot faster than she was. He shook hands with O'Hare. "We'd like to chat with Mrs. Malvado, Terry. Have you had time to consult with her? I'm ready now."

"Give me a few more minutes, Jared." He stepped inside the interview room.

Jared turned to Emma. She shouldn't be here and he told her so.

MARY MALVADO LOOKED EVEN MORE INFIRM DWARFED by the dull gray metal table she sat behind and O'Hare's bulk, which loomed like a Thanksgiving Day float beside her. A uniformed officer stood one foot behind her, his hands behind his back, seemingly at ease. But if Mrs. Malvado tried to bolt, he'd immediately subdue her. That wasn't a concern with this suspect.

Jeff leaned against the wall in the opposite corner, looking equally as relaxed. This was their technique, for one of them to grill the suspect while the other observed every nuance of movement or expression.

Jared made a show of sitting in front of her and consulting the pages in a manila folder he brought with him. It was too early for actual reports, but Mary wouldn't know that. He studied the Chinese takeout menu, flipped to a page of ten-codes, and then examined a three-page report from a case he closed last month, making sure to display a portion of the pages to show it was an official police document. Mary riveted her eyes to every movement. He exhaled loudly, closed the folder on the sheets and rested his folded hands on top of it.

"Mrs. Malvado, I'm Detective Jones. This is my partner, Detective Jeffrey Widows. I spoke to you earlier. Do you recall that?"

Her eyes remained glued to the folder beneath his hands. He barely heard her whisper yes.

"I'm going to record this conversation, if you don't mind. It's easier than trying to take notes, and more accurate. Do you have any objections to my starting this tape?"

She turned questioning eyes on O'Hare and he spoke. "No, we have no objections to recording this meeting."

Jared tapped the red button and recited the date, time and names of those present in the room. "We're on the record. Again, Mrs. Malvado, you have my sympathies. Please understand, you're here simply to provide information about the events of this morning. While you are not under arrest, protocol dictates that I advise you of your rights. You have the right to remain silent..." He repeated the Miranda warning by rote, watching for a reaction. Nothing. He inquired if Mary wanted anything and her eyes darted to an empty teacup before she shook her head.

He dispensed with his preliminary questions quickly. They were designed to establish a rapport between the interviewer and the subject and allow him to gauge her tone of voice, to hear the inflections used for normal questions like birthdate and level of education. What she majored in. How long she'd been married. She'd sound different when asked questions on-point, like did you kill your husband. A trained interrogator could learn a lot simply by listening, and he had the advantage of having briefly spoken to her at her home.

"What did your husband do for a living, Mrs. Malvado?"

"He was a businessman."

"What kind of business?"

She shrugged. "I-I'm not sure. He has a couple of rental properties, I know that. I wasn't involved in his dealings. There's a ledger on his desk in the upstairs office. That might help you."

By now, the ERTs searching the house should have that bagged and ready to transport back here to the station. "You don't know anything about his business interests?"

"No, sir."

"Who paid the bills?"

"He did."

"And if you wanted to buy something? Weekly groceries or new shoes?"

"I had money. He gave me money."

"Like an allowance?"

She cringed slightly. "I had money."

"Can you think of anyone who might want to hurt your husband? Did he have any enemies?"

A tight-lipped smirk crossed her face, disappearing in seconds. "I'm sure he did."

"Can you tell me who they are? Will you give me their names?"

She raised her folded hands from her lap and rested them on the table, looking him straight in the eye. No rosary beads this time. "No, I can't. I don't know who his enemies are."

"But you said he had them."

"I'm sure he did. He was that kind of man."

"What kind of man, ma'am? Can you be more specific? Anything you can tell us, even if it seems insignificant, could be helpful."

She spoke slowly, as if he was slow to learn. "He was the kind of man who made enemies."

Jared narrowed one eye, studying this newly widowed woman. Was she clever enough to be deliberately evasive? Had O'Hare instructed her to avoid direct answers? Or had Emma?

Mary reached into her pocket. The rosary beads reappeared. She held them with two hands, moving one bead at a time between her thumb and forefinger. This was multi-tasking at a new level, praying while discussing your husband's murder.

"What about his friends? Do you know if he argued with anyone recently?"

"No."

"No, you don't know if he had a recent dispute with someone or no, you don't know who his friends are?"

"The answer to both those questions is no, Detective."

"You two weren't friendly with other couples? Didn't you share a social life?"

"We barely shared a life."

"How did you feel about that?"

The stare she leveled on him jarred him. "I didn't feel anything."

"Can you provide a list of his acquaintances whom we can speak to?"

"He keeps his address book in the top drawer of his office desk. That might tell you. I can't."

He'd spotted that book. Full of names neatly printed on every other line. Malvado's penmanship was perfect.

"How long have you lived in that house, ma'am?" He'd already checked property records but the last few questions seemed to raise her hackles. Her posture reflected a fight response, hunched shoulders, fisted hands, tightened eyes. He backed off.

"Since we got married."

"Twenty-five years, is that correct?"

"Yes."

"I spotted several surveillance cameras posted outside your house. We're working on the theory that a random stranger might have entered your house. With your consent, we'll review that footage as soon as possible."

"That won't help you, Detective. Those cameras never worked, they were just for show. He thought he knew how to connect them, but he wasn't smart enough to figure it out. It was expensive equipment too, good money that he wasted."

"Did he do that a lot? Waste money?"

"He was too cheap to pay a professional to fix things properly. He always thought he could make the repairs and something always went wrong. Or he never got around to it. The roof has leaked for a year."

"Why did he feel the need for extensive security?"

"Who knows? For his own self-importance, maybe."

O'Hare bristled. "Don't guess, Mary."

"Sorry."

Jared studied her. "Were you fed up with him, Mary?"

O'Hare squeezed her forearm. "Don't answer that, Mary."

"Do you know how to handle a gun, Mrs. Malvado?"

She didn't blink. The beads stopped moving and she locked her hands tighter. Her knuckles turned white. "No."

Mary Malvado was one cool cucumber. Her voice never changed. Not when she recited the name of her church and its priest. And not when she described finding her husband dead. Either Terrence O'Hare prepped her well in the thirty minutes he spoke to her before announcing that his client was ready to be questioned. Or Emma had. But she'd only spent maybe five minutes with the woman. Hadn't she?

"Can you describe what you saw when you returned from church?"

There was no light in her eyes. "The back door was open. I—"

"Was that unusual for the back door to be open?"

"He never locked the doors, I always did. I was the one always turning off the lights to save money. Always making sure the garage door was closed and the windows were locked. When I left for church, I closed the door behind me."

"So you think someone was in the house?"

She stared at him. "I don't know." He locked his eyes on hers, waiting for more. But she didn't falter.

"Was there anything missing? Did you look around to see if anything was stolen?"

"No."

"Help me understand, Mrs. Malvado. You come home, find the back door open that you closed when you left and don't wonder about that? You don't come in and look around to see if someone is in your house or if anything is missing?"

"I did what I always do. I came home, put my bag down and went to ask my husband what he wanted for breakfast."

"But you didn't ask him, did you?"

"No, I couldn't."

"When you saw the condition he was in, weren't you afraid that the shooter might still be in the house? You didn't search for anyone?"

"No."

"You didn't fear for your life and run outside?"

"No."

"Why not?"

O'Hare stopped her. "Don't answer that, Mary."

Jared inhaled a calming breath. "Okay, where was your husband when you left for church?"

"Right where I found him."

"On the sofa?"

"Yes."

"Was he asleep?"

"No, he was watching TV."

"The TV was on?"

"Yes. He played it loud."

"Do you know what program he was watching?"

"Probably some old western. He—"

O'Hare interrupted. "Don't speculate, Mary. If you don't know what he was watching, say so."

Her head swiveled from her attorney to him as if in slow motion. "I don't know."

Silence prevailed, broken only by Jeff standing in the corner, suppressing a cough. Yeah, he and Jeff were on the same page. This lady was a block of ice. "Please continue, Mrs. Malvado."

"Sir?"

"You were saying you came home from church and you found the door open."

She hesitated. Was her story rehearsed and she was trying to remember the next part?

"I-I walked into the kitchen, laid my purse on the table and went into the living room. I usually cook breakfast when I come home from church. He always eats the same thing, eggs runny with toast, but I ask anyway. He watches TV sitting on the couch. He was right where he was supposed to be, waiting for breakfast."

"Could you tell he was dead?"

"Yes."

"Did you touch him to make sure?"

"No."

"And you called the police immediately?"

"Yes."

"Before or after you turned off the TV."

Her eyes widened. "I didn't turn it off."

"Who did?"

Seconds passed. At least thirty before Mary shrugged.

He stared at her, hoping the silence would be uncomfortable enough for her to offer more. Her gaze focused on her beads, sliding again between her fingers.

"How much time elapsed from when you found your husband to when you placed that call?"

"Not long."

"Can you estimate? Seconds? Minutes? How many minutes?"

She stared at him like he had two heads. "I can't say."

Later, he'd re-enact the drive home, enter the house and count the paces from the living room to the phone. Had she hidden the murder weapon first? The men on scene still hadn't located it. They'd found an air rifle, a pellet gun and two handguns on the first floor. None had been fired.

"Does your husband own any weapons?"

"Yes."

"Can you tell me how many and what they are?"

"No, I can't. He has a lot of them but I don't know what they are. I don't like guns. I don't know anything about them."

"Do you know where your husband kept them?"

"Everywhere. They were all over. There is a gun safe in the basement."

"Is it locked?"

"I think so."

He raised his voice, "You don't know?"

"I'm not sure."

"Do you know where the key is? What if there was an emergency? How would you get one?"

She was frightened, her eyes wide, her breathing more rapid. She tucked her hands beneath her thighs, the rosary beads slapping against the leg of the metal chair the only sound in the room. "I wouldn't."

"Have you ever fired one?"

"No."

"What was your relationship like with your husband?"

"We were married."

"Did you kill him?"

"No."

"Did you want to see him dead?"

Her head jerked backward and she blinked quickly. Her attorney interrupted again. "You don't have to answer that, Mary. Please confine your questions to the case you have, Detective."

That was the problem. He had no case. Only a dead body. No murder weapon. No one with a motive. No evidence whatsoever. Whoever killed Don Malvado took the weapon with them. And they were smart enough to take the spent shell. The coroner might have some luck identifying the type of gun used if he recovered anything from the head. Nothing was lodged in the wall behind the body, but that was no guarantee it would be found. Based on what he knew of gunshot wounds, his money was still on a shotgun.

"Did your husband own a shotgun, Mrs. Malvado?"

"I don't know."

"Have you ever fired a shotgun?"

Her shoulders stiffened. "No. I've never even held one."

The coroner hypothesized Malvado was shot up close.

Unless Mary covered herself in a tarp, she couldn't have avoided the back spray.

No trace of blood on her and no indication in the bathroom that she showered. He'd checked the tub and shower stall. They were dry. No discarded bloody clothes. And no witness except the woman who sat before him.

6

Emma slammed her palm against the side of the coffee machine. The damn thing never worked right. How much could it cost to replace it with an efficient dispenser? A second thump and the white Styrofoam cup dropped into place. She watched the juice of the gods stream into it.

Jared had been in the interview room with Mary for more than an hour. Was he grilling her? Reducing her to tears? She'd witnessed firsthand his ability to interrogate a subject. He was relentless. Mary wasn't strong enough.

But he also had a sixth sense about perps, one that let him see through the bullshit. He had to know Mary was innocent.

She'd been hovering in the hallway when he approached her. "Meet me for a drink later. I'll text you where and when. And get the hell out of this hall now. You can't be anywhere near this."

She hated when he was right, but he was. She strolled to the cafeteria, trying to appear indifferent. That was a posture she rarely achieved, and with Mary in there under Jared's scrutiny, it was impossible. A drink with him later would be good. She could tell him about the volatile marriage that Mary worked so hard to hide. She'd expose her brother for the bigot he was, hating women and people of color and anyone with a different sexual orientation. Put simply, he didn't like anyone who didn't look or think like him.

She laughed at the image. Overweight. Balding. Showing signs of the crippling arthritis that was their heritage. It was why she worked out at the gym six days a week, stretching, lifting, and running to beat time.

And Mary. She could tell him about her faith, her devotion to family and the sweet soul she possessed. He wouldn't learn any of that during his interrogation. He'd be focused on the crime. A crime of passion? No. Passion ceased to exist between those two more years ago than she knew. An opportunity for revenge? Not likely. She was fairly certain that, in Mary's eyes, her brother kept a roof over her head, paid the bills, and provided for her. Poorly, if you asked Emma. But nothing to deserve vengeance.

She emptied her coffee cup and banked it off the wall into the wastebasket just as her phone rang. Her niece. Dammit. She should have called her.

"Hi hon, where are you? Have you heard what happened today?"

"Is it true?" Vanessa's voice cracked. "Is he dead?"

"Yes. This morning. Where are you? How did you hear?"

"I'm working from home today. It's on the news. They reported they have a suspect. Is it Aunt Mary? Is she under arrest? Aunt Em, she didn't do it. I know she didn't. He antagonized so many people, me included, the police must have a list of people as long as their arms who could be guilty. Aunt Em, you have to tell them."

"Take it easy, Nessie. I'm here at the station. I—"

"Are you with Aunt Marry now? Is she okay?"

"No, honey, I'm not with her right now. The detectives are questioning her, but I'm sure they won't hold her. There's no evidence against her. I have to be careful, I just can't butt in. But I'll do as much as I can behind the scenes. I hired the best criminal attorney for her. It'll be okay, I promise. Keep your phone handy. I'll let you know when I know something."

"Will there be a funeral and stuff?"

She hadn't thought that far. The cause of death would be obvious, but an autopsy was still required. Autopsies were done in the mornings and Don might not be the first in line tomorrow. It could take a day or two before the coroner released the body. To whom?

"I'll find out all of that and let you know. You should call your mom and let her know what's happened. Mary is going to need a place to stay for the next few days. She'll feel comfortable staying with her sister." The two were like peas in a pod. Meek and afraid of their own shadows.

"Why?"

"Why what?"

"Why will she need to stay with my mom?"

The media must not have all the details. "He died at home, hon. It's a crime scene and probably will be for a few days." She didn't describe the state of the room. Vanessa would be terrified. "The police are going to have to allow Mary back in and that won't be tonight. I'll try to line up a service so the place is nice and clean for her. But it will take a couple days."

The silence on the other end broke her heart. Vanessa tried to find good in everyone, even Don. The idea of a bloody murder scene would never occur to her.

"Nessie, I've gotta go now. Reach out to your mom. I'll call you when they release Mary and let you know anything more."

She returned to the hall outside the interview rooms and walked the length of it, stopping at the end. Who was in there with Jared? He wouldn't be conducting his interview alone. What was Mary telling them?

Twice she jumped when other detectives came and went with folders and papers under their arms. The door might open any minute and Jared could exit. He'd be pissed if he found her waiting. Reluctantly, she left the building.

7

J ared motioned for Jeff to join him and the two excused
themselves from the interview room.

"Whaddaya think?"

Jeff eyed the closed door as if Mary would hear him
and covered his mouth with his fist. "She looks like I could
knock her out of that chair with a feather. All her responses are
spoken in a monotone. She's emotionless. Could be shock. I
think she's a victim of some kind of abuse and she's beaten
down."

"Enough to kill?"

He released a breath. "I don't see it."

Neither did he. Mary was open to the GSR test with her
attorney overseeing the swab. She didn't hesitate when asked if
a female detective could examine her chest and shoulders.
Nothing. Not even a mosquito bite.

Jeff covered his mouth again. "Is forensics having any luck?"

"So far, our evidence is the body. We need a helluva lot
more to charge her or anybody, for that matter. If she attended
church that regularly, anyone could have shown up at that
house and killed him. We have to filter through his business

associates and his friends for more information about him and the two of them as a couple. I want to release her for now, with the usual cautions. She can't go home, though. The basement alone will take days to sift through. I'm good with her staying with a friend or relative. I don't think she's a flight risk."

Please don't let it be Emma who gives her shelter. Jared didn't say that out loud. Jeff concurred there wasn't enough to detain Mary at this time.

"Right now, I don't see any other plausible motive except financial. You track down the business contacts, whatever they are. No one has said what the man did for a living. I want another look at that crime scene."

Mary's attorney assured them that she wouldn't flee and they released her with the caveat that they'd have more questions at a later time. She barely reacted when Jared informed her she was free to go but not to her home. A whispered thank you. She stood like an eighty-year-old lady instead of a forty-three-year-old. Almost feeble. Did she have the strength to hoist a shotgun?

He followed her and O'Hare out the door and scanned the hallway. At least Emma had the good sense to leave. Mary seemed uncertain about where she would stay but a woman with an amazing resemblance wearing a similar baggy sweater waited for her in the lobby. They didn't embrace. They barely acknowledged each other. Jeff's description popped into his head—emotionless.

How much light could Emma shed on her sister-in-law? They often discussed their cases and kicked around motives and possibilities. But this case involved Emma's family. He'd have to walk a fine line.

He texted her to meet him later at the Out-of-the-Way bar, a neighborhood haunt thirty minutes away from both their jurisdictions. It was a good place to keep their relationship low-key.

There was time to return to the crime scene. First, he drove to Mary's church where Father Greg confirmed her attendance at the morning service.

"What can you tell me about her, Father?"

"Is she in trouble? I'll certainly vouch for her. Why do you ask?"

"Her husband was killed this morning."

He crossed himself. "Dear Lord. May his soul rest in peace. What happened? Was there an accident? Is Mary all right?"

"It appears he was murdered."

Father Greg gasped and crossed himself again, muttering something Jared didn't catch. He paled. "Who did it?"

"We haven't determined that yet. Did you also know Mr. Malvado?"

"I-I, no, not really. Where's Mary now? May I see her to comfort her?"

"Her sister picked her up from the police station a short time ago. I don't know where they went. Would you know?"

How ingrained was this priest in Mary Malvado's life? Enough to provide an alibi for her while she killed her husband? Sanctuary for the soul and shelter for the body? Historically, churches were places where fugitives sought protection from the law. Was Father Greg part of her plan?

"You haven't answered my questions, Father. You understand I have to ask as part of an investigation into Mr. Malvado's death. You could help eliminate Mrs. Malvado as a suspect."

He might as well have shoved the man in the chest. Father Greg blanched and stepped backward as if his words had force.

"Surely you don't think Mary did it? That's unfathomable. She could never..." His voice trailed off.

Jared delivered the standard police line. "At this time, we're gathering as much information as possible about everyone involved. Anything you can tell me will be helpful. How would you describe her, Father?"

Sweat beads dotted his upper lip. "She's a wonderful

woman, very giving. Whenever we need volunteers for anything, her name is first on the list. Her devotion is genuine. God gave her a burden that she's borne with the help of her faith."

"What burden is that Father?"

He wrung his hands. "Her husband was not a God-fearing man. The sanctity of marriage was not foremost in his mind."

"Did Mrs. Malvado talk to you about that?"

"No, no, she didn't. She's not the type to discuss personal matters."

His response was a little too quick for Jared's comfort. "If she didn't discuss it with you, what makes you say that?"

He tightened the rope around his waist and looked past Jared down the hall. Then to the ceiling. Then out the window. Nervous about something.

"I-I sensed her unhappiness. He never attended church with her. She was alone all the time."

"He was a businessman. Maybe he didn't have time."

"That wasn't it."

"Then what was it, Father?"

He shifted from one foot to the other. "I don't know, Detective. I can attest to Mary's presence here today and every morning. Beyond that, I can't help you. If you'll excuse me, I have an appointment." Jared removed his notebook from his jacket pocket as the priest shuffled by and wrote, "Follow up on the padre."

Next, he set the timer on his phone and drove from the church to the Malvado home. For a more accurate test he'd make the drive in the morning, at the same time Mary did. Hell, he might even sit through Mass first. Maybe it would change his luck.

The church was twenty-two minutes from the house on a main road that wasn't heavily traveled, had no traffic lights and one stop sign. Morning traffic might not make a difference. He drove the circular driveway and parked next to an older SUV already identified as the vehicle Mary drove. One look inside confirmed that. The front passenger seat was trashed with tissues and water bottles, a sweater and pair of shoes, two umbrellas and a plastic rain hat spread across the passenger headrest. No visible blood on the sweater or shoes.

He slipped into paper booties, acknowledged Petrus posted at the door, walked inside and stopped at the kitchen table, pretending to place a handbag there. Softly, he said, "Hi honey, I'm home," and counted his paces to the living room. One, two, three, four...

Continuing the simulation, he raised his arms as he asked, "What would you like for breakfast, dear? Bang!"

He pivoted, strode back to the kitchen and placed his gloved hand on the wall phone, surprised that the Malvados still had a landline. Did she call from here or her cell phone? He'd have to check the emergency dispatch log. He tapped the stopwatch. Forty-seven minutes. A thirteen-minute discrepancy from Mary's timeline but there were several variables that might account for that. Maybe she was slower walking to the car. Maybe he drove the route faster than she did. Maybe she said hello to a few parishioners on her way out of church, slowing down her exit.

Or maybe she used the time to hide the gun.

8

Emma waited in their usual booth in the rear of the dining section of the bar, her mug of beer half empty. The usual lightning bolt that hit him every time he met her surged through his chest. Her record as a cop was exemplary. Her arrests always stood up in court and her memory for details was unwavering, even under cross-examination by the toughest defense attorneys. She knew the law and enforced it, but still maintained a sense of compassion for victims and suspects alike.

As a woman, her passion was uninhibited. Her zest for life shone in her eyes, like a child anticipating a trip to the county fair. Emma embraced every day with delight. He wondered if being locked into a uniform, a heavy utility belt and weapon weighing her down, was why when she was out of uniform, she felt so free.

He leaned in to kiss her hello before taking the seat opposite her, his desire already making itself known against his zipper. In seconds, their regular server set a beer in front of him and two menus.

He opened his menu. "I'm starving. I missed lunch today. Are you hungry?"

"Yeah. I didn't eat anything except a semi-crushed granola bar I found at the bottom of my purse. You look beat. How's it going?"

He studied Em's face. On duty, she wore minimal makeup and tiny blue balls in her pierced ears. He smiled at the gold hoops swinging from her lobes and the magazine-cover eye colors on her lids. She was beautiful. "Who's asking? The cop or my girlfriend?"

"Both."

The cold beer eased the tension in his shoulders and he relaxed back against the booth. "Too early to know how it's going. What can you tell me about your brother, Em, and his wife? This morning you snapped my head off, making sure I knew she wasn't a murderer. If not her, who wanted your brother dead?"

She shrugged. "I can't tell you anything about him. I haven't seen or spoken to him in years. We were estranged."

"How many years?"

She screwed up her mouth and nose and shrugged again. "Maybe ten. Maybe more. I honestly can't say. What I can tell you is that he was a prick and a poor husband. Look hard enough and you'll find dozens of people who are happy that he's dead, including me."

How odd to hear those words coming from her sweet lips. "How do you know what he was like if you haven't been in contact with him for so long. Are you close to Mary?" Was that why Mary was so collected during her interview?

Em's shoulders jerked backward. Why? It was a legitimate question.

"No, I'm not close to her. Today was the first time I've seen her in forever. I'm close with my niece. She's told me some ugly things my brother has said and done over the years and I grew up with him. I know what he's like. A leopard doesn't change its spots."

"Your niece? Your brother's daughter?"

"No. Mary's sister's daughter. Technically, she's not my niece or she's my niece-in-law or niece twice removed. We joke about that. For whatever reason, we bonded years ago. She's a beautiful young woman. It's a relationship I cherish."

"So she's kept you up to date on your brother?"

Emma took a deep breath. "Up to date isn't an accurate term." She swallowed a swig of beer. Was that a stall tactic to compose a response? Was the niece capable of murder? "We rarely discussed him. Once in a while she'd mention some outburst he threw at a holiday gathering or something her mother said that upset her. Like me, she tried to avoid him whenever possible. Only it was harder for her because family get-togethers included her mother, so she was expected to attend. And Don was usually there."

"Will she talk to me?"

"Of course. Nessie has nothing to hide."

Emma turned her attention to the menu when their server approached with two new cold brews. They both knew this menu by heart. What was she reading? Predictably she ordered a steak salad with no onions and extra dressing. Tonight he was in the mood for a hoagie. Something he could sink his teeth into and conquer. Unlike his murder case.

"So what did you think of Mary?" Emma was always full of questions about his cases. He supposed it was her way of learning, educating herself for when she was awarded that gold shield. She didn't realize her logistical skills were better than his. Several times, their discussions made him rethink the facts and see them in a different light. He valued her opinions.

"Devout."

"Yeah, she's really into that whole church scene. Way over the top if you ask me."

They'd never discussed religion. When he asked, Emma said she was raised a Catholic but was a non-practicing Lutheran. Catholic-light, she called it. "So your brother was a Catholic?"

She shrugged. "I doubt it. He fought going to church even when we were young."

He sensed his forehead wrinkle and Em confirmed his uncertainty. "What's the matter? You look confused."

"I don't understand why, if you had nothing to do with your brother and no idea what his life was like or Mary's for that matter, why you hurried over there today. What were you doing there?"

Emma laid her fork down and wiped her mouth with her napkin. She tugged on her earlobe, a tell that she was anxious. "Police instinct? I heard the call over the radio and recognized the address. It came in as a possible DOA and, I don't know, it was reflexive, I guess. I was on patrol and I contacted the day supervisor so, technically I took personal time. I wasn't there officially. I didn't mean to step on your toes." Her gaze remained concentrated on her plate. She never looked up.

"I'm not accusing you of any such thing. If you had nothing to do with the man, I don't get why you rushed there."

Now she made eye contact with him. "I wanted to make sure the DOA wasn't Mary."

"Did you have reason to believe it was?"

She ran her thumb along the side of her glass, spreading the condensation clinging to it. "I've always worried about Mary's welfare."

"Even though you weren't in contact with her for so long? Even though you had no idea what the conditions were in that house? Whether or not she was happy with the way things were? You know nothing about her, yet today, suddenly, you feel magnanimous toward a woman you claim you had no contact with? You check on her welfare when you haven't checked on her for years? I'm having trouble connecting those dots, Em. Come up with a better answer."

Her shoulders jerked back and her mouth dropped open for a quick second. "I don't need a better answer."

9

The direction of the conversation was uncomfortable so Emma redirected it. "Did you get A.J.'s wedding invitation? Are we going together to let everyone know we're a thing?" That made him smile. And moved him off topic. He'd been on a kick to "go public" for the last few months. She'd be the one whose career it would affect. People would imply she was sleeping with a detective to become one.

The truth was he pursued her for months and all but begged her on one knee to go out with him. He was regarded as the best criminal mind in his unit and admittedly, he was hot. He worked hard to keep his body in perfect shape, and she enjoyed every inch of it. She envied his metabolism that allowed him to eat whatever he wanted and magically burn it off while she mentally calculated the calories in every bite off of her fork. And from the minute they met, when those first sparks ignited between them, he treated her as an equal and supported any decision she made on and off the job.

His research was invaluable when she bought a new car, he'd cradled her when her longtime friend died in a tragic car accident, and indulged her spur-of-the-moment weekend getaway that used up his last vacation days. That was the weekend she fell in love with him. As life partners go, he was the cream of the crop.

None of that would matter once their relationship was out in the open. Her male colleagues would only see her sleeping her way up the ladder when, in fact, she belonged on that damn ladder. It was a dilemma she couldn't resolve.

Jared eyed her. "Is that an evasive tactic, ma'am? You don't want to talk about your brother?"

"I'm happy to discuss your case with you, Detective, like we always do. But I don't want to talk about my brother. Can you differentiate between the two?"

His hoagie stopped in mid-air. "Can you?"

"Absolutely. Here's what I know so far. Mr. Malvado's wife found him dead on his couch shortly before nine o'clock this morning. No witnesses, correct?"

"Correct."

"No official coroner's report yet but, from what I saw, a blast to the head. Unhealthy marriage makes wife a prime suspect but forthcoming interviews will negate that hypothesis." Her hand flipped over in the air, asking the question, what next. "You have a boatload of interviews to conduct. Friends. Business partners. What about a weapon? Did you find it?"

"Not yet. Do you know what she used?"

Her breath caught, startled by his words. "*She* didn't use anything. Mary didn't kill him."

"How do you know?"

That was a question she couldn't answer. "You interviewed her. Do you think she's capable of killing someone? I doubt she swats a fly when it lands on her kitchen counter. What'd she say to make you suspect her?"

"Not much. Nothing, really. She seemed easily intimidated, or in shock. I'm not sure."

"He's mentally abused her for years, I'm certain of it."

Jared leaned in on his elbows. "How can you say that when you claim you've had no contact with either of them for you don't know how many years?"

Her fist pounded the table before she realized it. The anger Don triggered in her—the fury she worked for years to dispel —was resurrecting itself. Again. "Because that's his M.O. He's a fucking bully. Always has been. You talk, he talks louder. You make a valid point, one he can't counter intellectually, he makes it personal. He calls you names. He puts you down with belittling words. He's loud and vulgar. Mary wasn't strong. Not against him. That's why I cut all ties. He's toxic. He should have died years ago."

She balled up her napkin and tossed it onto her half-eaten salad. "So. Are we going to the wedding together? Should I RSVP plus one or do you want to do it?"

The look on Jared's face said he was stunned. "You don't feel any sorrow that your brother was murdered?"

"Not one iota."

"Christ, Em, maybe I should include you on the suspect list."

"Maybe you should."

10

They avoided the subject of Emma's brother and the rest of the night surprised Jared. Emma ordered a shot of whiskey and threw it back without blinking. When she ordered a second one, he inquired what her plans were.

"I plan to go home with you and fuck the living daylights out of you." He suspected it was some form of remorse or shock or reaction to her brother's death that she refused to acknowledge. Once they arrived at his house, though, it didn't matter what motivated her. Emma's unrestrained passion blew his mind. At some point, she whispered she loved him, he was certain. But she was drunk, and he was drunk on her.

He woke her up in the morning with black coffee and aspirin, knowing that she wasn't a good drinker. And convinced he wanted to spend the rest of his life with her. She was quiet on the ride to the bar to retrieve her car. She brushed her lips across his before exiting, saying they would talk later.

He knew her well enough to know her head pounded and her stomach revolted. But she'd show up for her shift right on time in a clean uniform. He strode to his desk, smiling.

"Good night last night?" Jeff was a little too observant for his tastes. He suspected that Jeff knew about his relationship with Emma. It didn't matter. Partners always have each other's backs.

"How about making it a better morning. Got anything for me?"

The grin on Jeff's face disappeared, and he sat up straighter. "I spoke to a couple neighbors yesterday. They knew him only to wave to. Those homes aren't that close to each other. No backyard barbecues together. No get togethers to watch playoff sports. Told one of them once he wasn't a sports fan. Who the hell doesn't like football?"

Em loved sports, especially hockey. "What else?"

"Occasionally, the neighbor to the east would hear yelling. Always him. Never able to hear words, only shouts. He wasn't interested in establishing a relationship with Malvado. Said Mrs. Malvado seemed nice. From his kitchen window, he could see her leaving food for deer, milk for stray cats, and bowls for other critters. He never had a conversation with either of them."

"Neighbors across the road are so far from the Malvado house, they didn't recognize his name. Same with the homestead on the west side."

Jared ran his hand through his hair and Jeff read the gesture. "Yeah, pretty much a dead end."

Jared closed the folder marked neighbors. "What about business contacts?"

Jeff shifted his papers. "He owns three properties that he rents, one to a martini bar, one to a service station, and one in a small plaza with space for two offices. One of the office spaces is empty. I haven't tracked down the former tenant yet. The other is leased by a realtor who I spoke to briefly on the phone. She had minimal contact with Malvado. Barely remembered him. She's leased for close to three years. She

met him when she signed the lease, pays her rent electroni-
cally, and has had no issues in the building to contact him
about. She expects to be in the office all morning and available for a face-to-face. I figure we start there. Hope you're not
too hungover to pound a little pavement." He smiled at
his wit.

Jared reviewed the property pages Jeff had printed from
county records on the ride to the East Side, a section of the city
on the up and coming. New technology businesses were
moving in, bringing with them a tech-savvy younger generation
eager to share every detail of their ordinary lives on social
media and fascinated with the idea of congregating in groups to
talk about themselves. He'd been one of those kids once, ready
to telegraph his life to the world. Once he stepped on the law
enforcement path, his growing awareness of cyber security and
social media vulnerability stymied his public presence. The
only time he visited social media these days was in search of
suspects. Criminals were dumb and couldn't resist the urge to
brag about their misdeeds.

The service station bays had three eco-friendly cars inside
and a computer system along the back wall that rivaled their
crime lab.

A man whose physique indicated he was a gym rat introduced himself as Dutch Holmes. He wiped his hands before
shaking theirs.

"We didn't have much of a relationship with the guy.
Honestly, we despised him. Look at this place, it's more work
than me or my partner can handle. Don Malvado owns the
vacant lot that abuts ours in the rear and we've wanted to buy it
for years and expand. We tried negotiating a deal that was more
than fair that included a purchase price and higher rent, but
Malvado refused to sell. He tagged the property with an exorbi-
tant value and wouldn't budge, saying he could get his asking
price from any number of businesses. He was just blowing

smoke. I don't know who would pay triple the price that it's worth for a lot too small for anything more than a food truck."

"So he was a roadblock to business expansion?" Jared eyed him. Could be a financial motive.

"Yes and no. We started talks with the owner next door," he pointed toward the adjacent property, which appeared to house a single garage. Parking in this neighborhood was mostly on the street.

"It would be more costly, but we could expand in that direction and the owner seemed open to it. Maybe we won't have to. What happens to Malvado's businesses now that he's dead?"

No sense of loss here. That was a good question. Did ownership of these businesses fall to Mary Malvado? That could go to motive.

"You aren't sorry your landlord was murdered?"

Holmes grinned. "The world's better off with one less A-hole, don't you think?"

"Where were you Thursday morning, Mr. Holmes, between the hours of five and nine?"

Holmes waved his rag in the air. "Neither one of us killed him if that's what you're trying not to ask. We were right here. My partner and I open every morning at six except Sundays, when we open at ten. We're here by five-thirty to fire up the equipment. Sometimes these computers are fussy. We close the bays at eight, but the pumps stay on until midnight so myself or my partner are here doing paperwork. I can give you that day's invoices. You can see who brought in their vehicles and who picked them up. Is that a good enough alibi?"

It was.

They walked across the street to the martini bar. It wasn't open yet, but there was activity inside. They knocked and flashed their badges.

Graham Shultz introduced himself as co-owner, motioning to his husband and partner, Martin, wiping the bar.

Jared introduced himself and Jeff. "We'd like to ask you about your landlord, Donald Malvado."

Graham's hand flew to his chest. "Oh my Lord, we saw it on the news yesterday and we were shocked, shocked I say. We never knew someone who was murdered. We felt like celebrities." Jeff's head snapped up from his notebook.

"What was your relationship with Mr. Malvado?"

Graham flapped his hand at them. "Truthfully? Terrible. The man was a Neanderthal. He didn't approve of our lifestyle and he wasn't afraid to take cheap shots at us. Martin has a temper so I mostly dealt with him but after every conversation, I wanted to shower. He was insulting."

"Can you give me an example?"

"He'd refer to our customers as fairy friends, make remarks like could I tiptoe into the office for the rent check, and always, when he was leaving, he'd say 'bye girls.'"

Emma had called him a bully. This sounded like it. "How'd that make you feel? Mad?"

"Do you mean mad enough to kill him? Heavens no. I felt sad for the man, living in the dark ages. Look around you, Detective." His hand split the air. "Our business is booming. We walked Mr. Malvado's insults all the way to the bank. It didn't matter what he said to us because, beyond being our landlord, he didn't matter to us."

Fair enough. "Where were you Thursday morning?"

Graham laughed. "The bar closes at two but, by the time we get everything cleaned up, it's sometime around four. We go home and crash until noon, get up and do it all over again. The bar opens at three. Feel free to stop in any time. Bring your wife. The first drink is on the house."

The realtor provided little more information than she'd given Jeff on the phone and offered up her husband and her child's first grade teacher as her alibi.

The men returned to their car.

"They're not our killers," Jared said, snapping his seatbelt. Jeff concurred.

"Holmes asked a good question. What happens to the property now? Mary Malvado might be a rich woman if she sells all this. I sure don't see her as a landlord."

"I don't either. Guess we'd have to see the will to know that. I did a fast check of public records yesterday. Found a couple of business bankruptcy claims Malvado filed, and some minor lawsuits, people who slipped on an icy sidewalk at the service station, crap like that."

Jared sighed and reached for Malvado's address book. "I knew it couldn't be that easy. Guess we spend the rest of the day interviewing the names in this book." He leafed through the pages. "There seems to be some sort of system here. Some names are highlighted with yellow. A couple of names are starred. Wonder what it means. Let's start making phone calls when we get back to our desks. Some of these will be easy. Here's the number for his dentist. And an automotive place. He didn't trust his tenants to fix his car. Wonder if he expected a discount. If we call some of these, maybe we'll get into his head."

By lunchtime, two legal pads listed names of friends and foes. The friends column was shorter and included a handful of relatives, many who had little contact with Malvado beyond an annual Christmas card that Mrs. Malvado sent. The niece who Emma mentioned, Nessie, wasn't listed in his book.

The foes were the ones highlighted in the book. Speaking to them proved interesting. All had a similar story of befriending Malvado only to have him turn on them. Some with mutual investments that he defaulted on, others with loans that he failed to pay back. All willingly consented to in-person interviews and Jared had a list of appointments starting later in the afternoon. The character composite they were compiling was not a nice one.

Jeff shook his head and hung up the phone. "That was a female cousin who raved about him, his sense of humor, his willingness to help anyone who asked. She couldn't say enough good things about him. Her husband died several years ago and Malvado became her go-to guy for home projects. She looked forward to holidays with him. Doesn't understand how anyone could kill him. She's willing to talk to us. Says she has a lot of family pictures we could see.

"I heard similar praises from a longtime friend who tried a couple of business ventures with Malvado. They failed but he said Malvado would give the shirt off his back to a friend who needed it. He'll meet with us too."

Jared angled his head, surprised that he'd heard the exact opposite from the people he contacted. Anger seeped through the phone in their voices and none of them expressed sorrow that Malvado was gone. "This guy is a real Jekyll and Hyde. People either love him or hate him. There's no in between."

Jeff exhaled slowly. "The funeral ought to be interesting."

"Did anyone you spoke to fail to provide an alibi for where they were yesterday morning?"

Jeff held up a yellow legal sheet, checkmarks evident beside a column of names and places. "Everyone seems to be accounted for."

They would gauge everyone's truthfulness when they interviewed them in person. Meanwhile, Taylor and his uniforms could verify all the alibis via phone calls. Jared was certain they would all be solid. They were back to square one. Mary Malvado.

11

F orty-eight hours ago, Mary sipped hot tea in her own living room, reading the Bible and ignoring Don's snorts and snores from the opposite side of the room. The corners of her mouth dipped at the irony of this evening. Her sister, Ellen, slept in the recliner in front of the television. How many nights had she watched Don snoring in the same position, the tea in her cup as cold as her life?

On the ride here yesterday, her sister chatted about everything under the sun except the reason why she had to pick her up at the police station and why Mary had to stay at her house indefinitely. Their favorite cooking show. The TV drama they both watched. The weather. The city's baseball team. For Pete's sake, neither one of them liked baseball.

They ate dinner in front of the TV. She was grateful the game show negated the need for conversation. They both focused on guessing the correct answers.

Two hours ago, someone from the police department called to say Don's body was being released the day after tomorrow and she should advise a funeral home to collect him. She hadn't even thought about a funeral or what the obit should say or how she would feed the people who showed up.

Don Jr. was meeting her at church tomorrow for morning Mass and he planned to stay with her for the day, accompanying her to the funeral home and cemetery. Where should his father be buried? Logic dictated he go where her parents lay at rest but that would mean she'd be obligated to visit him whenever she was there to mourn them. She couldn't do it.

Somewhere she'd written the name of the cemetery where his parents were buried, but she couldn't remember where she filed that note. Emma should know. Maybe Don could rest there.

Her conversation with her son earlier today had been brief, mainly because she didn't have answers to his questions. She begged off the call, claiming she was too shocked to discuss anything. That was essentially true. She asked him to call his sister, who lived two states away. Diane left home when she was eighteen, refusing to endure her father's verbal abuse. Their relationship was strained after that and in recent years, had been reduced to holiday and birthday phone calls. Maybe now, that would change.

The only phone call she made before switching off her cell was to the rectory. She called Father Greg the minute she had a private moment at her sister's house. She excused herself to use the bathroom. Don was burning in hell right now, she was certain. But Father Greg offered the church for the funeral service, which he would preside over. What could he possibly say that would be complementary?

"It's difficult now, but God has shined his light on you this day, my dear," Father Greg soothed. He really had.

"Where are you, Mary? Do you want me with you?"

"I'm with my sister. Not now, Father, I'll see you tomorrow morning."

Church brought her comfort and she didn't dare deviate

from her regular routine. Her attorney cautioned that the police would be watching her. They'd find that assignment boring for sure.

How would she face the congregation at church tomorrow? What looks would she get from them, or would all of them who normally greeted her avert their gazes? People were fickle like that. Don's murder was the lead story on every news station. They referred to Don as a prominent businessman. Was he? The reports were short on facts, but were presented to imply that she was the chief suspect. Was she?

Father Greg had assured her God walked with her. At least Don Jr. would be by her side. Maybe he had some thoughts on his father's final resting place and service. For sure it would be a closed casket, which suited her just fine. She never wanted to look at Don again.

SHE'D BARELY CLOSED her eyes when the alarm jolted her awake. She dressed robotically in the same clothes she wore the day Don died. Yesterday she'd secluded herself in her sister's spare room and never got out of the borrowed pajamas. The police hadn't given her the opportunity to pack a bag. Perhaps she could swing through the house after church and pick up her clothes and toiletries.

Finding her sister up and sipping tea in the kitchen surprised her. She wasn't an early bird. "What are you doing up so early?"

"You don't have your car, remember? I'll drive you to church. You shouldn't be alone today."

Ellen's concern touched her. They weren't one of those lovey-dovey families who said endearing things to each other. She never heard her parents say they loved each other and once she was in seventh grade, they never said it to her anymore. She'd never expressed her feelings to her sister, whatever they were.

"Thank you. Is there more tea?"

Don Jr. waited for her at the bottom of the church steps, waved as they drove into the parking lot, and rushed to the spot Ellen drove to. He wrapped her in an embrace and held her tight for a good thirty seconds. He'd inherited her sensitivity, thank God.

"Mom, are you okay? Did you sleep? You look so tired."

Over his shoulder, Mary watched Detective Jones and his partner park their car at the curb. Her lawyer was right.

"I'm fine, Donnie, only weary. Sleep was elusive last night. It's all so unbelievable."

Flanked by her son and sister, both holding her elbows, Mary walked toward the only place she wanted to be. Father Greg bounded down the steps and encircled her in his arms. She relaxed into his hug, calm at last.

"Sister Mary, it does my heart good to see you. I was so worried about you. Stay after Mass for a special blessing." She smiled and climbed the steps holding his hand, her son still at her elbow. To her surprise, the parishioners gathered in a group in the vestibule, some crying, most clasping their folded hands in front of them. One by one they stepped forward, grasping her hands, pressing small Bibles, rosary beads and personal notes into them, whispering words of support and encouragement. And then, like a queen whose subjects worship her, she strode slowly to the front pew where she always sat, the group falling in step behind her to their usual rows. Tears filled her eyes. They knew. They understood.

Father Greg's sermon focused on sin and forgiveness. When she turned away from the altar after receiving Communion, Mary spotted the two detectives sitting in the back row of the church. Maybe they weren't Catholic.

As the worshippers filed out of church, Father Greg

reminded her to stay and directed her to his office. She turned to her son. "Donnie, those two men over there are detectives. Go ask them if I can stop at the house and pick up some things. And maybe take my car so Ellen doesn't have to haul me everywhere. I'll just be a moment with Father Greg."

Walking toward the priest's office, feeling the detectives' eyes on her back, she repressed a chuckle. Lifting her gaze to Detective Jones and smiling, she closed the door.

12

J ared stood beside Jeff watching Mary Malvado stroll toward the priest's office. "Is that the same woman we spoke with at the station? The one so intimidated it seemed a sneeze could reduce her to tears?"

Jeff didn't have time to respond. A young man, blond, with a straight nose like his mother, approached and extended his hand.

"Good morning, I'm Don Malvado Jr. My mother says you are police detectives. Is there a reason you are here this morning? I'm certain you're not regulars."

Jared shook his hand after Jeff. "It's police protocol, Mr. Malvado. A person capable of murder is capable of other unsavory behavior, including taunting his victims. We thought it prudent to observe your mother's routine."

"So, you're here to protect her?" The inflection in his voice sounded like he didn't believe that.

"In a manner of speaking. Sir, while this isn't the most opportune time, can you take a few minutes and speak with us? Can you tell us where you were the morning your father died, between say five-thirty and nine?"

He straightened his shoulders and glared at Jared. "You're right, Detective, this isn't the right time."

Jared felt his hackles rise. He was older, but he could go toe to toe with this guy. "Of course, of course. We'll be happy to talk to you at the station if you prefer. Would you like to follow us there or ride with us?"

The kid took a step back, his jaw agape. "Excuse me? Do you consider me a suspect? I was at my office all day, even after I heard the news. At least twelve people can confirm that."

"How'd you hear about what happened?"

"My executive assistant told me."

"And he or she knew about it ... how?"

"I-I'm not sure. Listen, detective, you are way off base if you think I or my mother had anything to do with shooting my father. I had nothing but the utmost respect for him. And my mother, well, she's been with him twenty-five years. It seems to me your time would be better spent searching for whoever *did* do it."

Jared shrugged. "To that end, do you have any thoughts on who might have killed your dad? Know of any recent disagreements he had with anyone? Any enemies that you are aware of?"

"No, I don't. I never discussed his business with him."

"What did you talk about? When was the last time you saw him?"

The skin above his shirt collar turned red and the color crept up to his cheeks. He stammered an unintelligible response and jumped when his mother touched his arm. "Donnie, did the detectives say I can take some of my things?"

Mary Malvado turned an innocent smile on the men. Donnie seemed incapable of speech.

Jared cleared his throat. "Good morning, Mrs. Malvado. What things are you referring to?"

"Good morning, Detective. What a surprise to see you here. Did you enjoy the sermon?"

She waited for his response.

"Yes, ma'am." Truth be told, he had no idea what Father Greg had preached. The cogs in his brain kept spinning about murder and motive.

Mary Malvado inhaled a fortifying breath. "As you are aware, I left my home Wednesday with nothing but the clothes on my back." She drew the baggy sweater forward as if he couldn't see it. "These clothes, as a matter of fact. I have nothing else to wear, no toiletries, not even my wallet. You haven't notified me that I can return home so I was wondering if I might take a few things from the house. I sent Donnie over here to ask. What were you talking about if not that?"

Donnie's beet red face was now ghostly white. She looked from her son to Jeff and then settled on Jared, her chin slightly elevated. In this church, with Father Greg's robes rustling as he made his way toward them, Mary Malvado was emboldened. The priest stepped up beside her and cupped her elbow.

"Good morning, detectives. I hope you enjoyed the sermon today."

If he only knew. A few parishioners lingered in the doorway. Nosy neighbors or allies? It felt like the troops were rallying around their leader.

"Good morning, Father. My apologies, Mrs. Malvado. Your home is still considered a crime scene. I'm afraid I can't let you in yet."

Father Greg spoke up. "Surely you can allow her some clean clothes. She has no money, no identification. Her husband has just died. If she isn't permitted inside at least send someone in to collect a few personal items. She needs better clothes for the funeral service. I'll volunteer if need be but, for God's sake, allow her some dignity."

Wasn't that an odd thing for a priest to say? There was

plenty in this conversation to hash over with Jeff, including the priest's willingness to rummage through Mary Malvado's underwear drawer. "I can authorize an officer to gather some items if you'll make up a list, Mrs. Malvado. I'm afraid that's the best I can do."

"I don't want a stranger rifling through my things."

That shined an interesting light on the priest, didn't it?

Donnie turned to his mother. "Mom, I can—"

Mary Malvado held up her hand to hush him as if he were eight years old, then folded her arms across her chest. "I'll give the list to Emma. I want Emma Hunter to gather what I need."

13

Emma smiled when caller ID showed Jared on the other end of the ringing phone. Yeah, she was starting to really like this guy. Well, more than like. A lot more.

It was rare for him to call when he was on duty. She began second shift this week and didn't need to report until three. Luckily, the schedule switched the day after the murder, otherwise she would have reported to work with one hell of a hangover. But the later starting hour had allowed her to catch more sleep and recover from her trip down shooters lane before clocking in. It had been a good night with Jared, though.

"Hey you, hi. This is a nice surprise."

"Hi. This is somewhat of an official call, Em."

She released the clothes she was loading into the washing machine and left the laundry room. Sometimes calls dropped in that little cubbyhole. "What's up?"

"I'm outside your sister-in-law's church. She—"

"What did you say? Where are you?"

"Listen to me please, Em. I'm outside your sister-in-law's church. Her house is still a crime scene and she wants some clean clothes. And her purse. It's a reasonable request, but I can't let her in there. She's requested that you gather the things she needs. She meets with the funeral director later today so it can't wait until you clock in. It has to be on your personal time, which is probably better anyway."

Jared's words spun in her brain. What was Mary thinking?

"She wants me? Did she specifically ask for me?"

Jared's exhaled breath filled her ear. "Yeah. You could've blown me over with a whisper. She said she didn't want a stranger going through her stuff. I thought that's what you were. You said you two aren't close, but she's asking for you. Her son is here and her priest, but it's you she wants. What are you doing this morning? Any chance you could meet us at your brother's house?"

She was at a loss for words. Jared could authorize anyone to walk in there and collect Mary's belongings. For that matter, he could accompany her inside. But the living room must still be a bloody mess and he didn't want to compound Mary's trauma. He'd be cognizant of that. But Mary must still be in shock to ask for her help.

Emma was trained to encounter accidents and death and yet her dead brother's image had haunted her last night. She didn't have a problem going into that house again but why her? She was the last person she'd guess Mary would reach out to. Mary hadn't said ten words to her since the moment she slid in beside her in the back seat of the freezing patrol car. A muttered "thank you" when she crawled out of the cruiser and another "thank you for your help" conveyed via Terrence O'Hare, her attorney, after his first conversation with her.

"Em? Are you still there? Hello?"

"Um, yes, yes I'm here. Sorry. Sure, I can come over there. Are you all right with this?"

"We'll discuss that later. How soon can I tell her you'll be here?"

"With crosstown traffic, it will probably take me thirty minutes. Maybe less. Do you want me to meet you at the house?"

"We'll wait here at the church. Text me when you get to your brother's."

"Will do."

"And Em ..." She stayed on the line. "Gloves and booties. It's still a crime scene."

"Ten-four, Detective. See you soon."

Hells bells. Jared was dragging her right into the middle of the case. The exact place he told her to stay out of. Aiding her sister-in-law with recovering her personal items deposited her smack dab into the defense's lap. If Mary was charged with her husband's murder, O'Hare could try to prove diminished mental capacity or temporary insanity. Asking Emma for help bordered on insane. She imagined the questions he might fire at her on the witness stand.

Isn't it true, Lieutenant Hunter, that you had no communication with your sister-in-law until the morning of the shooting? Didn't you in fact hire her defense team out of concern for her unstable mindset? Wasn't it you who she reached out to for personal assistance, a woman she hadn't spoken with in years, further exemplifying the state of distress she was in and her inability to think coherently?

Maybe O'Hare had planted this seed in Mary's mind, deliberately dragging Emma to the defense table. He was shrewd enough.

Traffic was light this time of day and she arrived at her brother's house in under twenty-five minutes. She drove slowly around the circular driveway and parked behind the patrol car stationed at the kitchen door. Officer Petrus stepped out of his unit and waited for her to exit her SUV. Emma held up her badge.

"Good morning, Officer Petrus. I'm here at the request of Detective Jones. He'll be here momentarily."

The patrolman nodded but remained standing in front of the kitchen door, both thumbs hooked into his utility belt and his fingers splayed in front. Casual but ready.

Emma shot a text to Jared, then strolled to the rear of the house, surprised at the junk in the yard and the trashy appearance. But not really. This was how her brother always lived. She didn't comprehend it. Their parents hadn't raised them to be slobs. Quite the opposite. Her mother wiped items before they went into the refrigerator or pantry and insisted shoes be stowed in closets and beds always be made before you left your room. She doubted Mary's upbringing was much different.

Jared's car appeared, followed by two other vehicles she didn't recognize. She saw Jeff in the passenger seat of the unmarked detective's car and squinted to see beyond it. Was that Mary's sister, Ellen? My God, she'd aged. Her heart skipped when she recognized the man who stepped out of the last car. Donnie Jr. He'd turned into a fine-looking man. She knew from Nessie that he was some sort of day trader, although how successful she didn't know.

Emma caught her breath. This was surreal.

Jared approached her. Jeff smiled when Jared said, "Thanks for coming, Lieutenant." Jared had shared that he suspected Jeff was onto them. She smiled at Jared and winked at Jeff.

"Good to see you, Emma." Jeff's grin said it all.

She turned to see Mary, Ellen and Donnie Jr. grouped in front of Ellen's beat-up green sedan, watching them. Dark circles rimmed Mary's eyes and she wore the same clothes Emma had seen her in Wednesday morning. Emma's feet moved involuntarily toward them.

Donnie likewise walked in her direction, his arms open. "Aunt Emma, it's been a long time." His hug felt genuine. "I hope you can help mom through this mess, no matter what's been between you two in the past."

Her brother, Mary's husband, had been between them.

She patted his upper arm, knowing Jared and Jeff were close enough to hear. "I'll do what I can, Donnie. It's good to see you." She stepped closer to the sisters. "Ellen," she nodded to her. And then, "Mary. How are you holding up?"

It wasn't a difficult question, but Mary had that critter in the headlights look on her face. Jared joined the group.

"Emma, Mrs. Malvado would like some personal items that are in the house. I'd like you to locate them and touch as little as possible. Did you bring your gloves?"

She did. She drew them from her back jeans pocket and waved them at him.

"Good. Did you make a list, Mary?"

Mimicking Emma's movements, she showed him the pages crunched in her fist. Jesus, she hadn't said a word yet. Emma stepped closer.

"Let me see, Mary. Are all these things in your bedroom?"

The handwriting was scrawny. Maybe she wrote it on her knee in the car. Three pairs of underwear and bras were listed. Three nightgowns. Mary seemed to think she'd be home in three days. Either that or she planned to do laundry.

Black and brown slacks and tops to match. In parenthesis, "you pick." Black flat shoes and her slippers. In parenthesis, "under the bed." Blue jeans, one or two it said. Polka-dotted pajama pants and sweatpants, one red and one black plus long-sleeved T-shirts that matched. Under a toiletry heading that said bathroom, she listed toothbrush, toothpaste, brush, comb, deodorant. The last line said prescription medicines—"you'll see them in the medicine cabinet with my name."

She wanted the book on her nightstand and her reading glasses. A notebook tucked in the back of the nightstand drawer—"you'll find it"—and her purse, which she thought was still on the kitchen counter. And finally, her Bible on the end table in the living room.

Mary's voice cracked. "If you think of something that I've forgotten, please pick it up."

Unkind thoughts peppered Emma's mind. This woman might as well be a total stranger asking her to "pick up some things that I like." How would she know? They were polar opposites. Emma's list would include jewelry and makeup, body splash or perfume. But Mary had declared herself 'plain' years ago, once comparing herself to Emma and saying she'd never be as fashionable.

Emma tugged on her black protective gloves and strode to the kitchen door, where Jeff waited with paper booties in his hand. He already wore both.

"What's he doing?" Mary almost shouted.

Jared stepped toward her. "Officer Widows is going to observe Emma while she's inside your home. It's for your protection, to ensure any evidence isn't tampered with, taken or even planted. Not that Emma would do that, but it's protective protocol for our officer as well as private individuals."

"I don't want him going through my things."

"No ma'am. He'll just keep an eye on Emma."

The rosary beads emerged from her pocket and began a nervous trek through her fingers. Jared signaled 'go', and Emma and Jeff entered the house.

Once again, Emma was struck by the uneasy silence. She heard Jeff breathing and her own shallow breaths. The refrigerator hummed. A clock ticked from somewhere, marking each second. The house had been locked up but was exceptionally cool. Someone had remembered to dial down the thermostat before leaving. It was, after all, a crime scene and needed to be preserved.

"Let's start upstairs. That's where most of the things on Mary's list should be."

Jeff motioned for Emma to take the lead. She stopped short

in the doorway of the master bedroom, taking in the disheveled room.

Jeff touched her arm. "Jared mentioned they didn't share a bedroom. I think hers is over here."

She moved to what used to be a guest bedroom and immediately saw signs of Mary. It shouldn't surprise her that her brother and sister-in-law were no longer intimate, but it did beg the question of why she stayed with him. Emma had a long list that prompted the same question.

Moving to the bureau, she began collecting the personal items. Jeff used his phone to record her and she detailed her actions.

"I'm opening the top right bureau drawer to find under—lingerie items. I'm removing three pairs of white cotton panties, three white underwire bras and three pairs of white socks."

Now her hands were full. "Jeff, do you see anything I can use to pack these items in?" They surveyed the room but nothing like a tote or suitcase popped out.

Jeff pointed to the double bed. "What about a pillowcase?"

It didn't seem right but Emma didn't see anything else to use as a container.

"I'm taking one yellow-flowered pillowcase from the left side of the bed to transport these items." This looked like the side Mary didn't sleep on.

It was easy to coordinate the tops with the pants. They hung side-by-side on a clothes rack. Once the clothing was added, the pillowcase was stuffed. Emma used the other pillowcase for Mary's shoes and slippers.

"Let's look in the master bedroom for a valise or something better than these pillowcases. Mary's been through enough. I don't want her to feel like a bag lady."

Jeff followed her into the master, crinkling his nose as she did. The room smelled stale. "This place needs some fresh air. I bet my brother never opened a window." Tennis shoes, slippers, and safety-toe work boots were piled in one corner, surrounded by rolled up dirty socks. She wondered where her brother wore those boots. They weren't cheap.

She opened the closet door to find the space jammed with clothes. No wonder there were piles of them around the room. One more shirt wouldn't squeeze in here. She knelt and dug through overflowing boxes and stuffed lawn bags, eventually laying her hands on a battered, gray suitcase. Crawling out on the floor, she remembered the video.

"I'm taking a suitcase from the master closet in order to transport the items Mrs. Malvado has requested. The suitcase is not on the list Mrs. Malvado provided."

Jeff gave her a thumbs-up. She was dotting every 'i' and crossing every 't'.

Emma collected the medicines from the bathroom then returned to Mary's bedroom nightstand. The book and her glasses were right on top. She opened the single drawer to a mish-mosh of items, including baby shoes, lace handkerchiefs, breath mints and pantyhose. Reaching into the back, she touched a small journal wrapped in a rubber band. Is this what Mary wanted?

Jeff looked around his raised phone. "Is that a diary? Something that could be useful to us?"

Emma shrugged. "I'm not sure. When the ERT team searched the house, what were they looking for?"

"Mostly a weapon and anything linked to Mr. Malvado. Practically everything in his office was confiscated. Mrs. Malvado was not the focus of the sweep."

Emma slid the band off the cover and thumbed the pages. She recognized Mary's handwriting from when she was still on the Christmas card list. Every page was filled with notes. From the back of the book, a slip of paper flittered to the floor. Emma bent, picked it up and unfolded it. She gasped.

"What's that?"

Jeff was still recording so she fought to control her voice and turned toward the camera. "It appears to be a copy of a birth certificate. The name on the certificate is Carson Gene Ganesh. G-A-N-E-S-H. The mother is listed as Isabelle Ganesh. There is no father listed but," she blinked to make sure she wasn't seeing things, "but a picture is stapled to it. It's my brother's high school graduation picture."

Jeff looked around his raised hands. "What? How old is it?"

Emma scanned the document. She looked at the date of birth and quickly calculated in her head. It was twenty-eight years old. Older than her nephew by two years.

"Do you recognize the woman's name? Was Malvado married before?"

Emma stared at the paper, sensing sweat pool under her arms. "No, I don't recognize her name."

She'd never heard the name Carson Gene Ganesh either. Was this her brother's son? Had he known about him? How could you have a son and not acknowledge him? What kind of man did that?

She eyed a second piece of paper behind the birth certificate. "There's something else here, a newspaper announcement about a Carson G. White joining a law firm." Her hand covered her mouth. Jesus. It was Don's younger face.

"What? What about it?"

"Oh my God, Jeff. The implication is obvious here. Look." She held up the school picture next to the picture in the newspaper. "They could be twins. Or...Jesus...father and son."

"Did you know about this? That your brother fathered another son?"

She didn't. But finding this in Mary's book proved she did. How long has she known? There was no date indicating when the copy was made. The imprint of a notary's stamp was visible, so it was valid. Had she known for all these years? And yet, she continued to live with him?

Emma removed her cell phone from her jacket and snapped a picture of the documents. Then she replaced them in the diary. The full sheets, folded in quarters, fit perfectly.

"I think that's pertinent evidence, Emma. You're not giving it back to Mrs. Malvado, are you?"

Mary had asked Emma to locate this book, but why? To ensure the police didn't find it? Had she wanted Emma to find this birth certificate? Did she think the rubber band would keep Emma from opening it? Was it an invasion of privacy, a violation of Mary's civil rights that she did open it without a warrant? This wasn't only a suspicion that Don had an illegitimate son. It was a motive for murder. When did Mary find out about this? Days ago? Before Don was killed? Years ago?

What about this kid? Did he know who his father was? Who was his mother?

"Emma?"

"Yes, I'm going to return it to Mary. And then I'm going to ask her to turn it over to Jared."

Jeff stopped recording and came toward her. "Are you okay? You look like you want to barf." He laid his hand on her shoulder. "This is a lot to absorb in just a couple of days. You're one of the toughest cops I know, but you're still human. Asking you to do this might not have been a good idea."

Her heart raced. "I keep finding more reasons to hate him, Jeff. I didn't think that was possible. There are only a few more items on this list. Let's find them and get the hell out of here."

He followed her downstairs to the living room but her step faltered in the archway. Cleaning crews hadn't been allowed in here yet and the dried blood was black as dirt. She gagged at the stench. The couch cushions remained concave, where his body had been. She thought about the impromptu memorials that spring up at roadside deaths or public murder scenes. No one would be rushing to lay a bouquet of flowers at the foot of this couch.

The ticking clock was louder. There, on the mantle. She remembered that gold clock with its spinning works underneath a glass dome. It had been her parents'.

"I'm recording, Lieutenant."

Jeff's voice snapped her back to the present. She spotted the Bible on the end table beside the love seat and reached for it with gloved hands. From there, she moved to the kitchen where Mary's purse was exactly where she said it would be. Emma unzipped it.

"I'm checking to make sure Mrs. Malvado's wallet is inside. She specifically asked for that," Emma recited to Jeff's phone. It was and she zipped it shut.

She closed the cereal box and slid it to the rear of the counter. The melted butter was probably rancid, but she snapped the lid on it anyway and placed it on the first shelf in the refrigerator. With her hand on the kitchen doorknob, she paused and spoke directly to Jeff's phone. "This is the end of the authorized retrieval of Mary Malvado's personal items."

14

Despite the cool temperature inside the house, Emma stepped outside and sucked in the fresh air as if it were an oxygen line to her lungs. It was a relief to be out of there.

Jared leaned against the front fender of his Ford. Mary, Ellen, and Donnie were right where she last saw them, gathered in a semi-circle in front of Ellen's car. Mary's hands were clasped, the beads weaved through her fingers glinting in the sunlight.

"How'd it go?" Jared posed the question to both of them.

"Duly recorded," Jeff said, eyeing the handwritten diary Emma still held in her hand.

Emma rolled the suitcase to Mary. "I think I found everything you wanted."

Mary plunged her hands into the pockets of her sweater when her gaze fell to the journal Emma clutched.

Emma raised it to waist level. "I looked in this, Mary. I probably shouldn't have but you weren't specific about the book you wanted from your nightstand and, well, it doesn't matter why but I looked in it. I think you should turn it over to the police."

Jared whispered to Jeff, "What's going on?"

"Shh, let this play out."

Mary rocked from front to back, drawing her bottom lip between her teeth. "There's personal writings in there."

Emma cocked her head. "There's more than that."

The color drained from Mary's face. "You saw it?"

"I did. It should be turned over to the police."

"Saw what, Mom? What's Aunt Emma talking about? What is that book?"

Mary hushed her son. "He doesn't know. No one knows except Father Greg."

"Knows what, Mom?"

His perplexity was genuine. The look on Ellen's face indicated she had no clue what Mary referred to either.

"The police should see it, Mary."

"Can you promise that only you will read what I wrote in there? You're the police."

Holy crap, Mary wanted her to drown in this case. Emma didn't want any more to do with it.

"No, I can't make that promise. I won't. This is information that could be made public in a trial if it comes to that. I've seen it, Mary. If you don't surrender it voluntarily, Detective Jones can obtain a warrant based on information received. That information will come from me."

She'd lapsed into cop-mode in an effort to protect herself. Even dead, her brother was sucking her into his secrets like quicksand. He'd always been toxic for her, so poisonous she'd severed all ties. And had been happier for it.

Mary crossed herself. "It will look bad, the things I wrote in there. My words aren't always benevolent."

"It'll be fine, Mary. I'm sure you can explain everything you wrote. You didn't kill Don. You have nothing to worry about."

She seemed to wither right before Emma's eyes. She reached for her son's arm, needing support.

"All right, if you think that's best. If you advise me to give it to Detective Jones, I will."

Whoa. Hold your horses. Emma raised her hand to stop any such notion. "I'm not giving you legal advice, Mary. Let's be clear about that. I'm not qualified and it's not my place. If you are more comfortable speaking with your attorney first, I'm certain the detectives will understand."

The screwed-up look on Jared's face screamed he didn't understand any of what was transpiring. He threw a questioning glance at Emma and then Jeff, who held up the wait-one-minute index finger.

Mary clung to Donnie Jr. now and waved a feeble hand in the air. Ellen stepped beside her.

"I don't need to speak to Mr. O'Hare," Mary said. "I want to return to the church. I need to talk to my son and I want Father Greg there when I do. Am I free to go? May I leave?"

All eyes turned to Jared. After a silent consult with Jeff who agreed, he said yes. Donnie moved to take the suitcase Emma nudged forward.

Emma raised the diary to shoulder level. "Mary?"

She turned to walk toward her sister's car and spoke over her shoulder. "Let the police have it. I'm done protecting him."

15

T he three of them watched the taillights of the two vehicles disappear. Emma's spirits sank with their descent down the drive.

"What the hell was all that about?" Jared asked.

"We found some pretty interesting stuff in that little book in Emma's hand." Jeff raised his phone. "Okay Emma, I'm recording."

Jared listened to her state the time, date and location where she found the book and, when she held it out, he eyed it curiously as he slipped on a pair of latex gloves. He waited for Jeff's signal that the phone was off before gingerly opening the cardboard cover.

"Is this her diary?"

He looked at her expectantly, but her guess was as good as anyone's.

Jeff peered over his shoulder, seeing the pages for the first time. "Something like that. Or a journal or personal log. Go to the back."

Just as she had done, Jared thumbed through the pages and stopped at the folded quarter sheets, which came loose. He tucked the book under his arm and unfolded the duplicate birth certificate.

"Holy shit. What is this?" His gaze jumped to Emma again.

"I'm the last person you should be asking." Even she heard the edge in her voice. The events of this morning angered her. Jared never should have let Mary drag her into this. She should never have been the one to find that damn birth certificate. The ERT team should have discovered it. Then she'd never know about it, never know how low her brother may have stooped. She thought the threatening letter he mailed her was the bottom of the barrel but this—the possibility of an illegitimate unacknowledged child—was the ultimate low. The certainty of Carson Gene Ganesh's biological beginnings gnawed at her. Various scenarios of how and when and why this happened spun in her head. Her chest heaved and her heart pumped erratically. She wanted nothing to do with any of this.

"I'm not involved in this case, remember Detective? Conflict of interest. If there's nothing else, I'll leave now. I have laundry to finish."

The fresh air and chirping birds suffocated her. The events of the last hour had shaken her to the core. She couldn't stop the questions ricocheting through her head. What the hell was going on? Who was Isabelle Ganesh? Who was Carson White? Why did Mary have a copy of that birth certificate? What had her brother done?

Without waiting for Jared's approval, she rushed to her car, digging the keys from her pants pocket as she did. Neither man tried to stop her when she cruised by them and drove down the driveway, clutching the wheel with sweaty palms. For a brief moment, she considered driving to the church. She wanted answers and Mary was rushing to her beloved priest. She turned the opposite way instead. Mary had a difficult time ahead of her telling her son about his father's bastard child.

This wasn't the time for Emma to intrude even though she was family. Well, at least she had been at one time.

She dialed her niece instead.

"Auntie Em, Auntie Em," Vanessa said between giggles. She loved imitating Dorothy's cry in the movie. It never got old.

"What are you up to, Nessie? Have a minute to talk?"

"Sure. I just finished one account and am opening another."

"And is it good news for a prospective buyer?"

"It is. They will be mortgaged to the gills in no time. It sounds like you're driving. What's up?"

Emma smiled at her niece's droll sense of humor. "I'm just leaving Aunt Mary's house. She wanted some clean clothes and other things and the detective in charge of the investigation authorized me to retrieve the stuff. I saw your mom. She was with Mary."

"How's Aunt Mary doing? And my mom for that matter? I haven't talked to her since you asked me to let her know what happened."

Vanessa's relationship with her mother was tenuous at best. She confided more in Emma than she did Ellen.

"They both looked tired. Mary is going to the funeral home today so we'll know those arrangements soon. I have a question for you that I'd like to tiptoe around." Why, she didn't know. It wasn't on her to preserve her brother's reputation. Especially not to Nessie. "Know any skeletons that might have been in your uncle's closet? Any that Mary might have shared with your mom? Something that would really shake the family tree?"

"They probably have a lot of them. Mom doesn't share much with me. Why? Did you find one? A skeleton, I mean."

"Um, maybe." Might as well be honest. The bond she shared with Nessie included being able to talk about anything. It had worked well when Vanessa was a teenager in the throes of battle with her mother. She'd always turned to Emma, once confessing that she eavesdropped on Ellen's calls, read her mail, and searched her purse regularly. When the conflict between mother and daughter became unbearable, Vanessa lived with Emma for several months after graduating high school.

So much like Emma, champing at the bit to leave home at eighteen. Only Emma's way out had been running away to marry Willy Hunter. Two stupid kids with stars in their eyes, weed in their pockets and not a clue about real life. They came to their senses in nine short months and dissolved the marriage, but her brother never let her forget she'd failed. He used to weave it into any conversation, how stupid she was, how immature, and on and on. It was one of the reasons she kept Willy's last name, to disassociate from him. Vanessa was much more sensible.

"I found a birth certificate tucked into a book that looked like a diary that Mary kept. There was no father listed, but your uncle's high school picture was attached to it. It was for a boy born to a woman named Isabelle Ganesh. Ever hear that name?"

"Whaattt? Are you serious?"

"As a heart attack. There's more. A newspaper clipping with a picture of the kid. Well, he's a man now, older than Donnie Jr. He's the spitting image of Don when he was younger. It shocked the hell out of me looking at it. Like seeing a ghost."

"Aunt Em, who is Isabelle Ganesh? I have a cousin, is that what you're saying? What's his name?" Even as she spoke, Emma heard Nessie's fingernails clicking on her keyboard. She'd already begun a name search.

"It still needs to be verified whether or not Don is the father. If Mary knows for certain, she isn't saying. You had no idea?"

"None. But you say Aunt Mary knew? She had the birth certificate?"

"A copy. Yes."

"Wow. That shines a whole different light on things, doesn't it? If Aunt Mary knew about this kid, maybe just found out or..."

She left the sentence unfinished.

"It's a complication, for sure. Listen, I'm heading home now. I'm on second shift through the end of the month. I'll see what I can find on these two. I know you're all over social media already. Let me know what you find. That will save me some time. And don't say anything to your mom or anyone until we find some answers."

"I doubt I'll talk to mom unless she calls with funeral information. Will you be at the funeral?"

"I wasn't planning to go, honey. I'm not going to be a hypocrite now and mourn my dead brother. He was dead to me years ago."

Vanessa's voice quaked. "Please go, Aunt Em. Please be there with me. Don't make me watch all the fake tears and listen to lies about what a good man he was by myself. Please stand beside me. We can stay in the back of the room. Besides, maybe this Ganesh lady and her kid will be there. As a cop, shouldn't you be on the lookout for that?"

Yes, she should, but Jared would have a fit if he discovered she was snooping around trying to learn about the woman. Vanessa was offering a chance to legitimately do that.

"All right. I'll go with you. Once we know the arrangements, we'll figure it out. Since he was my brother, I'm entitled to bereavement time."

"I'll call as soon as I know. Love you, Auntie Em."

"I love you too, Nessie."

∼

VANESSA SENT three text messages by the time Emma arrived at her townhome. She couldn't find any information on Isabelle

Ganesh. She wanted to know the boy's name. He was hardly a boy. He'd be twenty-eight. Don had married Mary when she was three months pregnant and they claimed Donnie Jr. was premature. Only the family knew the truth.

If Carson Gene Ganesh was his son, why hadn't he married his mother two years earlier, before he met Mary? When had he started dating Mary? The timeline in her head was fuzzy. Twenty-plus years ago, she barely paid attention to her older brother, caught up in her own life. Plus, she didn't like him even back then and didn't much care what he did.

Were Carson Gene Ganesh and Carson G. White one and the same?

By now, Jared would have requested a records search. Fortunately, one of her best friends from the police academy was currently working in the records room. She'd arrive at the station early today and make sure Nathan knew to keep notes of whatever he found.

16

"Is it too early to drink?" Jared checked his watch when Jeff laughed. It was barely after noon.

"Only if a liquid lunch is what you have in mind. What if we grab a bite and start to hash all this out? We might think better at an outside café than at the station."

It was a plan. They lugged their briefcases to a far patio table of one of their go-to sandwich shops. No one occupied the nearby tables, so they spoke freely, each lining up a yellow legal pad in front of them and clicking open their pens.

"Let's start with the priest," Jeff suggested. As if mimicking each other, the men wrote the word priest on their tablets and underlined it. "What's your take?"

Jared drew his pocket notebook from his jacket, flipped to the front where he'd written "follow up on the padre" and showed it to Jeff. "Pretty friendly for a man of the cloth. I wonder if he knows everyone's business as well as he knows Mrs. Malvado's."

Father Greg set off something in Jared's brain but, as yet, he couldn't pinpoint it. "Did you notice the change in her when she was in that church? It was as if the church fortified her. And the priest seems pretty touchy-feely for a man sworn to celibacy. Mary Malvado says she'd never break the sixth commandment but how about the seventh?"

Jeff tilted his head to the left. "I don't see it, to be truthful. Yeah, I think that relationship is odd, possibly not on the up and up, but I doubt it's sexual. White underwear and dirty sneakers hardly scream enticing. I don't picture Mary Malvado doing much on her knees besides praying."

"Yeah, I don't see it as sexual either but the word conspirators dances through my head when I see those two together. Let's run a background check on Father Greg, maybe interview some of his flock. We can ask about Mary Malvado at the same time."

"I like it," Jeff said. They both noted the strategy on their yellow pages.

Jared wrote the number two on the sheet and circled it. "We want to surveil the funeral. I'll check with the coroner's office and see where the body goes. The funeral home will provide us visitation and burial details. We should be there for calling hours as well as the Mass and graveside service. Traditionally, there's a luncheon or some type of gathering afterward. We should try to get into that too."

"You think there will be a Mass? Didn't the priest say Malvado wasn't a church member?"

"I think Mary Malvado wouldn't have it any other way and ole Father Greg will do her bidding. Wish we had enough for a search warrant at the church. The weapon could be there."

Jeff scratched his head. "But the timeline doesn't fit. He said Mrs. Malvado left him at the church and drove home."

Jared tapped his pen on the table. "We don't know if she drove home alone. The theory of an accomplice seems feasible." The notion that it could be Emma had surfaced more than once in his thoughts, which was ludicrous. But how had she gotten to the house so quickly?

Jeff jotted 'accomplice' in the margin of his tablet and punctuated it with question marks. "I'll focus on the church part. You take the family members, the ones we know and the ones we have to find."

Jared chuckled and reached in his briefcase for the newly discovered birth certificate. "Isn't this a monkey wrench in the works? A possible illegitimate son. We're living in a soap opera. No one who we interviewed mentioned this kid, did they?"

"Nope."

"It would be too simple to believe that Mary Malvado found out about him and blew her husband away in a heated argument. O'Hare would have a field day in court with that one. It certainly qualifies as a crime of passion. I want to bring her back in for questioning right after the funeral. First, let's see who shows up at this dog and pony show. We'll have to track this kid down. We can't hope he miraculously walks in the door to pay his respects to dear old dad, if Malvado is his father. Wonder what his relationship is with daddy? It's a viable theory that he just found out about his father and blew him away."

Jeff wrinkled his nose. "If he's an attorney, I think he'd follow a legal path, not a violent one."

Jared conceded to that logic. "Well, let's find him sooner than later. We have a window of time until the body is released. I doubt Mrs. Malvado can make funeral arrangements for the weekend so that gives us maybe two days to hunt down both mom and son."

More lines under the name Ganesh on his pad. "I'll swing through the coroner's office on the way back to the station and collect his report. Time of death will be crucial. It could give us a wide-open window for Mary Malvado to blow her husband away and still be on time for Mass. What else needs our immediate attention?"

Jeff scratched his head. "We haven't inventoried Malvado's items from his office yet. Have the IT techs had any luck with his computer password?"

Jared wrote that reminder down as well. "I'll check."

"What about Emma?"

His heart fluttered. "What about her?"

"Under normal circumstances, she's the sister of the victim, and we'd interview her as a matter of course. Finding that birth certificate surprised her but, for the record, one of us should officially ask her about it, and her relationship with her brother. There should be a report for the file."

He and Emma were getting along so well, Jared dreaded the idea of bringing up the topic. He'd seen snippets of hate in Emma's eyes, heard it in her voice when she discussed her brother. It was a side of her new to him. And unsettling.

"I can talk to her," Jeff continued. "That way it's not personal."

Jared met his gaze. Partners confided details of their lives without fear of judgment or betrayal. He could easily tell Jeff about their relationship, especially since he was certain Jeff knew. But Emma had been adamant when they began dating and remained convinced that she would take the hit if they went public.

He'd wanted so badly to stand beside her last month when she received that Catholic Ministries commendation for saving a three-year-old's life. He was so damn proud of her. But she'd begged him not to attend the ceremony because the focus would be on them together and not on her accomplishment. He could see her point, but he didn't want to keep their relationship in the shadows forever. Jeff might have some insight if he discussed it with him, but he'd promised Emma secrecy.

"I'm lead detective, Jeff. I should be the one to interview the victim's sister."

"Then do it here at the station, on company time. Don't do it over drinks or dinner or in the bedroom. Keep it business."

Involuntarily, the corners of his lips edged upward. He couldn't hear the words bedroom and Emma and not smile. Jeff grinned at his reaction.

"You're right. We'll interview her together. She's not high on the priority list, though. She's on second shift through the rest of the month. We can always find her."

"Right. What else?"

Jared reached into his briefcase again. "Let's take a look at this journal." Leaning back, he opened the cover and scanned the first page. "Jesus, the first date is three years ago. There can't be three years of entries in this book. It's too small. Let's see... her handwriting is not as neat as her husband's. Page one. *'I should have started this journal at the beginning of my cancer journey but I'm not much for writing. It's supposed to be therapeutic and help with my healing so here goes. Today I'm cancer-free, according to my five-year medical evaluation,'*" Jared read. "*'I wanted to celebrate but Don said he was busy so I went to the church. The building was locked so I called Father Greg. He held my hand for an hour while we prayed. He's a wonderful man.'*"

Jared looked up to find Jeff's eyes wide.

"The next entry is," he flipped the page back and forth, "four weeks later. She's happy. *'What a wonderful picnic with the whole family, even extended relatives. Don couldn't make it so Donnie Jr. drove me. Everyone seemed more relaxed without him around. It was a good day.'*"

He skipped a handful of pages. "This looks like some holiday entries. *'I worked so hard to make this a nice Christmas. I picked presents for Don that I knew he'd like. He gave me two gift cards.'* Not the most thoughtful of husbands."

Jeff chuckled. "My wife would kill me if I gave her a gift card unless it was stapled to a clothing catalog."

Jared jumped to the back of the journal. "The latter entries are briefer." He sat up straighter in his chair. "Listen to this. *'Father Greg says this will work. I'll try.'*" He flipped the page. "*'He's despicable.' 'I hate him.' 'I wish he would die.'*" On the next page. "*'I could kill him. God, please, guide me. I want him dead.'*"

Jeff leaned in toward him. "What's the date?"

"Two weeks ago."

17

M ary shooed Ellen, Donnie Jr., and Father Greg into the priest's office. Sitting on the metal folding chair in the restroom, she collected her thoughts. Revealing Don's secret was going to cut like a knife to her soul.

Had it only been two weeks since she'd learned about him? It felt like a lifetime of weight on her shoulders. A newspaper announcement about a young man joining a law firm and his picture. The resemblance was unmistakable. The copy of the birth certificate folded beneath it. She almost fainted.

No return address. Nothing else in the envelope. Mailed from somewhere here in the city.

She didn't ask Don about it, knowing he'd deny it and not wishing to subject herself to his rage. He'd distort her question into an invasion of his privacy.

She didn't tell her sister or her son. How could she tell Donnie he had a half-brother somewhere? The veracity of the birth certificate was never in doubt. The face smiling back at her from the newspaper clipping was a younger version of Don. It was the face she fell in love with.

Betrayal wasn't new to her. She'd long suspected there were

other women and couldn't be sure when she stopped caring. But this was a dagger to her very being. They'd gotten pregnant before they were married, and Don pledged his life to her. He was over the moon about the news. How had he reacted when this boy's mother told him she was pregnant?

She'd swallowed her pride and showed the clipping and birth certificate to Father Greg, sobbing in his arms and praying for strength. The name Isabelle was familiar, not that she knew the woman. Was she "the other woman" in Don's life or was Mary the other woman? She'd heard the name back when she and Don first dated, when he was tender and loving and she was important to him. An old girlfriend he mentioned once after she asked about several hang-up calls at the house whenever she answered. "I ran into her sister last week and she probably told her," Don had said, never looking away from the television. "She wants to talk to me but I don't want to be bothered. If you give those kind of people an inch, they never go away."

"What kind of people," she'd asked.

"Trash," he'd answered. "She was nothing but a fling. A friend with benefits. You don't have to be concerned about her. If the phone calls don't stop, we'll change the phone number."

Don had a reputation as a player when they met, so prior girlfriends didn't surprise her and Don said Isabelle exaggerated their brief encounter as something it wasn't.

She'd believed him and the phone calls stopped. The name Isabelle faded into the recesses of her mind.

Based on the news clipping, the mysterious Isabelle was much more than a casual friend. It had taken a full hour to regain her composure after opening the anonymous envelope. Her heart raced so fast, she collapsed onto the desk chair trembling, rubbing her sweaty palms against her thighs, up and down, up and down, and looking around the kitchen as if seeing it for the first time. Had her whole life been a lie?

It took every ounce of strength to drag herself up the stairs, yanking on the banister for each step. She searched Don's desk drawers, tried to break into his locked filing cabinet, read each page in his address book, inspected every piece of paper she could find. Nothing.

For more than a week, she looked at him differently when he came home. Coldly. She found the courage to ask where he was going when he picked up his keys and when he'd be back, scrutinizing his every move, smelling his clothes when he finally did walk in the door, even kissing him to smell his breath. She held every envelope the mailman delivered up to the light and began logging the mileage on his truck each night.

She enlisted help from a college student working at the public library to search public records and social media sites. She peered over the student's shoulder while he searched different apps and groups she didn't know existed, hoping for tweets and pictures and proof. But they were phantoms. Not a trace of the woman or the child, beyond the news clipping.

She toyed with the idea of confronting Don. Father Greg asked if she really wanted to know if Don had another family. The information would only make her life more miserable. For all she knew, Don had a private bank account established to support them. She hadn't found a bankbook but that didn't rule out the possibility. She'd wondered if they lived in a nicer house than she did, if when he walked out of it, he went to her, if Isabelle was happy.

She imagined different settings about Isabelle's life and about Don's role in it. All of them ended the same way. It didn't matter if Don supported Isabelle and her son or if he had nothing to do with them. It didn't affect her one way or the other. She admitted to Father Greg that she was unhappy no matter what the circumstances.

That conversation turned her heart to stone. After that day, she no longer cared whether Don took his blood pressure pills or ate healthy meals. She confessed to Father Greg that she wished him dead. And now he was. But not his secrets.

Father Greg tapped on the bathroom door. "Mary? Are you all right?"

"I'm coming, Father. In a minute."

All eyes turned to her when she entered the office. She gratefully accepted the three-ounce Dixie cup of water Father Greg extended.

Since receiving that cryptic envelope she'd been empty, devoid of emotion. Sappy neglected dog commercials didn't even yield a tear. But seeing Donnie Jr. drop his head into his hands then jump up and punch the wall screaming obscenities broke her heart. So much like his father when he lost his temper. Did his other son have the same trait?

Her sister sat silently, her jaw slack, tears rimming her eyes. Donnie Jr. asked questions she couldn't answer. Why hadn't she confronted his father about this? What else did she know about the woman and her son? Where did they live? Had she tried to contact them? Why not?

Through his tirade she prayed, her beads so tight between her fingers, they pinched. "I-I didn't have the strength to learn the truth. What difference would it have made if you knew, Donnie?"

He looked incredulous. "What difference? I would have moved you out." He pounded his chest. "I would have challenged him on it. I wouldn't have backed down, not this time. What kind of man walks away from his own child?" His arm flailed toward her. "And you, you just stayed with him. Were you planning to live happily ever after with him? You haven't been happy in years. You deny it but I see it. I've watched you wilt. Why didn't you tell me? Together, we could have figured something out."

"Your reaction is exactly why I didn't tell you. He's still your father. He deserves your respect."

"No! Hell no, he doesn't. He deserved what he got. I'm glad he's dead."

Mary crossed herself. "No, Donnie, please don't say that." It was one thing for her to give thanks that Don no longer lived, but his son should mourn him. Honor thy father and mother.

Donnie fell to his knees in front of her and grasped her hands. "Mom, did you do it? Did you kill him? I understand if you did. Everybody in this room would understand. If I had known, I might have done it. I'll get you the finest lawyer. I'll take a second mortgage if I have to. We can—"

"I already have a fine attorney. Emma sent him. This isn't the time—"

"Aunt Emma? You two haven't talked in years. Did you call her? When? You didn't even call me."

This conversation drained her from head to toe. She longed to sit in her spot in the front row of the nave and pray that this whole mess could be over. "I didn't call her. She just showed up."

"With the detectives?"

"No. Before."

She hadn't given a second thought to Emma's arrival at the house. After calling the police, she'd run out the kitchen door and vomited in the hedges. What a mess there was to clean up. The first man to arrive introduced himself as Officer Petrus, placed her in the back seat of his car and relocated it to the far edge of the driveway. Hearing a car door slam, she twisted to look out the rear window and watched Emma walk into the house. She assumed it was her job.

"None of that matters right now, Donnie. Your outrage has to wait. It's giving me a headache." She pressed her fingers to her forehead. "Funeral decisions must be made. We should plan a lunch and, and there are business decisions I'll need advice on. You need to keep your temper in check and help me."

Father Greg's hand settled on her shoulder, telegraphing a wave of comfort through her. "The ladies auxiliary will handle all the luncheon details, Mary. You don't have to give that a second thought. The service can be standard. I'm familiar with your favorite hymns, I'll choose them. Do you have a cemetery in mind? I'll call and make the arrangements. You look so tired. You should rest."

Funny. She'd slept better in the last few nights than she had in years.

18

The resemblance between Carson Ganesh White and Don Malvado was remarkable. Everything about the kid's face was a younger version of the driver's license photo Jared had in his files.

He went by Carson G. White, taking the surname of a man his mother married when he was still a baby. It hadn't taken Jared long to back track to the marriage certificate once he searched Carson's social media friends and found his mother. The marriage hadn't lasted long.

Jared arrived at the law firm unannounced, knowing his badge would open the door and grant him a few minutes of Carson's time. When Carson walked into the conference room Jared caught his breath, as if seeing a ghost.

"Mr. White, thank you for seeing me."

His handshake was firm. "I'm not sure what you're doing here or how I can help you Detective. What's this about?"

"I'm investigating the death of Donald Malvado." Jared watched his face for a reaction, but Carson only raised his hand and slid it down his multi-striped tie. "Do you mind if I ask you some questions?"

"Like I said, I don't know how I can help you."

"Do you know Donald Malvado?"

The slightest tremble of his lips betrayed Carson's composure. "I don't know him, no. I've never met him. The only thing I know about his death is what was reported on the news."

"You've never met him?"

"No sir."

Malvado was shaping up to be a bigger piece of shit than Jared thought. "Do you know who he is, Mr. White?"

Carson filled his lungs and exhaled slowly. "He's the man who got my mother pregnant and then turned his back on her. Biologically, he's my father but that's the extent of it. I've never known him or needed him. The fact that he's dead now doesn't matter to me."

"You knew he was your father yet you never met him?"

"No, sir. I never had a desire to. Who wants to meet a man who abandons his own son? All Donald Malvado ever did for me is teach me the kind of father I want to be if one day I'm blessed with children. Believe me, it will be nothing like him. Beyond that, he's nothing to me or my mother."

His inner strength and conviction surprised Jared. He admired the kid. "May I ask where you were Wednesday morning?"

"Right here. I entered the building at five-fifty-five, my usual arrival time. I didn't leave until after seven that evening. My badge swipes will verify that."

"That's a pretty long day."

He smiled and revealed the same gap in his teeth that Malvado had. "Yes sir. I'm a grunt right now. Long days are in my future for the next five years at least."

Jared returned his smile. "It will be worth it in the end."

"Yes sir."

"May I ask you about your mother? Has she had any contact with your—er, Mr. Malvado that you know of?"

"I highly doubt it. She hasn't had any contact with him since I was born. He threatened to sue her for harassment and ruin her life if she even hinted that he was the father of her baby. My mother struggled for a lot of years, working two jobs to provide for me. It destroyed her. She's little more than a shell now, still working as a waitress at a family-owned restaurant but she has no life. Only me."

"I'm sorry to hear that. How long have you known who your biological father was?"

"I think I was about eight years old when I started asking questions. My mother was blunt and told me my father didn't want me. It didn't matter. I have two uncles who are like fathers to me, and an aunt who raised me while my mother worked. I looked him up when I got older, even drove past his house one day. But I had no interest in meeting him. Well, I guess that's not possible now anyway."

"Did your mother's siblings know who your father was?"

Carson shrugged. "I guess so. You have to understand, he wasn't someone we talked about. Ever. He was nothing to any of us."

"How did your mother react when she heard the news about his death?"

"I don't know."

"You didn't talk about it?"

"Never mentioned it."

"I'd like to speak to your mother."

Carson straightened. "You can do that, but I insist that I be present. Come to my cubicle and I'll see what I can arrange."

Isabelle Ganesh White was working the early shift and was unavailable to meet with Jared until four-thirty. Jared shook Carson's hand and accepted his invitation to meet them both at her restaurant, but he left the law building knowing he was spinning his wheels.

The time for Isabelle Ganesh White to kill Malvado was twenty-eight years ago when he left her alone and pregnant, not now when she and her son had risen above it and succeeded. His father's existence wasn't news to Carson. But was Carson's existence news to Mary Malvado?

19

Emma shrugged into the jacket of her black pantsuit mulling over the new information she'd collected after receiving Nathan's notes. Isabelle Ganesh married and divorced Douglas White shortly after her son was born. She'd kept the White name, which was why every trace to her as Ganesh led to a dead-end. Her son, Carson, kept a low profile until college, where he excelled. He went by the name Carson G. White, even though no adoption papers were on record.

Emma dragged her favorite black stilettos from the closet and smiled as she slipped into them. These shoes always made her feel sexy. Not exactly the right attitude for a funeral service, but who cared? Jared would be there, and she wanted to make sure he noticed her. Seeing each other while she worked three-to-eleven was difficult and soon, she'd be on midnights. The red silk camisole underneath her jacket was purely for spite. She wasn't mourning this passing.

As agreed, Nessie waited for her in the parking lot and, clutching her hand, they entered the funeral home together. Mary had arranged for friends and relatives to pay their respects two hours before the one o'clock service at the church, which sat a block away from this building. Emma had memorized Isabelle and Carson's driver's license photos. She'd also found a chess championship photo of Carson from college. He was the spitting image of her brother when he was younger. If either of them showed up, she'd recognize them.

Jeff stood at the far wall of the lobby entrance, nonchalantly noticing everyone who arrived. Only Emma knew it wasn't so casual. She covertly acknowledged him when they made eye contact and drew Nessie into the main viewing room. Mary stood at the front beside the closed casket, the ever-present beads shifting through her fingers. A picture of her brother propped on top of the coffin stared back at the mourners. Father Greg moved among the grievers like he worked a bingo game, clasping hands and chatting softly.

Jared's eyes widened when he saw them. She drew Nessie with her to the back of the room.

"What are you doing here?" His voice was gruff. "You hate funerals and, if I'm to believe you, you have no sympathy for your dead brother. Once again, I'm surprised to find you rushing to him."

She ignored the attitude. Jared always became irritable with a problematic case. "Detective Jones, I'd like you to meet my niece, Vanessa. Nessie, this is Jared, the guy you keep wondering about when you pry into my social life."

Vanessa displayed her most charming grin, eyed him up and down and shook Jared's hand. "It's nice to meet you. Don't worry, my lips are sealed." She moved her fingers across her lips as if zipping them closed and grinned wider. "Auntie Em wasn't planning to come, but I begged her not to let me go through this alone. I hate these things almost as much as her, if not more. And this one especially."

Jared was in investigative mode. The vein in his neck pulsed, a telltale sign. "Why this one especially?"

Vanessa's face sobered. "I didn't like my uncle very much. Not at all, really. He wasn't a nice man."

Emma didn't want Jared interrogating her here. She reached to touch her arm. "Why don't you go up front, hug Aunt Mary, let your mom know you're here and then come back to us if you want?"

The grown woman morphed into the child she remembered. She wrung her hands. "Aren't you coming with me?"

"No, honey, I'll stay back here. Mary knows I'm here. She saw us walk in. Go on, you'll be fine."

Vanessa frowned and moved away from them at the pace of an ancient tortoise.

She turned her smile on Jared, but it dissipated when he scowled at her. "You've had no contact with your brother or his family for years and yet recently, you can't seem to stay out of their affairs."

Her heart sank. "For Christ's sake, Jared, I wasn't going to come. Nessie asked me to be here with her. She was expected to show up, and she didn't want to do it alone. Stop reading something more into my presence. If you want the truth, I thought maybe this surprise illegitimate son and his mother might be here. I'm very curious about them. And contrary to what you think, I'm not rushing to my brother *again*."

"You don't know the woman or the kid?"

"Never heard of them."

"How long do you think Mary knew about them?"

A question she'd asked herself a dozen times. "I don't know."

He inclined his head toward Vanessa who chatted with Donnie Jr. off to the side of the room. "What about your niece? Did she know?"

"No. She was shocked." She crossed her fingers against her thigh, silently hoping Vanessa wasn't asking Donnie about his half-brother. The conversation looked amiable. Had Donnie Jr. known too?

Jared tapped her elbow. "Are you going up to pay your respects?"

"Hell no. Respect is the last thing I had for him. His wife and family are better off." She scanned the room. No signs of Diane, their daughter. She'd had plenty of time to drive here.

"I'm tempted to lift the coffin lid just to make sure he's in there," she said. When Jared swore under his breath, she chuckled. "Will you relax? I'm on my best behavior. Five-O is watching."

His face softened. "Sorry. This is a new side of you I'm not used to. I've seen you be kinder to criminals."

She discreetly brushed her fingers across his side. "No, I'm sorry. My brother brings out the worst in me. Always has. Are you staying for the duration?"

"That's the plan."

"Mind if Nessie and I sit in the back with you and Jeff at the church?"

"Your niece doesn't want to be with family?"

"My niece doesn't want to be here at all. We'll buy you lunch afterward. You can't turn down an invitation from two sexy women, can you?"

"Don't you have to be at work at three?"

She chuckled. "I've had a death in the family. I'm entitled to three days bereavement." She winked. "And three nights."

20

So many people trudged into the funeral home. More than Mary ever would have imagined. Many of them introducing themselves for the first time. All expressing sorrow that Don was "gone too soon." Seriously? Were they truly sorry about that?

Standing beside his casket, her feet hurt, and her belly growled. Breakfast hadn't appealed to her earlier but now, the hot tea was crying for a piece of toast or muffin to absorb it. The nonstop argument with Donnie had done little to ease her nerves. He'd phoned someone at his office—computer guru, he called him—and instructed him to search for Miss Ganesh and her son. He'd pounded the table when Mr. Guru came back with nothing, ordering the poor man to look harder.

She wasn't spared his wrath either, insisting she must know more. So much like his father, it saddened her.

Mindlessly, she shook hands as unfamiliar faces filed past her, smiled at the kind words directed toward her, and kept Father Greg in sight. He'd assured her God would give her the strength she needed to survive this day. It didn't feel like it. Her back ached. The floral sweetness of the room gagged her.

Where had all these baskets and flower displays come from? How would she send thank you cards if she didn't know who sent them?

Two cousins stood off to the side whispering so loudly she heard them marveling that she appeared so resilient, withholding her tears until a private moment, they guessed. They'd be surprised.

Emma stood in the back beside Detective Jones. She looked elegant in a sleek pantsuit. Why wasn't she in uniform? Donnie told her Detective Widows was in the outer room watching everyone who walked in the front door. Donnie was angry the police were there, intruding on their grief, but Detective Jones fed him the same line as in church. His father's killer might be among the mourners.

She wished she knew he was. That was one hand she'd like to shake.

At least the funeral allowed her to see some relatives she hadn't seen in what, maybe two years. No one visited them or invited them for dinner anymore, all busy with their own lives she supposed. Maybe that could change now that...

JARED STOOD between Jeff and Emma whispering, "Should we look at who's here or who isn't? I admit to being at a loss."

"There's the business acquaintances on that side," Jeff's gaze moved toward the right. The bar owners looked rather flamboyant chatting animatedly with the two burly service station guys wearing work boots and their sleeves rolled up to their elbows. They all walked up to Mary Malvado, shook her hand and spoke a few words. But none of them made use of the kneeler in front of the coffin or even glanced in that direction. Malvado's other tenant, the realtor who leased office space, sent flowers.

Once everyone vacated this room for the church, he and Jeff would write down the names on all the cards and take pictures of the register the visitors were signing.

Emma leaned into him. "That's Mary's family on that side. The woman with the wad of tissue in her hand is Mary's cousin but they grew up like sisters. I remember her at several family functions. The others milling around are distant relations.

"Those two men near the door are friends from Don's high school days. I used to have a crush on the one on the left."

Jared's heart jumped and he leveled his gaze on her.

Emma's smile tingled his toes. "I was ten years old. Every young girl has a crush on at least one of her older brother's friends." She winked at him.

"I don't see any of the neighbors I spoke with," Jeff whispered. "Considering the proximity of the homes, that's not suspicious."

Emma cleared her throat. "Since no one is going to mention the elephant in the room, or rather the one that isn't, I don't see the mystery mother and child. I suppose they could show up only for the service."

A laugh escaped him before he could stop it. His attraction to Emma existed on several levels. Physical for sure. The dip of that red camisole was driving him crazy. It was also the sensual undertone of her voice on the phone when they spoke privately. And her penchant to call a spade a spade, to get right to the heart of the matter. She and Jeff anxiously awaited the appearance of Isabelle Ganesh White and her son.

But based on Jared's meetings with both yesterday, he doubted they'd make an appearance. Emma wasn't aware that he'd met her nephew and his mother. There'd be time to talk about that later. He hadn't been able to brief Jeff either. Only a hastily whispered, "dead-end."

Isabelle Ganesh White burst into tears when he met her,

kissing her son on the cheek and motioning for Jared to sit in the vacant booth.

"I'm sorry, Detective." He leaned forward to hear her soft voice. "Don was a bastard. A son of a bitch. There aren't enough curse words to accurately depict him. But he was the love of my life. My heart is broken."

Isabelle Ganesh White had no sooner gotten her emotions under control when he asked his first question and the dam broke again.

"When was the last time you saw Don Malvado, Ms. White?" Her son reached for her hand, more support than Donnie Jr. had exhibited.

A sad smile graced her face. "Twenty-seven years ago, Detective. Carson wasn't quite one year old when I showed up at his gas station. It was still a filling station then. He'd said he wanted nothing to do with me when I told him I was pregnant. I thought maybe, if he met his son, he'd change his mind. Carson was an adorable baby." Her eyes misted and her lips trembled. "But he turned us away. He denied that Carson was his son and threatened to sue me if I claimed publicly that he was. He even called the police and reported me as a trespasser. He threatened to take out a restraining order against me."

She talked at length about when they were young teenagers experimenting with love and sex for the first time, her first kiss and more. Her eyes shone while she recalled those days and Jared felt a pang in his heart for this woman so harshly discarded. But her information was about the past. She'd had no contact with Malvado since that emotionally wrenching day. Still her heart broke that he had died. Jared's instinct was right. She wasn't their killer.

He returned his focus to Mary Malvado at the front of the room, meeting and greeting. He hadn't seen her cry at all, not like Isabelle. Her husband was dead. Wasn't her heart broken like Isabelle's? Don Malvado had married and provided for her. Where were her tears?

Emma tugged on his fingers and leaned in. "Their daughter Diane isn't here. She's three years younger than Donnie. She left right after high school. I thought she'd show up to support her mother at least."

"Were they close?"

"No one in that family is close."

Terrence O'Hare strutted in, scanned the room and headed straight to Mary, his arms open. His size dwarfed her. She endured his bear hug and introduced him to her son. Donnie Jr. launched into a verbal diatribe that apparently made Mary uncomfortable. She blanched and drew her son off to the side, shaking her head. Jared would've loved to hear the conversation, but the facial expressions were just as telling. Donnie Jr. was angry and Mary was madder than a pitcher who throws the home run ball that loses the championship.

O'Hare shook hands with Father Greg. When did those two meet?

He glad-handed a few other people and strolled to them. "Detectives. Doing your due diligence, I see."

Jared reached for his outstretched hand. "Terry, how are you?"

"Fine, Jared." He eyed Emma. "Private citizen looks good on you, Miss Hunter. May I speak with you for a moment? Outside?"

"Sure."

Jared followed her exit with his eyes and so did Mary, taking in every step until they disappeared.

His attention returned to the group when Father Greg clapped his hands. "Everyone. Everyone, may I have your attention please." Mary stepped up beside him. Emma's niece searched the room for her, coming to stand beside him. "Where's my aunt?"

"She stepped out for a minute. You're fine here, hon."

"Thanks. There are some intense vibes bouncing around up there. It feels safer back here."

Jared faced her. "What do you mean? And remember, you're talking to a detective."

"Yeah, but you're cool, like my aunt." Her shoulders lifted and lowered. "My mother is mad. She thinks Aunt Mary killed him. She's worried Mary will be arrested. She couldn't survive going to jail. My mom never cared for my cousin Donnie. He's like a chip off the old block, just as callous as his dad. She thinks he's going to abandon his mother. She's not happy that I'm with Aunt Em. Those two never really liked each other, I'm not sure why. Mom didn't have any nice things to say about you, either."

Jared smiled.

"They'd both have a bird if they knew you and Aunt Em had a thing."

He pursed his lips and Vanessa laughed. "Remember?" She zipped her lips shut with her fingers and threw away the imaginary key.

"Donnie is pretty pissy too. I don't get why he's angry. His dad was mean to him all his life. But he's got his shorts in a knot about something. Do you think they told him about the newest member of the family?"

Jared eyed her. "What do you know about that?"

"My aunt told me. She wondered if I'd ever heard my mom and Aunt Mary talking about him. I was a credible sleuth in my younger days. I snooped through all my mother's stuff." She grinned with pride. "But I never heard about the b-child." Air quotes punctuated her words.

"You're pretty close with Emma then?"

Her eyes glistened. "I wish she were my mother."

Involuntarily, he smiled. Emma as a mother was a role he'd

never considered. "That's quite a compliment. I'm not sure your aunt would like the idea of having a kid."

"Well she'd be good at it, trust me. She has a knack for talking to me, calms me down, lifts me up, motivates me, whatever it is I need. I tell Aunt Em things I've never told my mother." She jabbed Jared's shoulder. "Maybe you two could have a kid. I'd be a great aunt. I've had the best role model."

Beside him, Jeff chuckled. To Jared's relief, Emma returned to them, reaching for Vanessa's hand and kissing her cheek. "You okay?" This was the Emma he knew, soft and loving.

Emma's influence over the girl was obvious. She was spunky, with a quick wit and a bring-it-on attitude. Her mother cowered in the corner, so Vanessa hadn't learned that from her.

"Aunt Mary is having Uncle Don cremated, did you know that?" Emma's face said she didn't. "My mom said Mary doesn't want him buried in a grave she has to visit. I get that, but isn't that against the Catholic faith?"

The same question crossed his mind. What happened to the resurrection of the body?

Father Greg's voice boomed through the room. "If you would all please gather in a circle, I'd like to lead you in a few prayers before we move to the church for the funeral service. Please, please, everyone gather around. Let's take each other's hands."

Mary's hand slipped into her priest's.

The four of them remained against the back wall, incurring stares from Mary and Junior. Emma didn't bow her head. Her eyes roamed the room, following every sniffle and sob. As a grieving family member, she fell way short. But she'd make a helluva detective someday.

21

Father Greg's voice droned on and on, describing someone's husband who was dead. Certainly not hers. Mary didn't recognize the benevolent, enterprising, loving father and husband who Father Greg described. He wasn't lying—that was a sin—but he put a spin on the truth that surprised her.

Yes, Don had rushed to her rescue in the pouring rain when she had a flat tire on the way home from the dentist. Father Greg failed to add that he screamed at Mary for waking him up, threw his auto club card at her and left her standing in the downpour. Sure, he kept a roof over her head and food on the table. He didn't reveal that the roof leaked and so much food was wasted in the meals he walked out on or turned cold when he was hours late for dinner.

He absolutely attended all of Donnie's little league football and baseball games, screaming from the stands that Donnie played like a faggot and the referees and umpires were blind, stupid or idiots. Donnie didn't pursue sports in high school.

She stood when everyone stood, knelt with them, sang the

hymns by rote. She only wanted it to be over. Through the entire service, Donnie's rage simmered, so much so that her left arm felt warm standing beside him. Her sister's aloof attitude cooled her other arm. The knot in her back had to be Emma's eyes riveted on her. The stiffness across her shoulders was from the detectives' scrutiny. They suspected her of killing Don. Ellen thought so too. Probably half the people praying behind her wondered if she'd finally found the nerve. She squirmed. It didn't matter. After today, she was free.

Emma keeping her distance at the funeral home and standing in the last row now made sense. But why was Vanessa back there too, instead of up here with her mother? What had Don done to her? She couldn't ask. He'd never had a kind word for her once she moved out on Ellen. In Don's mind, a woman didn't leave home unless she was getting married and leaving to take care of her husband. He shunned his daughter after she left. Don often said Mary had done it right. A virgin who moved straight from her parents' home to the one he died in to take care of him. It was over.

Mercifully, Father Greg was wrapping up the service with a final prayer. Thank God. Seriously.

Ever the gracious hostess, she stood in the church vestibule as people filed out to thank them for coming and direct them down the stairs to the community room. The aroma of fried chicken and rigatoni sickened her. Only a couple more hours of this charade.

No lunch invitation for the detectives, but they weren't walking out of here without her speaking to them. She waited. The looks on their faces hinted they thought the vestibule was empty when they finally exited the sanctuary.

"Detective Jones? Thank you for paying your respects. Or are you here because you believe my husband's killer walks among us?" If she sounded bitter, she was. Why wasn't he out looking for whoever murdered Don? Not that she cared much who or why her life was drastically altered seven days earlier. But these men watching her every move was unnerving. They should spy on someone else.

She peered over his shoulder. Emma and Vanessa sat with them in the rear of the church for the service, but where had they disappeared to? "Wouldn't your time be better spent finding the person responsible for all of this?"

The vein in his neck visibly pulsed. His partner avoided eye contact with her. "I'd like to go home, Detective. This afternoon. Is there any reason why I can't?"

By now, all that blood on the floor and sofa was dried and hard. It would be impossible to clean. New carpets would be a nice change. Easier to rip up that room than to try to preserve the rug. Same with the furniture. The way the sun flooded that space in the afternoon, a new brighter pattern would pop in there. In fact, the entire house would feel lighter without Don. His presence created a heaviness wherever he sat.

Father Greg's footfalls ascending the stairs straightened her shoulders. "Detective? Do I have to say please?"

"No ma'am, no." His cell phone appeared. "Allow me a minute to check that the premises are clear." He stepped outside and his partner followed.

Father Greg turned his sparkling hazel gaze on her. "Is everything all right?"

"Yes, Greg. I'm ready to move forward with my life."

THE RAZOR sharp scent of antiseptic smacked her in the face the second she opened the kitchen door. She tugged her sweater tighter. They never kept the house this cool. Five steps into the kitchen and she gasped. It was spotless. The stainless steel sink shone. The dish drainer was empty. The desk beside the refrigerator that she left her purse on was cleared except for a pile of mail bundled with a rubber band. Hadn't there been food on here last week?

Bracing herself for the mess that waited for her in the living room she moved forward and gasped. How could this be? The room was immaculate. The knick-knacks on the mantle shined. Someone had washed the windows. The coffee table held only the TV remote. And the sofa. The sofa looked worn but almost new. There were no bloodstains, no discoloration of any kind.

She stepped farther into the room and stared at the wall behind the couch. Clearly there was a spot on the wall where the drywall was repaired, but care had been taken to minimize the contrast to the rest of the area. Only a discerning eye could find it. Who had cleaned these rooms? She'd expected to spend days doing it. The corners of her mouth lifted. The house was lighter already.

She took the stairs two at a time to the second floor, a box of heavy-duty trash bags tucked under her arm. She glanced into the office, surprised to find it empty. Don's computer was gone, his desk cleaned of everything that was on top of it. She opened the desk drawer. Good, the address book she told them about wasn't there. In fact, every drawer in the desk was empty. All the boxes that crowded the floor were gone. The room looked so much bigger. The police took everything but the furniture. Would they return all his files? Other than current records for his businesses, she didn't need all the crap he kept. They'd done her a favor. No need to clean out this room.

She headed to the master bedroom, crinkling her nose at the stale air and throwing open the window. Don kept this room a mess. His cell phone and keys were missing from the nightstand. Where was his wallet? Tucked in a back pocket of a pair of jeans, maybe. Damn, she'd have to search his clothes before throwing them and everything in this room in the garbage. There wasn't anything here she wanted to keep, not even the bedding. She snapped on a pair of black latex gloves and grinned. Just like Emma wore.

22

J ared and Jeff returned to the office after a late lunch with Emma and her niece. That had been a fun two hours sitting beside her in the booth listening to Vanessa tell tales about a younger Emma. They'd easily laughed at Emma's feigned embarrassment over secrets Vanessa spilled and Emma's threats to never confide in Nessie again. He liked her.

Back at the office, they tackled the bags and boxes of evidence collected from the sweep of Malvado's office and bedroom. Jared looked at Jeff over the mound of files and folders removed from Malvado's filing cabinet. "I'll say one thing for the guy. He kept meticulous records. Some of these receipts go back ten years. I'm not an accountant, but I think he was cheating the IRS. But I doubt the feds killed him." He moved the income tax returns to the side and picked up Malvado's folder marked tenants.

"The tenant leases look standard. There's an automatic five percent rent increase every year. That's a little steep, but those businesses are thriving. They must not have been deterred."

Jeff raised his gaze from the laptop screen. "Even if they

were, where else would they find such prime commercial property to operate from? Malvado had them between a rock and a hard place. Find anything from the so-called business partners who he stiffed?"

"Not really. Two contracts that look valid. One for a private charter business out of Florida and one for what looks like a security business, both with the same man, Lester West. He's the Rhode Island guy who admitted to a rocky relationship with Malvado, an on-again-off-again enduring friendship he called it. His alibi checked out. He hasn't left the state in months."

"Doesn't mean he didn't hire someone."

"Yeah, but these business deals went south years ago. That's a long time to carry a grudge. And it doesn't feel like a professional hit, even though whoever committed this crime was savvy about leaving evidence behind. Not a fingerprint, strand of hair or shoe imprint from anyone except Mary Malvado. Tell me you're having better luck finding something on his computer that's helpful."

"Not really. His computer skills aren't all that great. It looks like he used this like a word processor and not much else. I'm not finding any electronic payments, no social media accounts, no personal files with photos or notes. His recent online searches are for different weapons, mostly high-powered rifles. Wonder what he wanted with them."

"Based on a partial shell he recovered from the head, the coroner said the murder weapon was definitely a shotgun. Was Malvado searching for any shotguns?"

Jeff shook his head.

Jared turned a ledger page. "Looks like he still wrote checks for everything. And he balanced his checkbook every month. I haven't balanced mine in years. I don't find anything out of the ordinary in the personal account or the business. No payments to Isabelle Ganesh White or her son."

"I don't know, Jared, maybe we're looking in the wrong direction. Our focus has been on Mr. Malvado, but maybe we need to look a little closer at the missus. Does she have a computer? Where is it? We believe we found her journal by happenstance, but did we? She specifically told Emma to look for it in her nightstand. Why mention it if she didn't want us to find it? Is she deliberately misleading us to cover for someone else? You've suspected something like that all along. Neither one of us thinks she did it herself. Our initial search warrant allowed us to seize any articles belonging to Donald Malvado deemed pertinent to his murder. The ERT agents looked everywhere a weapon might be concealed, but they couldn't search that house for items related to Mary Malvado and motive like a laptop or tablet. What's in her car? What's under her mattress? Is that the only journal she kept or is there another one?"

The more Jeff talked, the more Jared liked the logic. He'd witnessed Mary Malvado transform from meek, helpless widow to empowered survivor of a tragedy. She was a chameleon for sure.

"You might be right. Let's bring her back in for a chat. I'll call the judge. Her wishes recorded in the diary justify a follow-up search warrant. I want her cell phone records too. Maybe they're more revealing than her husband's, although his substantiates there was no love lost between the two. Maybe we'll get lucky and find a thread with her conspirator, whoever that is."

Jared tossed the phone company logs across the table in frustration. "Malvado's phone records aren't any help. He rarely texted. Maybe he was smart enough to delete conversations. I guess we could check the cloud to be sure. A couple texts to the bar owners telling them when he'd swing by for the rent check. His texts are mostly back and forth with his wife, some of them rather brusque. The more I get to know this guy, the more I want to applaud whoever whacked him."

Jeff chuckled. "Emma will be happy to hear that. I think the funeral disappointed her. It was a non-moment for sure. Have you told her yet that you met the Whites?"

Jared frowned. This was a dilemma for him. "No. The lead detective in a homicide case wouldn't ordinarily keep a family member informed about the investigation, would he? Her mind is brilliant, Jeff, and there have been several cases that she's talked me onto the right path. But when the subject of her brother comes up, she mutates into someone I don't recognize."

"We haven't interviewed her yet. Want to do that tomorrow? Does she come on at three?"

"No, she's off three days for bereavement leave."

Jeff burst out laughing, and Jared shrugged. "She hated her brother but she's taking advantage of paid personal leave. Go figure. I'm seeing her tonight."

"Find something else to talk about besides Malvado. Dial her up now and give me the phone. I'll schedule a time for us to meet with her here."

EMMA WAS QUIETER than usual at dinner that night. "Everything okay?"

She shrugged. "Nessie and I stopped for a drink after lunch."

That surprised him. She had another drink in front of her. "A little early to hit the sauce, wasn't it?"

She laughed, the creases in her forehead momentarily disappearing. "It was, for both of us. I'm ready for a nap. But we needed to settle our nerves and, I hate to say, toast my late brother's departure. It wouldn't have been appropriate to do it in front of you and Jeff. And neither of you was imbibing.

"So, after we split from you two, we stopped. Nessie asked me about my feelings and," she paused, "and I couldn't find them. I have no feelings one way of the other about my brother's murder. I mean, I know he's dead but I'm not saddened by his death."

Odd that Mary Malvado said almost the same thing, that she didn't feel anything for her dead husband. Maybe the man really was a prick.

Emma swallowed a large gulp of beer. "Do you think this job has jaded me so much that I've grown cold? That I can't feel anything anymore?"

"You're absolutely capable of feeling, Em. I can attest to that first-hand." At the idea of making love to her later tonight, he smiled. She'd be anything but cold.

She smiled too. "I guess my Catholic upbringing is resurrecting itself. The Catholics thrive on guilt, you know."

"You have nothing to feel guilty about, do you? You said you cut yourself off from your brother because he was toxic for you. You said you didn't regret it. If that's true, then it's not unreasonable that you don't feel anything. *If* that's the truth."

She emptied her mug without responding and signaled for another. For not feeling anything, she sure was drinking a lot more. "How come you didn't embrace your sister-in-law today and express your sympathy?"

"What d'you mean?"

"You didn't give her the time of day at the funeral home."

"I wasn't going to pretend to mourn him. I'm not a fraud."

"That's not what I'm saying. You rush to the house when the call comes in because you say you were concerned about Mary. You declare at the scene that Mary isn't guilty, like some momma bear protecting its cub. You retain the slickest lawyer in the city, on your dime. O'Hare isn't cheap. Yet you stand at the other end of the room from her at a time when I would imagine she needs the most support, and you don't even acknowledge her. And now, for the second time since he died, you're getting drunk."

She lowered her glass to the table. "I'm not getting drunk. Mary knew I was there. I didn't have to make a show of it."

"What about your nephew? The two of you embraced at the house and you promised to help, yet you didn't say one word to him this afternoon. It was obvious he was rattled, probably because of the news his mother gave him. He was ready to go ballistic. Your niece, who isn't really your niece, tells me you are a calming influence for her, but you ignored your biological nephew's blatant foul mood."

"I have a different relationship with Nessie."

"You're still Don Jr.'s aunt. None of it makes sense. What's really bothering you, sweetheart?"

She lifted her hands, palms up. "What doesn't make sense? I'm a cop. I was a cop the day of the murder, and I was a cop today waiting and watching. I wasn't there to grieve or to console anyone." She picked up her beer again and ignored his question.

"How's the case coming? I'm being officially interviewed when I return to work. Jeff called today. I doubt I'll be much help, but I understand the protocol. Any of his acquaintances raise your suspicions? Maybe I know them."

He ignored Jeff's caution. "So far, no one. Not many people liked him, but everyone seemed to tolerate him."

Emma pursed her lips, looking beyond him at some unknown spot. "Yeah, that's right. Until he broke that final straw, uttered that one last damaging statement, leveled that ultimate threat that pushed you over the edge until tolerance was impossible. Until he forced you to..."

As if snapping back from a horrific journey, she shook her head and looked around, surprised at her surroundings. "I, ah, sorry. I kinda got lost there. I shouldn't day drink." Despite her disclaimer, she emptied her glass and caught the waitress's attention for another.

"I know you don't want to discuss your brother, Em, but maybe it would help if you talked to me about him. You—"

"No it wouldn't."

"You don't have to snap my head off. He really does bring out the worst in you, doesn't he?"

"You have no idea."

23

J ared paced his office. Emma was coming in first thing this morning for her interview. He was never nervous about interviewing family members, but this one had him on edge. Emma was more than the sister of the victim. She was a smart cop. He suspected she'd ask as many questions as Jeff would. She had a knack for flipping a conversation, which he warned Jeff about.

She breezed into the police station wearing his favorite flowered sundress and red high-heeled sandals. She was like a sexy garden of color. The scent of her perfume teased him. His pillowcase still smelled like her. She chuckled when Jeff recited the time, date and people present.

"This feels so weird, doesn't it?" She crossed her legs, giving him a sneak peek at her thigh, and he gulped. "I'm used to questioning victims, trying to learn the circumstances of what happened to them. I never stopped to think about what it feels like to be on this side of the table. This is good to give me the victim's perspective. It will be educational."

Jeff cleared his throat. "We're on the record, Miss Hunter. Tell me about your brother."

"What would you like to know?"

Typical Emma.

"What was your relationship?"

"We didn't have a relationship. Not for at least ten years, maybe more."

"And why was that?"

"What do you mean?"

"What caused you to be estranged? Did something happen?"

"Something like what?"

"That's what I'd like you to tell me."

Emma looked around the room, then shrugged. "It wasn't any one thing, Detective, it was a culmination of years of his bullshit that I walked away from. Being around him was unhealthy for me."

"So, you had no contact with him or his wife in how many years?"

"As I already said, at least ten years or more."

"And you aren't familiar with his routines or his acquaintances?"

"Not at all."

"Where were you the morning your brother was killed?"

"I was on patrol in Zone Six. I reported to work about seven-thirty and went out on the road about seven-fifty. I was on duty when the emergency call transmitted."

"On the road? Do you remember the neighborhood or the street?"

"Well, I was actually ten-seven, grabbing a coffee and an egg sandwich. I heard the call on the portable. And, for the record, I paid for breakfast."

He and Jeff chuckled. Leave it to Emma to include that in the statement.

"And what did you do then?"

"I checked with my supervisor, clocked out, and drove to

the location. I received permission to use the squad car, since it was an emergency."

"That's your take-home car, right?"

"Yes sir."

"Why did you feel the need to respond?"

"It was instinctive, I guess. I recognized the address as my brother's house."

"But you were estranged from him."

Emma laughed. "Ah, yes. Family is the other F-word, Detective. But he was family."

Suddenly, Jared didn't recognize this woman. What kind of answer was that?

"What did you observe once you arrived at the crime, er, excuse me, at your brother's house?"

"There was a cruiser running at the far end of the house, but I didn't see any uniforms outside so I went inside, expecting to find someone there."

Jared reached for his notebook and made a note to confirm that with Petrus.

"How did you gain entry?"

"I entered through the kitchen door. They've never used the front door, always that door."

"How did you know that hadn't changed? It's been ten years since you were there."

She blinked and blinked again. "My brother was a creature of habit. He resisted change. But to answer your question, I didn't know for certain that the kitchen door was the usual means of entry. It's how I always entered the house, and it's how I entered it that morning."

"What time was that?"

Involuntarily, she checked her watch. "I don't know the precise time but I believe it was about five minutes before you and Detective Jones arrived. I spoke with Officer Petrus and Sergeant Taylor that morning. Perhaps they noted the time."

She reached for her left earlobe. She was anxious. "Have you checked with them?"

"We will." Jeff wrote a note on the pad in front of him.

"So, you drive up to the house, see a patrol unit parked there but, instead of approaching whoever is in the cruiser, you enter the house."

"That's correct. I wasn't concerned about who was in the car."

"What were you concerned about?"

"The ten code."

"The possible dead body?"

"Yes sir."

"Did you know it was your brother?"

"No, I didn't know who it was."

"Were you surprised to discover it was your brother?"

Her left earlobe had to hurt by now. She twisted it. "No. No, I can't truthfully say I was surprised."

"Why is that?"

"He wasn't a likeable man."

"Couldn't he have changed in the ten years since you'd seen him?"

"He hadn't."

"How do you know?"

"I'm still in touch with other family members. My niece, to be specific. I'm very aware of the rants my brother has thrown in the last ten years and his conduct toward other family members that was just plain mean and spiteful. He hadn't changed."

"So, you weren't surprised to find your brother brutally murdered in his living room. What were you?"

"Excuse me?"

"How did it feel seeing your brother dead? You weren't surprised, but were you saddened? Relieved? Angry that someone ended his life that way?"

Emma folded her hands in her lap and smiled. "I wasn't anything, Detective. I didn't feel anything at all."

"That's a little disturbing, don't you think."

Emma grinned. "No, I don't."

"What did you do when you saw him?"

"What did I do? What do you mean?"

"Did you burst into tears? Did you scream? Did you look for the patrolman who belonged to the squad car? Did you wonder what happened?"

"I-I didn't do anything. I just stood there until Officer Petrus asked me to leave."

"Did you hear Officer Petrus enter the house?"

"No, no I didn't."

"Where were you when Officer Petrus found you?"

"In the living room. I didn't go into any of the other rooms."

Jeff leaned in closer, his brows knitted. "You just stood in the living room staring at the dead body of your brother?"

A brief grin crossed Emma's face again. "Actually, I was staring at his high school picture, thinking back to our childhood, thinking that the picture reflected his true colors even then."

"How so?"

"It was his eyes. All those years ago, they displayed his meanness. I never saw it until I looked at that picture that morning. It was validating."

His head jerked faster than Jeff's. "You don't think that's an odd word to use after finding your brother dead? What did you find validating about it?"

Emma stared at him, her dark brown eyes hard. "That I-I-I cut him out of my life."

She continued to stare until Jeff looked away.

"Take me back to when you arrived at the house. You saw a police car there but ignored it and went into the house through the kitchen door because ten years ago, that's how you used to walk into their home."

Emma smiled. Jared did as well, knowing Emma like he did. If the roles were reversed, she'd pose the question exactly the same, implying that what she did was somehow wrong. She wasn't thrown.

"When you phrase it like that, it sounds rather sinister but yes, that's what I did."

"Was the door opened or closed?"

She paused and tugged on her left earlobe. "It was...the screen door wasn't locked and...the door was...the inside door was...open I think."

"You're not certain?"

She laughed a nervous laugh that sounded like a stutter. "If you're asking me if it was open, I'm not sure. If you're asking if it was locked, no, it was unlocked otherwise I couldn't have gotten in."

"So, you remember the door was unlocked but you can't recall if it was open?"

"No, do you believe that?" She chuckled again. "I'm trained to observe but I'm not certain about the door. That surprises me."

For a quick second, Jared's breathing suspended. It surprised him too. Emma was keen on details, even when they watched crime shows on TV. She was always the one noticing the time on the clock, the woman's chipped fingernail polish, or the dead flowers in a vase in the background.

"And what did you observe inside?"

Emma let out a puff of air. "The kitchen was a mess, but they never kept a clean house that I remember. I walked into the living room and saw my brother on the couch. He was dead."

"What made you walk directly to the living room?"

"Pardon me?"

"You entered via the kitchen door. What made you walk to the living room? How did you know to go to that room and not the family room or an upstairs bedroom?"

Emma used her hands to demonstrate her words. "It's a galley kitchen. When you walk in the door, you either turn right," her right hand flipped to the right, "or you go to the left." Her other hand demonstrated. "The family room on the right was only used on holidays. I went left into the dining room, which leads directly to the living room. That's where I found him."

"How did you know whoever was possibly dead wasn't upstairs in bed? It was still early morning."

Her head shook slightly. "I didn't. That was the natural path for me to take."

Jeff paused to make more notes. Emma propped her elbows on the arms of the chair and folded her hands in front of her. She avoided looking at him and watched Jeff instead.

Her body language displayed confidence. Except for the earlobe habit, she didn't fuss or fidget. She made direct eye contact with Jeff when she responded, and with him when she glanced his way. He'd expected no less.

Jeff inhaled. "Okay, you walked in the house and by some divine guidance, knew to go straight to the living room and—"

Emma rolled her eyes. "It wasn't divine guidance, Jeff. It was a normal entry."

"So it seems to you. All right, you stroll into the living room and find your brother. Did you immediately know he was dead?"

"Yes."

"How did you know that?"

She readjusted her position in the seat. "It was pretty obvious. His brains were splattered all over the wall. Imagine my surprise that he had brains." She released a nervous laugh.

Jared again wondered what happened to the Emma he knew.

"Did you touch him to verify he was dead?"

"No sir."

"Did you touch anything in the room?"

"No sir."

Jared interjected. "Why did you go there, Lieutenant?"

She canted her head. "I recognized the address as that of my brother's."

"Yes, but why did you rush there if you were estranged?"

Her reaction after hearing dispatch broadcast a possible DOA still bothered him. She said it was reflexive. He wanted it on the record.

There was a sting in her words when she responded. "As I already said, Detective, he was family."

That sure as hell wasn't the answer he expected. He glared at her, pressuring for more. Most suspects squirmed under his scowl, especially if they had something to hide. But Emma was too smart for that. She returned his piercing gaze with her own, daring him to blink first.

After a few tense seconds, Jeff interceded. "Let's get back to my questions. You say you were estranged. Maybe ten years, you said. How did it feel walking back into the house again after so many years?"

She shrugged. "What do you mean?"

Jeff also shrugged, keeping it informal. "You hadn't been there in a decade. Had the place changed? Did you look around to see if there was anything different? New curtains in the kitchen? New wallpaper?"

"No."

"You weren't curious?"

"That wasn't my focus."

"What was?"

Emma released an exasperated breath. "As I already told you, my focus was the emergency call about a dead body."

"That you knew was in the living room?"

She smiled again. "That I found in the living room."

Jeff grinned. "All right. What about earlier that day? Between five-thirty and six-thirty?" Her gaze darted to him and then returned to Jeff.

"Why? Is that the time of death?"

"The estimate."

"I, um, I was at home. My alarm is set for five-thirty, but I usually wake up before it goes off. I woke up by myself that morning." She glanced at him again and he felt a blush cross his cheeks. "You'll have to take my word for it."

"So what time did you wake up?"

"Um, about four-thirty, I think. About then."

"What did you do before you reported for work?"

Her shoulders rose and fell. "My usual morning routine. I made coffee, I showered, I read the newspaper on my phone. I checked my mail from the day before. I dressed in my uniform, and I drove to work."

"Did you speak to anyone?"

"No, sir. No one can corroborate my story."

"What else did you do?"

"Excuse me?"

"That's a lot of time from when you woke up to the time you reported to work. The drive from your place to the precinct is less than thirty minutes. What else did you do?"

"I-I didn't do anything else. That was my morning."

"And no one can verify that?"

"No sir."

An uncomfortable silence settled over the room.

Emma took a deep breath. "Is there anything else, gentlemen?"

Jeff shook his head. "No. Thanks for coming in, Emma."

The gaze she pinned on him said she wasn't happy. Jared strived for damage control.

"I'll walk you out, Em."

She waited until they were in the parking lot to explode. "What the hell was that, Jared?" Her voice rose. "I thought you wanted my help finding a killer. That was a goddamn interrogation, and I didn't like it one bit. What were you thinking? You think I killed him?"

He was the calm to her outrage. "No, we don't think that. It was just an interview, Em. You're the victim's sister and one of the first people to see the body. You saw it before I did. You couldn't have expected softball questions. You said it yourself, you're a trained observer. You could have seen something vital to our investigation. That's what Jeff's questions were designed to discover."

They'd reached her SUV and she whirled on him, poking her finger at his chest. "Don't you think I would have told you that morning if there was something odd about the crime scene? You see me almost every day. You could've asked me about it ten times since then."

"When, Em? When we were in bed? We keep professional and personal separate, remember? That was your rule."

"We've always discussed our cases with each other."

Now his temper flared. "Yes but I've asked you numerous times to talk to me about your brother and you continually avoid the topic. Your brother's murder *is* my case and you've made it clear you *don't* want to discuss it."

She opened her mouth to reply but shut it quickly. She pivoted and opened her car door. "I have to go."

"How about if I meet you for dinner? Someplace fast since you're back on duty. Let me know what a good time is."

She started her car and rolled down her window. "I'll try to call you, but I'm not promising."

Staring at her taillights, he doubted he'd hear from her.

He returned to the conference room to find Jeff reviewing his notes. He'd hoped Em's interview would clear his mind about her actions. It hadn't. "What d'you think?"

Jeff laid his pen down. "I hate to say it, Jared, but if we're looking for motive, she moves near the top of the list. Her answers dripped venom."

"Yeah, but she was on duty. We could easily check her GPS history to track her movements."

"What if she drove her personal car to her brother's before she went on duty?"

"That puts her at the house while Mary Malvado is still home."

"Maybe she's the accomplice we've wondered about?"

Jared's heart sank hearing in Jeff's voice the nagging thought he'd had. "Nah, I don't see it. Emma is all cop. She lives and breathes the job. She wants to advance in the department. She wouldn't jeopardize all that for some asshole she walked away from years ago."

24

Emma slammed her steering wheel as she sped home. What the fuck. Jared must have nothing, no leads, no suspects. Except her, of course. How crazy was that?

He had no evidence. Not a fingerprint, not a clue. And no weapon. She knew that for certain.

Were those the kinds of questions he asked Mary? Jeff's tone was designed to intimidate her. It didn't, but Mary wouldn't be tuned into the tactic, wouldn't know it was a bluff. It was just a matter of time before Jared called Mary in again for another round of questioning. Especially after finding out about her brother's illegitimate son. He had no other options, no other clues.

The wife was always the prime suspect in a case like this. Maybe she should call and warn her. Jared would be incensed if she did. And she didn't want to engage Mary in any kind of conversation like that, knowing that O'Hare would learn of it and use it. He'd be beside Mary when they questioned her again. He wouldn't let the detectives bully her. The idea to speak to Mary's priest was tempting. But again, it probably wouldn't stay confidential. Unless she did it in the confessional.

She burst out laughing. That was a hard pass.

Should she tell Jared what she knew? Solving this would be a huge feather in his cap. At the same time, it would alter her life forever. Why ruin her career just to solve her brother's murder? He wasn't worth it.

25

The windows were wide open, and sunlight filled the living room. Mary eyed the carpet samples spread on the floor that Donnie Jr. tramped on as he paced. "What do you mean you don't know if there is a will? Don't you remember signing one? You would have had to sign one."

Mary twisted her wedding band. Since yesterday it bothered her, as if it no longer fit. She'd been able to delay this confrontation with her son for two days, telling him she was tired after the funeral, unwell and needed to be alone. That was essentially the truth.

Like his father, he was happier to do other things than be concerned about her. Was Isabelle Ganesh crying for Don? Was her son comforting her instead of interrogating her? "I don't remember. I could have. I'm his wife. Everything passes to me, doesn't it?"

"Not necessarily. When someone dies without a will, their assets are frozen until the court system combs through every detail of the estate. That could take a year. The court decides where a person's possessions will be allocated. That's why it's imperative to locate it as soon as possible, to avoid legal entrapments."

"Don't use that know-it-all tone with me."

Don Jr. huffed at her but softened his voice a decibel. "What about his papers and his files? Is there a life insurance policy? That could pay for the funeral. Have you looked in his files?"

"I haven't looked anywhere, Donnie. It hasn't been foremost in my mind. Besides, the police took everything out of his office. If he had a will in the file cabinet, they have it now."

"They what?" Thunderous again. She shivered at his tone, so much like his father's. She didn't see one bit of her in him anymore. "How could you let them take everything? What the hell is the matter with you?"

She bolted out of her chair. "Nothing is the matter with me that a break from all you people who think I don't deserve respect won't cure. You have no right to talk to me like that. I put up with it for too many years from your father, and I won't stand for it anymore. Not from him. Not from you. Not from anyone. I warned him and now I'm warning you."

Donnie stopped short, his mouth agape. They stared at each other, Donnie's chest heaving and she remarkably tranquil. It was liberating.

"Enough about the will. Listen to me, I want you to do something and I don't want you to mention it to anyone." Donnie's jaw clenched but she wasn't backing down. "Your father's cremains will be ready tomorrow. I'd like you to pick them up and take them to the martini bar. There's a crawl space above the second floor that your dad stored who knows what there. I'd like you to place the box with his ashes there."

Donnie's mouth formed into a small circle. "You're not going to bury his ashes? I thought—"

"No, I'm not going to waste money on a gravesite for him. Do you plan to visit him there? I hardly think so since you hated seeing him when he was alive. Do you think your sister will visit his grave? She was a no-show for his funeral, so I doubt it. And I certainly have no desire to pay my respects."

"But why the martini bar?"

"I'd love to flush him down the toilet but I can't take the chance that those nosy detectives won't inquire about his final resting place. And Father Greg implied the church might frown on that. So I want him to spend eternity among people he despised. That bar fills every night with lesbians and gays who I'm certain are wonderful people. But your father looked down on them. He never said one nice thing about those boys who lease that place. It's a fitting spot for his perpetual resting place. You don't have to tell the owners what's inside the box, just that I'd like it stored there."

Donnie rolled his eyes. "Why do I have to do it?"

"Because I'm telling you to."

Another face-to-face showdown. Her cell phone ringing in the kitchen sliced the tension between them.

"Hello Mr. O'Hare, how are you today? I haven't written all my thank you notes yet, but the basket you sent was beautiful. Thank you."

"The police will be knocking on your door shortly, Mary. They have a warrant to search your house again for additional evidence. You must let them in and it's best that you do. They also want to interview you again. They want to talk to you this afternoon. I committed to have you at the police station by three o'clock. Are you available then? If not, you have to make yourself available."

Her throat tightened. "What? Why do they want to talk to me again? There isn't anything more that I can tell them. What evidence do they think they'll find? There's nothing here for them."

Donnie came up beside her to ask who was on the phone.

She whispered, "Mr. O'Hare."

He spoke again. "It's not unusual for them to question

witnesses more than once, Mary. They very well may ask you the same questions as last time, just to see if you answer differently."

"But my answers won't change. I-I don't know anything more. I—"

"It's just a conversation, Mary. I'll be there. Don't work yourself up about it. Remain calm and composed. Shall I send a car for you, or can you meet me at the station?"

"No, that's not necessary. My son is here. He can drive me."

"Drive you where, Mom? I have things to do today."

She rolled her eyes at him. "I'll meet you there, Mr. O'Hare. Thank you."

She disconnected the call and turned to her son. "The police want to speak with me again. I'd rather not go alone. You'll have to go with me."

Donnie removed his phone, tapped his calendar app and scrolled his screen. "I have to make a call, but I can take you. I hope they don't take too long. This will be good, Mom. You can ask them about the will and get a copy of it."

MARY MALVADO BLANCHED when she opened the door to Jared's knock. It was understandable. A dozen men in bullet proof vests and police jackets emblazoned with the letters ERT stood behind him. He smiled, trying to appear friendly. But this was far from a friendly visit. Somewhere in this house lay the clue to a murder.

She stepped back to allow them inside without saying a word.

Donnie Jr., on the other hand, resembled that wind-up bunny whose battery never runs down, bouncing on the balls of his feet and babbling. "I don't see why you have to search the house again, Detective. Are you looking for something specific?

My mother has nothing to hide. You can see she's being completely cooperative. Perhaps if you tell us what you're looking for, we can find it for you.

"Speaking of looking for things, I'm trying to locate my father's will. Do you by any chance have it? My mother says you took the office files. It might have been among them. What about his cell phone? She couldn't find it. I'll need his contacts. I don't understand why you'd take his phone. Did you already look through all his paperwork? Did you find the will? I'd like a copy of that. We have his properties to manage. It's critical that we know his intentions."

He didn't remember seeing a will but now he wondered who stood to gain from Don Malvado's death. They hadn't found a life insurance policy either. He texted Jeff to check again for both, not to make Junior happy, but to satisfy his own curiosity. Meanwhile, Jared opted to ignore his incessant blabber.

Carson White had shown more compassion for his mother than Junior was demonstrating toward Mary. Wasn't it more important to find his father's killer? Jared resisted asking that and instead, directed his inquiry to Mary. "Mrs. Malvado, the warrant authorizes us to take your cell phone. Do you have a tablet or personal computer? We'd like that as well."

Her hand flew to the base of her throat. "What? No! That's an invasion of privacy."

"No, ma'am. It's a murder investigation."

"I assure you, Detective, there are no calls from whoever killed my husband on my phone."

"Nevertheless, ma'am, I'm asking you to turn it over to me."

"How will someone reach me?"

"We'll return it as soon as possible." He eyed the phone hanging on the kitchen wall but decided not to point it out.

"Where's your iPad, Mom?"

"In my car."

Junior rushed out to find it.

"I don't appreciate this intrusion, Detective."

"No ma'am." He averted the evil eye Mary leveled on him, thankful that one of the search team summoned him from the stairs to the second floor.

"Jared, our warrant describes a woman's bedroom at the northwest corner of the house but it appears to be vacant. Just so you know."

Jared took the steps two at a time and headed to the room Mary Malvado used as a bedroom, only to find the racks of her clothes gone, the bureau cleared, and her slippers no longer tucked under her bed. "What the hell?" The room was wiped clean. He pivoted toward the master bedroom. "Well, I'll be damned."

The bedroom was tidy and clean. A new bedspread covered the king bed and matching valances hung over the opened windows. He walked to the closet to peek inside. Mary Malvado's clothes hung neatly from the rod. And there were the slippers. None of Don Malvado's clothes were there, the shoes and other crap that had covered the floor were gone, replaced by fresh vacuum tracks. A grin spread across his face. "I'll be damned." He retained that smile while he walked down to the first floor to look at the other rooms.

The company that specializes in body and blood clean-up did an outstanding job. The house wasn't this neat the first time Jared walked into it. At the bottom of the steps he glanced into the living room and spied the carpet squares on the floor. The living room looked immaculate. He barely noticed the scent of deodorizer. She'd purchased new furniture and rearranged the layout. Where the sofa had been, a recliner and reading lamp stood and the television now hung from the opposite wall, an oversized loveseat positioned for viewing. The room looked larger, less cluttered. The coffee table was gone, replaced by matching end tables in the corners.

Were those paint samples on the dining room table? He chose that route to return to the kitchen, stopping to inspect the color swatches. She was opting for lighter, brighter colors.

Mary Malvado stood in front of the kitchen sink with a glass of water in her hand.

"Looks like you're redecorating."

She gulped. "We've been talking about re-painting for a while. The cleaning company... the wall behind the couch looked...odd."

Jared nodded that he understood. Maybe he did. After all, the wall had been covered with her husband's blood. It was natural to want to paint that away, wasn't it?

Junior returned with the iPad, which Jared motioned for Officer Petrus to accept. "Is there a passcode for it?" Mary shook her head.

One of the evidence men stomped down the steps with a stuffed bag. Mary Malvado screeched. "What are they taking? Are those my things? Detective, I demand to know what's going on."

"You'll have a receipt detailing everything we take pursuant to the search warrant, Mrs. Malvado."

"I'd like to know what you're looking for."

"We're searching for your husband's killer, ma'am."

"Well he's certainly not in this house."

"Yes ma'am, but clues to his murder may be."

Her shoulders straightened, but she stifled her response. Instead, Donnie spoke up.

"About that will, Detective Jones. Could you check for it? If we're coming to the police station this afternoon, we could pick it up."

"Why do I have to go to police headquarters?" Mary Malvado whined. "If you have questions to ask, why can't you ask them now? I've already told you everything I know."

"We're not permitted to interview you without your lawyer present, Mrs. Malvado."

"I consent to it."

"Thank you, but that's not how it works." He wanted her on an uncomfortable metal chair in the interrogation room waiting, worrying, and wondering what would happen. Her cell phone lay behind her on the desk and startled them when "Amazing Grace" played in chimes. The screen displayed the name Father Greg.

"You haven't confiscated my phone yet. May I answer that?" Without waiting for his approval, she rose, snatched the phone off the Formica, and stormed out the door. He took one step toward her when his cell phone vibrated in his back pocket. A text from Jeff. "No will. Better—wait until you see what we found on the priest. Wrap it up fast."

26

They had an hour before Mrs. Malvado's interview. Jared re-read the notes Jeff carefully organized and highlighted. Father Greg was a member of a local sportsman's club, which Jeff had visited. Not only was the padre an excellent shot, but he also owned and practiced with several weapons according to the club owner. Here in Pennsylvania, firearms weren't required to be registered, so there was no way to determine exactly what weapons he owned. The club owner confirmed he was proficient with handguns and a rifle. He couldn't recall ever seeing the priest with a shotgun.

He didn't recognize a photo of Mary Malvado either and had never seen the priest on the range with anyone else, either male or female.

State records didn't identify Father Greg as having a concealed carry license. That didn't mean he didn't wear one under his robe. The idea of a pistol-carrying priest amused Jared. "It certainly puts a different spin on passing the collection plate, doesn't it?"

Jeff laughed. "Yes but unfortunately, marksmanship expertise is not enough to search the rectory."

"I know, but we can use the information to pressure Mary Malvado. Let's take off the kid gloves for this little chat. Like you said, we focused on Malvado and his enemies when we first questioned her. I want to examine Mary's relationship with her priest. How familiar is she with the guy? What does she know about him on a personal level? Maybe we can shake her up if she thinks we think her precious holy man is our suspect. I don't think she'll let him take the fall for her unless he's part of it.

"And one other thing. Like Emma, she has no one to confirm her early morning activities. I want to know what she did before she went to church that day if she wasn't busy whacking her husband.

"And when we're done with her," Jared added, "let's have a chat with Father Greg again."

Terrence O'Hare rose to shake their hands when they entered the room. Mary Malvado crossed herself and kissed her rosary beads.

Jeff leaned against his usual back corner. Jared dropped the file he'd carried with him onto the table. This time, it contained real reports and crime notes. Mary Malvado jumped when the folder hit the metal.

"Thank you for coming in again, Mrs. Malvado. I—"

"I told you I'd answer your questions this morning. This is a waste of my time." The clear blue eyes he'd seen the day her husband died had turned dark and malevolent. That was okay. He wasn't in the mood to play nice.

"Tell us about your relationship with Father Greg."

She paled. "What? He's my priest."

"Is that all?"

Her spine straightened. "What are you implying?"

"Is he a friend?"

"Yes."

"A trusted friend?'

"Yes."

"A confidant?"

Her chest rose and fell more rapidly. "He's my confessor. And that's private, Detective."

"Is he your accomplice?"

She gasped. "Wh-what? I don't know what you mean."

"What about conspirator? Different word, same meaning."

She whirled on her attorney. "I'm not sitting here to listen to this. Why are you allowing it?"

Jared didn't give O'Hare time to respond. Shoot the questions at her like bullets. Stun her. Throw her off guard.

"Is Father Greg concealing the murder weapon for you? Is he the one who showed you how to shoot it? Did you know he's an excellent marksman?"

The wide eyes and puffed cheeks on O'Hare's face showed surprise, but Mary Malvado didn't blink.

"He's your alibi for where you were the morning your husband was murdered." He leaned in closer to her. "Shot to death in your living room. Isn't that right, Mary? Weren't you in church that morning?"

"I was and Father Greg told you so."

"That's pretty convenient to have your friend, your confidant confirm your whereabouts. The only problem is, the two of you have the timing all wrong."

Mary Malvado had fire in her eyes. "That's an outrageous thing to say. There is no timing to get wrong. I was at seven o'clock Mass. I left my house at six-thirty like I always do. Father Greg greeted me at the door. You already know that."

"And was your husband alive when you left the house?"

The beads weren't moving today. They stayed stagnant in her hands. "Of course he was."

"Well now, there's the problem, Mary. The coroner places the time of death between five-thirty and six-thirty that morning. You say you left the house at six-thirty and your husband was alive, but that can't be, can it? In fact," he drew a typed page from the manila folder and referenced it, "you said when we first spoke that your husband was alive and watching television. You were ready to guess what program he was watching before Mr. O'Hare stopped you. Only the TV wasn't on when I walked into that room. It wasn't on when the first officer arrived on the scene. How do you explain that, Mary?"

O'Hare touched her forearm. "Don't answer that, Mary. Only tell him the facts that you know."

Mary's eyes penetrated Jared's face. Her stare burned his cheek.

"Where'd you get the shotgun, Mary? Was it Father Greg's? Does he have it? We can search the rectory, you know. We can run through your treasured church in full uniform letting everyone know we're looking for the shotgun we believe you used to kill your husband. Is that what you want, Mary? You can keep that from happening, Mary. Tell us where the shotgun is."

She jumped to her feet. Her chest heaved. "Go to hell, Detective."

"That's not very Christian of you, Mary."

"Mr. O'Hare, do I have to tolerate this? I'm here to answer questions, not listen to baseless accusations or to hear Father Greg's reputation impugned. Am I under arrest? If not, I'd like to go home."

O'Hare stood. "Detective, my client is right. We came here voluntarily to reply to specific questions, not hypothetical ones. I think we're finished cooperating."

Jared stood as well, eye to eye with Mary Malvado, using Emma's ploy, goading her to look away. "Sit down, Mrs. Malvado. You too, Mr. O'Hare. We're not through yet."

O'Hare sat as if in slow motion. Mary's eyeballs rounded to the size of quarters, but she sat back in the chair. He remained upright and leaned forward on his hands. "Tell me about that morning, Mrs. Malvado. What time did you wake up?"

"What?"

"The morning your husband was killed. What time did you wake up? Did a gunshot awaken you?"

"No! I didn't hear a thing."

"Well then, what woke you? What time was it?"

The rosary beads found life in her fingers. "My alarm wakes me up every morning at five. Sometimes I wake up on my own. Don gets mad if I make too much noise and wake him so I try to beat it. Most days, I do."

"What about that day?"

Her gaze fell to the table. "I-I don't remember."

"Don't you?"

"No sir."

"What time do you *think* you woke up?"

"Before the alarm."

"And what did you do then?"

"What do you mean?"

"What's your morning routine?"

"I don't know. I get up. I brush my teeth. I say my morning prayers. I make a cup of tea. I get dressed and I go to church."

"Every morning?"

"Pretty much."

"Did you eat breakfast?" He remembered the melting butter and open cereal box.

"No, I don't usually eat in the mornings."

He felt his eyebrows come together. "Did your husband snack in the mornings?"

O'Hare interjected. "You can't know that Mary, if you didn't see it."

"I don't know."

Jared paused, deciding not to dwell on the mess in the kitchen.

"Where is your husband in the mornings?"

"Sometimes he's in his room." Her cheeks turned a deep red. "He prefers his own room."

"Yes ma'am. And if he's not in his room?"

"He falls asleep on the couch. He watches TV late. I tiptoe downstairs so as not to wake him. If I boil water on the stove, he doesn't hear it. The microwave is too noisy."

"Where was he that morning?"

"The television was playing. I assumed he was in the living room."

"Did you wake him that morning?"

"No, the TV was on loud. He didn't hear me."

"Did you look in on him?"

"No."

"What did you do?"

"I went upstairs and got ready for church."

Jared recalled her outfit, the oversized sweater and the dirty sneakers. On her worst day Emma had never looked like that.

"And what time did you leave for church?"

"I already told you, Detective, I left at six-thirty."

"And you never looked in on your husband?"

"No, why would I do that?"

"Oh I don't know, maybe to see if he was dead or alive."

She caught her breath.

"So, no one can corroborate your story?"

"It's not a story, it's what I did."

"You got up, you brushed your teeth, you drank some tea, and you killed your husband, is that correct?'

Her fisted hands flew to her mouth.

"Here's the problem, Mary. From the time you say you woke up to the time you arrived at church, no one can verify what you did. You brushed your teeth and drank a cup of tea, which takes all of twenty minutes at most. Plenty of time to shoot your husband between the eyes and clean up. You claim—"

"That's not true!"

"You claim he didn't hear you because the TV was loud. But when we first interviewed you, you said the TV was off when you came home from church. You said you didn't turn it off. So who did, Mrs. Malvado? If you didn't walk into that room, blow your husband's head off, turn off the TV because you're the one who was always locking the doors and turning off the lights, then who did?"

She burst into tears. Terrence O'Hare jumped to his feet. "That's enough, Detective. This interview is over."

"I don't think so, Terry."

Jared and Jeff had discussed this moment. Combed through their meager evidence wondering if it was enough. Debated whether to show their hand or investigate further, looking for what they didn't know. That was Jared's favorite conundrum to quote—"we don't know what we don't know." It was all circumstantial, but damn if it wasn't convincing. Time wasn't their friend. The longer this case stayed open, the colder it got. She had the motive and the means, whether or not someone helped her. She did it.

"We're leaving, Detective."

"Not today, sir. We're arresting your client in connection with the murder of Donald Malvado."

27

Mary Malvado screamed and fell back into her chair.

Terrence O'Hare stuttered for one second before clasping his hands in front of him, assuming the pose he took in the courtroom. "What are the charges, Detective?"

Jeff stepped forward. "Mrs. Malvado, please stand up." She rose automatically. "You have the right to remain silent." He produced a pair of handcuffs from his waistband and reached for her left wrist. The rosary beads fell to the floor. "You have the right to an attorney."

"She has an attorney, gentlemen. What are you charging my client with?"

Jared stood to meet him eye to eye. "We are detaining her on suspicion of murder. As you know, we have forty-eight hours to formally charge her. When we do, you'll be the first to know."

Jeff took Mary Malvado by her handcuffed arms and eased her toward the door. She looked at O'Hare over her shoulder. "Please contact Father Greg. Let him know I won't be in church tomorrow."

Jared thought that was the perfect walk-off line. They were headed to the church next.

JARED RANG the bell at the rectory three times before an elderly priest answered. He flashed his badge and introduced himself and Jeff, asking to see Father Greg. The priest showed them into a library and offered them coffee.

Father Greg's step faltered when he entered the room. He wiped his mouth on a wadded napkin in his hand. "Gentlemen, this is unexpected. Is this about Mary? Is something the matter?"

"What is your relationship with Mrs. Malvado?" They'd decided on the ride over to go for the jugular. Jared watched for his reaction. "I ask because we've just arrested her and her only concern seems to be you and missing Mass tomorrow."

He took a step backward, crossed himself and sought support from a nearby chair. "Arrested? You can't mean it. On what charge?"

"She's a person of interest in her husband's murder."

"That's absurd. You can't possibly believe—"

"Where were you the morning Don Malvado was killed?"

He tightened the rope around his waist. "Really detective, you know the answer to that question. I was here, presiding over Mass."

"What about before Mass, Father? What preparations are involved prior to the service?

His skin turned a whiter shade of pale. "Before? What do you mean? Mass is at seven o'clock. Before that I rise, shower, and have breakfast. And morning prayers, of course."

"And what time does all that happen?"

He blinked once, twice, three times. "In the morning, of course."

"Can your fellow clerics confirm your presence at prayers?"

Father Greg settled on the arm of the chair, running his hands through his hair. "What's all this about, Detective? Why do you ask me where I was?"

"You didn't answer my question, sir. Can someone confirm your presence?" In his heart, Jared already knew the answer.

"I-I don't know. It's not group prayer. I prefer to be alone before Mass, sort of a meditation time to prepare my heart and my mind."

"So no one saw you that morning?"

"I don't know."

"We understand you're quite proficient on the shooting range. Do you own a shotgun Father?"

All the air left his lungs. "Wh-what?"

"Don Malvado was killed with a shotgun. Sometime between five-thirty and six-thirty that morning. I don't believe Mary Malvado could hoist a shotgun, let alone hit what she aimed at. She had help. Was that you, Father?"

"Dear Lord, no!"

"Do you own a shotgun, sir?"

"I-I used to have one. But-but I no longer have it. It was stolen or something, I'm not sure."

"Did you report that theft to the police?"

"No, no I didn't. I'm not certain when it disappeared. I may have misplaced it. I haven't—"

"Was it really stolen, Father, or did you dispose of it after you helped Mary Malvado kill her husband?"

Father Greg let out a small yelp and crossed himself. "That's a wild accusation and most definitely unfounded."

"I'm a simple man, Father, and I've learned that the simplest explanation is usually the best explanation. I think poor Mary Malvado was in a bad marriage and she turned to you in faith first, and then for guidance. Poor Mary took her vows seriously so 'til death do us part' was her only way out. I think you helped Poor Mary with that. Did you teach her to handle a shotgun? That would be my guess. Did she shoot him? I don't know. Did you pull the trigger? Again, I don't know. Were the two of you conspirators in his death? I'd bet my next paycheck on it."

"That's enough!" The priest jumped to his feet. His jaw tightened and he spoke through clenched teeth. "I did not kill Don Malvado and neither did Mary. You can leave now, Detectives. Don't ring this doorbell again and don't show up in my church. If you do, I'll file a harassment complaint against you. The next time you wish to speak to me, call my lawyer."

He power walked to the door and swung it open wide.

Jeff and Jared headed to the exit. Jared stopped in front of him. "Who's your attorney, Father?"

"Terrence O'Hare."

28

The steel handcuffs were cold on her wrist. Not too tight, thank goodness. Guided by the slight pressure from a policewoman's grasp on her elbow, Mary walked down a hall and through a door marked Employees Only in red letters. Then through a second door where a large woman sat behind a metal desk piled high with papers and books. The policewoman called her Rosalie. She had a nice, wide smile.

They asked for her belt, but she wasn't wearing one. They took her tennis shoes, replacing them with paper slippers. They asked for her jewelry. All she wore was the same cubic zirconia squares that she never took out of her ears and her wedding band. Removing the earrings bothered her. She felt naked without them.

Rosalie assured her they'd make her stay a comfortable one. How were they going to do that when it was so cold in this lockup? Rosalie called it a holding cell, but it was probably the same as a jail cell. It wasn't big. She'd read once that the average cell was six by eight feet. She placed one foot in front of the other and counted. One. Two. Three. Four. Five. Six. Seven. Eight. She faced the back wall.

Fat studs anchored a steel cot with slats instead of springs to the wall, topped by a thin, striped mattress. The thickness couldn't be more than three inches.

Her nose wrinkled at the faint fragrance of Lysol. How clean was this place?

A stained steel sink smaller than the one in her powder room was also anchored to the wall beside a steel toilet that she'd already thrown up in. There was no toilet seat. The side walls were solid, but the front of the cell was all bars from floor to ceiling.

Mary touched the crossbar, but the grime on it repulsed her and she jerked her hands back then jammed them into the pockets of her sweater.

Wildly, her fingers searched the insides. No beads. Dear God, she lost her rosary beads. Tears filled her eyes. Think, Mary. You had them at the police station.

Was she allowed to call out to Rosalie? She wanted to ask the police to search for her rosary. She *needed* them. "Rosalie! Rosalie!" She yelled and another woman's voice from farther down the hall mimicked her, "Rosalie. Rosalie. She ain't no maid that you summon when you want her, girlie. Where you think you is?"

Mary slumped to her knees, cradled her head in her hands and cried.

What was she supposed to do now? Mr. O'Hare knew she was here so the one phone call a person always was allowed on TV didn't matter. Was she still permitted to call someone? She longed to hear Greg's voice, but she wanted to talk to Emma.

Would Emma know she was arrested? Did police share that information? Would she arrange for her release? She promised everything would work out. She promised it would be fine.

29

Emma choked on her coffee reading the daily reports. Jared arrested Mary. No charges filed yet. He was playing the intimidation game he was so good at. He didn't have any goddamn evidence, so he was pretending he did. Locking her up, frightening the pants off her, trying to scare her into confessing to killing Don.

She'd seen him do it before and when she questioned his tactics, he merely shrugged and said, "it's a means of persuasion. Better than a light bulb hanging from a string and a rubber bat."

How could he arrest her?

It was eleven-thirty and she went on shift in a half hour, but she yanked her phone from her pocket and dialed him. His groggy voice told her he'd been asleep.

"What the hell, Jared? You arrested Mary?"

"This isn't the time, Em. Take your shift and we'll talk about it later."

"Just answer my question. On what grounds?"

"Go to work, Lieutenant." He disconnected the call.

Infuriated, she called the county jail and inquired about

Mary's well being. She'd been upset earlier in the evening over lost prayer beads, the night guard said. She was calmer now, huddled in the corner at the back of her bunk. The guard hadn't seen her sleep.

Rosary beads. Mary was worried about her fucking rosary beads? Where the hell did you buy those things? Especially at this time of night? It was twenty minutes until her shift. But she was concerned about Mary.

She woke up Nessie. "I'm sorry, honey, I know it's late. I desperately need a favor."

"What is it, Aunt Em? What's the matter?"

"Aunt Mary's been arrested."

Vanessa released a small scream. "No! How could you let that happen?"

"I didn't find out about it until just now when I came on duty. She's in the county jail and she's not doing well. She lost her rosary beads, and I guess she's pretty upset about it."

"Seriously?"

"Yeah, I know, it doesn't register with us, but it's important to her."

"Why are you calling me? I don't have any rosary beads."

"Neither do I or I'd send you to my place. But I did a search and, believe it or not, Walmart sells them. You're close to one that's open twenty-four-seven. Please go buy a pair for Mary. They may be children's First Communion beads, but at least they're a rosary.

"It's a lot to ask, honey, but it's important that we keep Mary calm. I'll call the squad in that district and ask them to ride through the parking lot so there will be a police presence. Shopping at that hour of the night isn't the safest."

"I don't even like going there during the day."

"I know and I'm sorry to ask you to do this, but it's important. Buy a set of beads and drop them off at the county jail. I'll text you the address and I'll notify them at the jail that you'll be swinging by."

"Do I have to go in?"

"No, Nessie, it's too late for visitors, and I wouldn't want you to do that. It's a lot I'm asking now, I know, but trust me, it will help Aunt Mary. She's having a bad time in there and we both know how strong her faith is. The beads will help her get through the night."

"What about tomorrow? What happens then?"

"I'm not sure, honey. I'll see what I can find out. I'm getting ready to go on duty now, so I have to hang up. Text me when you're back home, okay. And remember how much I love you for this."

"Yeah, yeah. If I didn't love you, I would have hung up five minutes ago. Promise to call me tomorrow and tell me what's going on."

"I promise."

Emma found minimal comfort in knowing at least Mary could cling to rosary beads through the night. She doubted Mary would sleep unless she passed out from sheer exhaustion.

She'd gotten Mary into this. How was she going to get her out?

30

J ared expelled a huge breath of air once he rounded the corner toward his desk. Emma waited for him, leaning on it with her arms crossed over her chest. He carried two cups of coffee for he and Jeff, and a box of pastries. Despite his Glock in his shoulder holster, with his hands full like this and that look on her face, he felt defenseless. He braced for Emma's fire.

"Good morning, Detective."

"Good morning, Lieutenant. I would've expected you to be home catching some sleep. You must've had time to nap last night while on duty." He liked to tease her about sleeping on the job when she worked midnights, which she didn't do. He placed the box on Jeff's desk without looking away from a scowl that said she wasn't in the mood for levity.

"Did you find Mary's rosary beads?"

"What?"

"Mary's rosary beads. You know she always has them with her. She's missing them."

His anger flared. "How do you know that? Let me guess, you checked with your supervisor, clocked out for personal time, and dashed to the jail last night. It was instinct, right? You're going to tell me she's family, right?"

Emma's shoulders straightened. "No. I did not."

"Then how do you know about the beads?"

Her hands flopped wide, palms up. "Okay, I admit I called the jail to check on her but really, Jared, you had no grounds to arrest her. What on earth are you thinking? And what evidence do you have to support a case?"

"I'm not going to discuss my evidence with you, Lieutenant. Good morning, Jeff."

"Morning." Jeff sat down to inspect the goodies without another word.

"C'mon Jared, what's going on?"

"As I said, Miss Hunter, I'm not discussing this. You, like everyone else, will hear our case at the preliminary hearing tomorrow."

Jeff's head snapped up faster than Emma's mouth opened.

"You're going to make her spend another night in jail? Jared no!" Her screech raised heads around the squad room.

This wasn't the time or place to argue with her, and he didn't want to. Not about this. They hadn't seen each other in a handful of days, had barely spoken. It was always difficult when Emma worked the midnight shift but this time around, it felt different. More distant. This damn case was coming between them.

"Lieutenant Hunter, I'm not in the mood to argue my case with you. The district attorney will be a hard enough sell, so unless you have another reason for being here, please let my partner and I get on with our work."

He watched anger flash in her eyes and then, disappointment. He was treating her like every other male who tried to make her feel inferior. She wasn't.

He stepped forward and grasped her elbow. "Let's take this somewhere private. Please?"

Emma's back was ramrod straight, her chin high while he walked her to the interrogation room, closing the door for privacy.

"What's going on, Em? You've never questioned my actions like that."

She slumped into a chair. "Jesus, Jared, you can't possibly think Mary killed him. Keeping her locked up is like torturing her." At least the ice in her voice was gone. She sounded tired.

"She's tougher than you think. I checked on her this morning and she's fine. The guard said she fell asleep sitting in the corner of her bunk. Her neck is probably stiff but she's okay. She's being treated as if on suicide watch. The guards are checking on her every half hour. I ordered that because of you, Em."

She looked at him in surprise.

"I think she's a cold-hearted killer but you, you seem to think she's some kind of saint. I don't understand why because you hardly know the woman, but you've been on point on a few of my cases so, out of deference to your instinct or inside information or whatever, she's not in with the general population, and she's being monitored. She was grateful for the rosary beads you sent."

Emma started to speak, but he cut her off. "The jail called me last night to authorize giving the things to her. Even I know they're important to her. Whoever I spoke to didn't know who requested the special delivery, but I allowed it. I reviewed the camera footage outside the jail this morning before I came in. I recognized your niece. I doubt she would have known about the missing rosary beads, so you had to be behind that."

He strode to the table and looked down when his feet scraped something on the floor. Mary's rosary beads. He reached for them.

"Here. She must have lost them here yesterday. You can return them to her."

Emma shook her head. "No, I'm not going to do that." She sounded defeated, her voice low. "Will you make sure they find their way to her?"

"Sure."

"You give me credit for insight with your cases but on this one, you doubt me. She didn't kill him, Jared."

"Then who did? Because someone waltzed into that living room and shot the hell out of Don Malvado."

He raised his index finger. "Mary had motive. Text messages reveal a marriage in discord and you, yourself, say he treated her like shit. Those texts were on his phone, by the way. No corresponding texts on her phone. Doesn't that strike you as odd? She doesn't seem knowledgeable enough to erase her digital footprints, does she?"

He added his middle finger. "She had opportunity. Just the two of them in that house every day."

Now his ring finger. "She has no alibi for the time the coroner says the death occurred. Sure, her priest-boyfriend or whatever he is establishes her presence in church for seven o'clock Mass but, like you, no one can swear to her activity in the early morning hours."

Last, his pinkie. "I have a time discrepancy, a window that gives her plenty of time to hide the weapon, which we still haven't found. As you know, the lack of a weapon goes to planning, which screams pre-meditation."

The index finger on his left hand joined the group. "No other fingerprints or footprints were found anywhere in that house except his and hers."

The middle finger. "She hasn't reported anything missing, so we can rule out a random burglar."

The left ring finger. "There are no other suspects."

His last pinkie shot up. "And I haven't even mentioned the illegitimate son. Goes back to motive."

She stared at eight fingers splayed in front of her and swallowed hard. "Every bit of that is circumstantial evidence, Jared. Even I know there's no proof on the table."

"That doesn't make it inferior evidence. Do I have to remind you of your Academy training?"

The passage was fresh in his mind. He'd rehearsed it in anticipation of needing to convince the district attorney today to file murder charges against Mary Malvado. At the preliminary hearing, the DA had to argue in front of the judge that the evidence was substantial enough to go to trial. Jared had to persuade the DA first. Convincing Emma would be a dress rehearsal.

"Unlike direct evidence, which proves a material element of a legal action, circumstantial evidence proves other facts from which one may infer the existence of material elements. The law does not discriminate between the two in terms of their weight. A criminal conviction may rely solely upon circumstantial evidence. I've done my homework. There are studies that show certain kinds of circumstantial evidence are more accurate than direct evidence."

He still had to explain this all to Jeff.

Emma stared at him with tear-rimmed eyes. Tears for her sister-in-law or because on this one, he'd outsmarted her. That would be unlike her. "You make a good case, Detective. Will you consent to bail?"

"I don't think she's a flight risk so yes, I'll suggest it to the district attorney. But the charge is murder so the judge will likely set it high if he grants it at all."

Emma's shoulders slumped. "I'll manage it, whatever it is. Thank you, Detective."

The steel in her voice was back. She stood, her eyes downcast. "I'm going home to get some sleep."

"I know you're on midnight, Em. What day are you off? Can I see you?"

"I'll call you." The door closed behind her.

M r. O'Hare explained a preliminary hearing was a proceeding to establish what he called a prima facie case, essentially a hearing for the detectives to show what proof they had that she killed her husband. How could they possibly have proof?

"Very rarely does the judge fail to bind the case over for trial, Mary, especially when it involves murder." A chill ran down her back. "By law, the judge is required to believe the prosecution at this stage. He—"

"What does that mean?"

"He or she usually sides with the police. It's a way to show support and it's politically smart. They have to run for re-election. I don't want you to panic when you hear that."

Too late.

"This could work to our advantage. The police and the district attorney have to produce what evidence they have against you so I'll know what to argue. I think their case is weak and there's a chance the judge could think so too and dismiss the charge. But you shouldn't expect that outcome. Once we're at the defense table, we'll know for sure. I will caution you now that once this is determined to go to trial, the DA will probably offer you a plea deal."

"A what?"

"He will try to bargain with you. Reduce the murder charge to manslaughter in exchange for your confession. I don't want to know if you did this, Mary. I'm asking if you're willing to fight."

"What choice do I have, Mr. O'Hare? I didn't kill my husband. I wished he would die but I didn't kill him. I'm innocent, I swear."

He bowed his head in a very paternal way. Did he believe her?

"I'll enter a not guilty plea on your behalf. I'll request you be released on bail but again, since this is a murder charge the DA might contest that."

"You mean I might have to stay in jail?" The thought nauseated her.

He patted her hand like he always did. "Just let me handle it. Don't be concerned."

How could she not be? She'd spent two miserable nights in jail with only her attorney taking the time to visit her. Why hadn't Emma come? Why the hell hadn't her son shown up? Someone delivered her a pair of rosary beads late last night, which she was thankful for. They weren't hers, but they were comforting. She'd wondered if they were blessed.

When she asked, the guard said she didn't know where they came from, but the detective in charge authorized their delivery. They had to be from Father Greg. He also managed to send her a message that he was praying for her, relayed by another guard.

The facility was cold. Not just the temperature, but the atmosphere of the place. The walls were gray, the floors were a darker gray and once the sun went down, the place was dank and lonely. At night, there was always someone moaning or crying. She'd cried too. The wool blanket on the cot was rough, the deodorizing laundry soap used for the sheets stung her nose. She'd barely eaten in two days. She had no appetite, which didn't matter because the food didn't appeal to her. Scrambled eggs and a piece of dry toast in the morning. A sandwich of cold cuts and canned fruit cocktail for lunch and meatloaf for dinner last night that looked as gray as the walls.

Don often criticized her for gaining weight, ignoring the long-term impact of the cancer drugs and instead implying she was too lazy to exercise or eat right. She could afford to drop a few pounds.

Mr. O'Hare wanted her to dress for today's preliminary hearing as if it were a special event at the church and asked for a description of an outfit her sister could assemble. It had taken some thought, but she opted for the dress she wore at Easter, a floral print with a lace collar and fluttery cap sleeves. She'd even purchased new shoes to complement the dress with a small heel. The ensemble made her feel pretty and Father Greg had complimented her on it.

She listed the items she'd need to a guard, embarrassed to mention underpants and a bra. The county-issue undergarments were basic white cotton, not unlike what she normally wore. But she preferred her own.

Showered and dressed, she perched on the edge of the bunk clutching the child's communion beads she received, waiting for the guard to tell her it was time for her court appearance. She prayed she wouldn't vomit. Or cry. Ellen had included a handkerchief with her clothing.

The effect the dress had at Easter wasn't present today, with her hands cuffed in front of her and wedged between two uniformed men wearing guns. The sun warmed her face on the walk to the van and the men practically lifted her into the vehicle. She couldn't spend the rest of her life in jail. It was a sin, but she'd take her own life if necessary. Father Greg would understand.

She watched out the window as they drove to the courthouse, wondering if everyone could see her inside and what they thought. But people on the streets were going about their everyday lives without a concern about her or what her future was. Finding Don dead had given her hope for a better life. The sun glinting off the handcuffs was like a lightning bolt torching that hope. A tear escaped and rolled slowly down the left side of her face. She couldn't reach her pocket, but the guard heard her sniffle and handed her a tissue.

The van rolled to a stop behind the courthouse. Mr. O'Hare and Father Greg waited for her. She was never so happy to see Greg. A group of people with cameras stood farther back. They began shouting questions to her the minute the door slid open.

"Mary, did you kill your husband?"

"Why'd you do it Mary?"

"Mary, you're a martyr for all abused wives. How does that make you feel?"

"Mrs. Malvado, are you innocent?"

The guard sitting beside her touched her forearm. "Do yourself a favor, ma'am. Don't say anything to the media." With that, he stepped out and turned to help her out.

Father Greg and Mr. O'Hare reached for her as well. Father Greg's strong hands on her arms conveyed immediate strength.

"Sister Mary, how are you? I prayed you'd have the strength to survive this."

"Let's not dawdle out here," Mr. O'Hare said, nudging her toward the opened garage door. The reporters continued to fling questions at her.

"How are you going to plead, Mary?"

"What'd you use to kill him?"

The two men rushed her into the building, into the basement with more police and police cars than she'd ever seen.

With the men propelling her forward, they reached the elevator in record time. Fast enough for the door to close and lock out the media mob. She breathed a sigh of relief.

They emerged into a hallway with marble floors. Mr. O'Hare shoved them toward a door marked private and urged them inside. "These proceedings rarely start on time and our case isn't first on the docket so it could be a while. You can wait in here until a deputy comes for you. Would you like some water?"

His head canted toward a water cooler in the corner.

"No thank you. Can Father Greg stay here with me?"

"Well, he's in here now, so I'd say yes. There will be deputies in the hallway assuring that you don't try to escape. Father, I'd advise you not to stick your head out the door or they might realize you're here and tell you to leave. This room is designated for pris—er, arrestees only. I'll go see what's going on in the courtroom. I'll see you there."

Her jaw hurt from locking her teeth all morning. Her neck and back ached from sleeping against the wall. Her belly ached from the knots in it. Somehow, the shoulder massage Father Greg began once the door closed made it all bearable. She closed her eyes and dropped her head backward.

"Mary dear, what can I do? How can I help you?"

"You're helping more than you know, Greg." She drew his hand to her lips and kissed it. "This is such a nightmare. I don't know what to think anymore. I never imagined I'd be arrested and jailed. You have to be careful. The police think you helped me kill Don."

"I know that, dear. They questioned me. You shouldn't be thinking about me right now, you should be praying for a miracle."

"I'm so sorry about this, Father. You don't deserve—"

"Mary, don't say that. None of this is your doing. Where's

your faith? This is just a test the Good Lord is giving you, giving both of us. You have to stay strong and see this through."

"I don't know if I can, Father. I was happy to find him dead. Elated. God is punishing me for those feelings."

"Nonsense. He's not a vengeful God. I've always believed he has a plan for you. This is the hardest part of it, I'm sure. You have to believe." He pressed her hands to his chest. His heart pounded beneath her fingers.

"You're just as frightened as I am, Greg."

He blinked tears away. A sharp knock on the door separated them and Father Greg jumped toward the wall. A female deputy poked her head inside. "Your attorney said it will be about a half-hour longer, ma'am."

The door closed before she could say thank you.

P anic glued her to the chair when the guard said it was time to move to the courtroom. Father Greg and the guard lifted her to her feet, but her steps faltered. A cold sweat covered her body. Her knees buckled. "Greg, I can't do this."

"Yes, you can, Mary. The Lord will carry you."

"Sir, you'll have to go out into the hallway and enter the courtroom through the public doors. I can't let you use this private entrance."

"Of course, of course." Father Greg enfolded her hands. "Have faith, Sister."

A feeling of emptiness engulfed her when he left her side. The guard propelled her forward.

Entering the courtroom through the side door, she became lightheaded. So many people. Like an audience at a concert. All sitting reverently, as if they were in church. Ellen and Vanessa sat in the front row beside Donnie Jr. They smiled when they saw her. Donnie Jr. kept his head lowered. Probably on his phone.

Mr. O'Hare stood in front of the crowd at a long rectangular wooden table, nodding toward her. He smiled reassuringly, waiting for her to close the distance between them. It felt like a mile. Detective Jones sat at a table to the right with a young man in a sharp looking three-piece suit. Probably the prosecutor Mr. O'Hare warned her about. "Don't concern yourself with what he says, Mary. He's not the one who testifies."

Detective Widows sat behind his partner in the front row. A wooden banister separated the spectators from the tables. A few of the reporters who yelled to her in the back lot perched behind Detective Widows, raising their cameras to record her entrance. Her gait wasn't steady.

Not many faces in the crowd were recognizable. Who were these people? Gossip seekers? A few women from church held balled up hankies to their mouths when they saw her. She probably looked terrible. Thank God, the guard removed the handcuffs before she made this appearance. Lester, Don's long-time friend from Rhode Island, leveled such a mean glare on her, she cringed. Why was he here? Did he know Don's secrets? Whose side was he on?

Father Greg entered through the back double doors and made his way to the second row, settling in behind Vanessa. He gently patted hers and Ellen's shoulders.

The doors opened again and Emma walked in, taking a seat in the last row. She wasn't in uniform. Was this like a wedding? Friends of the bride on one side, friends of the groom on the other? Emma sat on her side.

The long trek to the table ended and Mr. O'Hare reached out, tugging her to stand beside him and then sit. He leaned in and whispered, "Don't look so frightened, Mary. This is mere formality." He reached into his coat pocket. "Here."

Her rosary beads. She pressed them to her lips.

Deputies were positioned all around the room, along the walls and at the doors, all of them staring at her. The judge's seat looked massive with a state seal behind it as big and round as a truck tire. Two flags larger than the American flag Don used to fly at the house hung in neat folds beside it. The room looked so much larger in person than on TV. In contrast, the court stenographer was dwarfed by the wall. He sat ready to type, thankfully looking at a legal pad instead of her. The eyes of everyone behind her bore into her back. She sensed it. What they must think.

"All rise."

She jumped to her feet along with everyone else. The judge glided in from a concealed door, his black robe flowing behind him. "Be seated."

The commotion made by everyone resuming their seats was short-lived.

When he spoke, the judge's voice was deep and low. "I call Case Number two zero two one twenty-seven, the Commonwealth of Pennsylvania versus Mary Louise Malvado on a charge of murder. All parties appear to be present. Mr. O'Hare, does the defendant have a plea?"

Mr. O'Hare rose and buttoned his suit jacket. "We plead not guilty, Your Honor." A low rumble rolled through the courtroom.

"Your plea is duly noted. Is the state prepared to present its case, Mr. Artemus?"

The young man in the sleek suit jumped to his feet and strode to a podium. He adjusted the microphone, opened a binder, and laid it in front of him. "We are, Your Honor." His response boomed to all four corners. "This is a case of cold-blooded murder." Someone behind her gasped. "Mary Louise Malvado was in a marriage she no longer wished to be in. It was old and cold and lifeless. She and her husband of twenty-five years, Donald Malvado, were two strangers living under the same roof. She wasn't happy."

His hand swung in her direction. "By all accounts, Mrs.

Malvado is a deeply religious woman so a divorce, the path a normal, upstanding, adult couple would take—"

"Objection, Your Honor." Mr. O'Hare jumped up so quickly, it scared her.

"Sustained. Limit the editorializing for trial, counselor."

Mr. Artemus tightened his tie. "My apologies to the court. Divorce was not an option for Mary Louise Malvado as it is frowned upon by the Catholic Church. But so is murder. Yet the state maintains that murder is the option Mary Louise Malvado opted for to exorcise herself from a loveless, abusive marriage." More gasps from behind her.

"On the morning of June fourth, while her husband relaxed on the living room sofa and before she left her home to worship at her local church, Mary Louise Malvado fatally shot Donald Malvado, ending years of her perceived pain and frustration. Unphased by the act of murder she'd just committed, Mary Louise Malvado calmly attended her regular seven a.m. Mass where her fellow parishioners and even her priest noticed nothing unusual about her demeanor while her husband bled to death at home. I call Detective Jared Jones to the stand."

By the time Detective Jones finished responding to Mr. Artemus' questions, Mary was convinced she killed Don. She was the only one who could have. The way he spelled everything out, she didn't look innocent. Not at all. He said it and she believed it. Her life was over.

Mr. O'Hare rose, tapping his fingertips on his legal pad. He cleared his throat, buttoned his jacket, and walked toward the witness stand.

"Detective Jones, did you find a murder weapon?"

"Not yet."

"Not yet? You're optimistic that one will turn up? Where?"

The breath Detective Jones exhaled into the microphone

echoed through the courtroom. "We haven't recovered a murder weapon."

"Did you perform a gunshot residue test on Mary Malvado within twenty-four hours of her husband's death?"

"Yes."

"And what were the results?"

"They were negative."

"So, she didn't fire the magical missing murder weapon?"

The prosecutor objected to that question.

"You have no proof that Mary Malvado killed her husband, do you?"

"Not yet."

Mr. O'Hare argued that the charges against her should be dropped because there was no proof, but as he predicted, the judge ruled in favor of the prosecutor. He believed there was enough suspicion to have a trial. Mr. O'Hare patted her folded hands and whispered, "They're trying to buy more time to prove their case. This was expected."

Maybe he expected it, but she'd prayed for a miracle, just like Father Greg suggested.

Mr. O'Hare rose again. "We request bail, Your Honor." He described her as an upstanding member of the community, a God-fearing woman and an unlikely flight risk. Wasn't that the truth? Where would she fly to?

To her surprise, the prosecutor sided with him. Ten percent of a million dollars bail might as well have been a million dollars. She didn't have that kind of money.

And then miracle of miracles, Mr. O'Hare informed the court the bail would be posted that afternoon. It didn't matter who or how. She'd be allowed to sleep in her own bed tonight.

33

The outcome of the hearing pleased Jared. He'd encouraged the DA to consent to Mary Malvado's bail. She wasn't going anywhere, and they could keep an eye on her if she was out and about living her everyday life. One of the female detectives had already begun attending Mary's church, wearing plain clothes and introducing herself as a new resident. Besides befriending Mary, Shirley's assignment was to endear herself to Father Greg and the congregation.

Every murderer makes a mistake, especially when they think they've gotten away with something. It was just a matter of time.

The look on Mary Malvado's face when her attorney guaranteed her bond was genuine surprise. Either she didn't know her house could be used for collateral, or she wondered who would guarantee the one-hundred thousand dollars on her behalf. He wondered that too.

After the ruckus died down from the galley when the judge granted bail, the people interested in Mary Malvado's case filed out. Jeff had exited immediately after adjournment and stood in the hall, his phone discreetly recording everyone who left.

Often, the killer, like the firebug, sticks around to see the consequences of his work. They might get lucky.

Jared gathered his files and turned toward the back of the courtroom, surprised to see Emma waiting for him. And Isabelle White and her son Carson, still seated in the last row. If he spoke to them, Em would ask. He couldn't ignore them.

When he neared their row, he winked at Emma and turned toward them. "I'm surprised to see you here." Ms. White wiped tears from her eyes. Her nose shined bright red. Carson held her close around the shoulders. Junior hadn't uttered one word to Mary Malvado, hadn't even acknowledged his mother when she entered the courtroom. The difference between Malvado's two sons was night and day.

"I didn't want her to come, but she insisted," Carson White said, extending his hand. "You spoke very well, Detective, but from where I sit, legally you don't have much of a case."

He smirked. "To be truthful, I don't. Not against her."

Emma stood off to the side, not bothering to hide her curiosity. She craned her head to hear better.

Isabelle White drew in a fortifying breath. "Did she kill him?"

"I'm not certain of it." He stepped toward Carson, turning his back to Emma and lowering his voice. "That's his sister waiting for me. Your biological aunt. Do you want to meet her, or would you rather I leave with her before you and your mom make an exit?"

Too late. Emma approached them. "Detective Jones, I was hoping to speak to you before you go."

Carson eyed her from head to toe and smiled. She looked gorgeous in a tailored three-piece pinstriped suit, cocoa brown with pale blue stripes. Another silky camisole, blue like the stripes and cut low to the top of the vest, peeked out from the jacket. So did pale blue stilettos from the hem of her pants.

He stretched to draw her closer. "This is Lieutenant Emma Hunter. Don Malvado was her brother."

A high-pitched squeaky mew like a kitten's escaped Isabelle White. "You're Emma?" Her hand flew to her mouth. "I remember you when you were this high." She measured two feet from the floor.

Emma squinted.

"Emma, this is Isabelle Ganesh White and her son Carson."

Emma was so stunned, her face turned ghostly white and her body inclined backward. He and Carson reached at the same time to steady her. She held onto his arm, studied Carson for a brief second, and returned her gaze to Isabelle. "You know me?"

Isabelle's chin quivered. "I met you a long time ago. You probably don't remember. It was only one time. I went by Belle back then."

Emma's head shook slowly, her eyes riveted on Isabelle's face. She was scraping her brain for a memory, mentally opening childhood doors to recollect the name. Her jaw locked her teeth together. Jared saw the muscles in her face tense.

"I'm sorry, I don't remember."

Isabelle's smile was forgiving. "That's all right. I'd like you to meet my son." Without faltering, she added, "Carson this is your Aunt Emma."

Tears rimmed Emma's eyes when she refocused on Carson. "Oh my God, you're the spitting image of him." Her voice was higher. "I'm...I'm so...I'm so so sorry. I-I didn't know about you. About either of you."

He'd never seen Emma unnerved like this. He drew her closer and wrapped his arm around her waist.

"That's the way we wanted it, Emma." Carson's voice was steady. "It's nice to meet you though, even in these unusual circumstances. I'm sorry for your loss."

Jared was struck by Carson's sincerity. His father was dead, yet he was consoling a woman he just met. He liked these two and hated Don Malvado all the more for abandoning them. If he never found Don Malvado's killer, it might not be so bad.

"Thank you, but there was no love lost between us. We didn't get along. Quite frankly, I didn't like him. I don't need your sympathy. I have a hundred questions I'd like to ask, and I have no right to ask one. Is there anything I can do for you? Do you need anything?"

Tears rolled down Isabelle's face. Carson hugged her. "No, thank you. We've always been fine, and we will continue to be."

Emma leaned into him. Rejection didn't sit well with her. He hoped she didn't push the matter.

Carson turned toward him. "Thank you, Detective. Good luck with your case."

He liked this kid's strong handshake. "May I suggest we leave the courthouse by the downstairs entrance? There were reporters outside who might get nosy if they see the two of you. They're desperate for information about this case."

Carson guided his mother in the direction he led Emma. Once outside, Emma stopped them. She drew her card from her purse. "If I can ever help you, this is my work and my cell number. Please take care of yourselves."

She took his hand and they watched mother and son walk away.

34

She was a jumble of emotions. Jared's hand holding hers helped. She stared in the direction the white sedan exited the parking lot. "It's uncanny how much he looks like him. The same smile, the same space between his teeth. I feel like I'm looking at a clone of a younger Don." She leaned into Jared's side.

"She seems so strong, yet weak at the same time. It's always been just the two of them and it shows. They're a family. I bet she was beautiful at one time. I wish I could remember her. When did you meet them?"

He tugged her toward his car. "Last week. I spoke to Carson at his law office, and I met Ms. White after her shift was over at the eatery where she waitresses."

Her heart skipped. "She works as a waitress?"

"That's always been her career."

He opened the passenger door and waited for her to settle in her seat. The idea that the poor woman raised a child on her own tore at her. She allowed Jared to back out of his parking space and head toward the exit before asking, "How much time did you spend with them? What did you think of them? What did she say about my brother?"

"She hasn't heard from him since her son was born."

Her insides plummeted. "He knew about him? And he ignored them? Jared, how could a man do that? What kind of a man does that?"

"I've wondered the same, especially after meeting them. I liked her. Life dealt her a shitty hand and she stayed in the game anyway. He's a good kid, a fine young man. I'd be proud if he were my son. And you're right, the bond between them is pretty strong."

She shook her head. "Belle. I'm wracking my memories, but I don't remember anything about her."

"From the stories she told me, she and your brother had quite a thing. She had a crush on him from kindergarten, where they first met."

Emma's interest piqued. Old yearbooks were on file at the library. She could search the pictures. "Did she tell you what happened?"

"Just that he refused to claim the baby and threatened her with legal action if she revealed he was the father."

"That sounds like my brother. His M.O. was always to threaten to sue. He'd raise his voice and scream, 'I'll take you to court. Everything you have, I'll own.'" She waved her hand, pointing in the air like he always did. "And Isabelle just walked away? Pregnant and alone?"

"She contacted him after the baby was born, hoping to sway his position once he saw Carson. Same outcome. They had a strong family network. Carson made it sound like he had a good life, despite not having a father. He's known your brother's identity for years and had no desire to meet him. He's the exact opposite of your nephew, Donnie."

Emma chuckled. "Yeah. I find it funny that Carson is the spitting image of Don while Donnie is fair and takes after Mary.

It's also ironic that Carson is an attorney. Don always wanted Donnie to be one. I can't believe Don knew about him and didn't support them. That bastard."

He smiled. "Isabelle doesn't share those feelings. She's still in love with him. She cried for him. In front of me and today. I haven't seen your sister-in-law do that yet."

Neither had she. "Mary has always been stoic. It was hard to tell when she was happy. Take a look at her wedding pictures. She smiles but it doesn't reach her eyes."

"Oh, I don't know, I saw genuine emotion in the courtroom when I described how she committed murder. I saw realization that she's not going to get away with it. Even her priest appeared shocked hearing the details."

She reached to caress his thigh. "You were great up there. I love watching you testify. Very convincing too, with all your circumstantial facts. Except for one thing. Mary didn't do it."

The car stopped in front of a Mexican restaurant she liked. "Are you buying me lunch?"

"I am."

"I'm not sure I can eat, but I sure could use a drink. Today has been a shocker."

They hadn't spent time together lately. She'd missed him. She held his hand as they walked inside and to their table. Once they were seated and drinks ordered—iced tea for him and a margarita for her—Jared peered at her.

"Are you on duty tonight?" He eyed her glass.

"Yes. I plan to nap before I go out some," she checked her watch, "nine hours from now. One drink isn't going to stay with me that long, not with food." That placated him.

"Mary seemed surprised when the judge granted her bail. Were you?"

She shrugged. "I wasn't sure. After all, it's a murder charge, which isn't a bailable offense ordinarily. Did you have a hand in convincing the district attorney to allow it?"

Jared gave her the slightest smile. "She's not going anywhere. I'm not sure she's our killer." He grinned. "I must be hanging out with you too much."

She returned his smile. "Not too much lately. Thank you for that recommendation. I discussed with Terry the likelihood of bail, but he wasn't sure how it would go."

"You what?"

"Relax, Jared. I couldn't ask you, for fear you'd think I was trying to influence you. I wasn't sure my brother's house was mortgage free, although it certainly should have been. They've lived in it forever. I reached out to Terry to say that in the event bail was a possibility and Mary's house was not, I would step up."

He sighed. "Em—"

"Let me finish. I suggested if my brother's house wasn't viable, her sister Ellen could use her house for bond guarantee and if neither of those worked, I told him to contact me. I didn't want Mary to spend any more time in jail."

"I can't believe you contacted him in the first place."

"In case you've forgotten, I'm the one who hired him. Technically, I'm his client."

"I wish I could forget it. I don't understand you, Em. Once again, you're going out of your way to help a woman you've had no contact with for years."

She couldn't explain what she felt. "I don't know what to tell you. Maybe it's obligation. Sympathy. Admiration that Mary endured so much for so long. Anger that she'd had to. Belief in her innocence. Or maybe it's all about me. Maybe it's guilt. If I hadn't severed ties, if I'd stayed on the fringes of her life, maybe she wouldn't have gone through any of that. Maybe she wouldn't be facing a murder charge today."

"That's bullshit. You didn't walk away from her, you walked away from your tyrant of a brother. Mary's happiness was not on you. She had the option to leave him any time she wanted. You did what was necessary for your self-preservation."

She'd told herself that from the minute she received her brother's hostile letter. The one that sat on the kitchen counter for days before she opened it. With no return address but that distinctive printing that she recognized. It was self-preservation. She shut her eyes and dropped her head backward.

"Please let's not go into this again, Jared. I'm doing—I did— what I believe in my heart was the right thing to do. For everyone."

"All right. Let's talk about something else. Did you hear that RayKay is retiring?"

A butterfly took flight in her chest. "Ray Kayson? Retiring? He's certainly old enough but I thought he'd never give up his desk. When did he announce?"

"His wife's health has become an issue. He told me yesterday. I'm not certain anyone outside our division knows yet."

"I'm sorry to hear that."

"You realize what this means, don't you? You should be next on the promotion list."

She didn't dare hope. "I was next up last time a position came open and it didn't seem to matter. So far Shirley and Carol are the only two who cracked the old boys' network and it took them half their careers. I'm quickly approaching that point."

He reached across the table for her hand. "And you outshine both of them. You've paid your dues. You scored in the top five on the test. Plus there's a new administration in place this time around. You would be the youngest female detective joining the roster. That's a feather in their caps. You should be a shoe-in."

"Yeah, well, I'll believe it when I see it." She licked the salt off the rim of her glass. "How would that affect our relationship, Jared? We can't be partners who sleep together."

Jared's hand shot back to the edge of the table. "Is that all we're doing is sleeping together? Christ Emma, I thought it was a helluva lot more."

His words stung, because it was. "It is more than that, we both know it, even though we dance around it. But your buddies and the higher ups won't see it that way. I'll always be the underling sleeping her way to the top."

"Jeff doesn't see it like that."

"He's your partner. He'll always have your back."

"And we'll always have yours. Anyone who doubts your qualifications, you'll prove them wrong. You shouldn't have to, but one week on the job and it will be obvious. You'd be an asset to the group and none of the detectives would judge you because of our connection. You couldn't work the homicide squad with me, but that doesn't matter. You'd be good on the white-collar squad, bank robbery and even the drug squad. You're a top-notch investigator. You are still interested in the job, aren't you?"

She sighed. "Of course, I am. I'll mention it to whoever tomorrow morning."

"You look tired, sweetheart. Midnights killing you this month?"

She was tired. Exhausted in her bones. "Not really. I never sleep well in the daytime. You know I'm a night creature. But when I try to sleep, I dream about him. I see him on that couch, alive, snarling at me, insulting me and I—" she paused, reached across the table for his hand and said, "I killed him. I'm the one who shot him."

Jared closed his hand over hers. "That's an odd dream to have. You're supplanting yourself into the killer's shoes. Probably because of your intense dislike for your brother. And your self-inflicted guilt. Maybe you wished you did it instead of Mary." He chuckled. "You are pretty competitive, you know."

She didn't say anymore. Couldn't risk it.

"How about doing me a favor? Next time you're in that dream, pay attention to where you hid the weapon!" He laughed at his own joke.

She faked a smile and nodded. She knew exactly where it was.

35

The whirlwind of activity around her baffled Mary. One minute, she was convinced she was a murderer doomed to spend the rest of her life in the six-by-eight entrance to hell. That jail cell was the doorway to it, she was sure.

Then suddenly, the guards escorted her back to the waiting room and handed her the few items she'd been allowed to have. Her Bible, the clothes she arrived in, her jewelry. Terrence O'Hare arrived, sat her at the table and directed her to sign surety papers guaranteeing her re-appearance in court and using her house to secure the one-hundred thousand dollars bail. She didn't understand the legal terminology.

"It's like a promissory note. Your house is a promise that you won't disappear. It guarantees that on the appointed dates for any court appearances, you'll appear. If you fail to do so, the bail bondsman will own your house."

Dear Lord, where would she live? "I won't go anywhere."

"I'm sure you won't." O'Hare scrolled on his phone. "I want you in my office..." he studied the screen, "at nine o'clock on Thursday. Be prepared to give me names of friends and relatives who will serve as character witnesses for you. I'll need a handful of parishioners from church who saw you that morning. Try to mix it up, women and men. And your priest, of course. He's like our shining star on the witness list."

Her head spun. "Is that all you need, names from church?"

"I don't know yet. Now that the case is set for trial, I'll have discovery of the state's evidence. That means everything they have in their files, every report they've written, fingerprints, blood samples, witness statements, test results, everything. Right now, your husband is the victim, but by the time we walk back into court, you'll be the injured party. The negative GSR test will work in our favor. I'll prepare subpoenas for the female guard who examined you and whoever else might not willingly cooperate. And—"

She smashed her palms against her forehead. There was no air in this room. "Please Mr. O'Hare, I need a minute to breathe, to think. Please, I can't do this right now."

His eyes widened as if she'd struck him. Didn't he understand what she was going through? Her life was...was...she had no idea what it was. But she couldn't deal with any of it right now. She wanted to be alone to think. To brood. To scream.

He looked stunned that she interrupted him. Embarrassed by her tone, she acquiesced. "I'm sorry. Don't worry, I'll be there on Thursday, and I'll tell you whatever you ask. I simply can't think about it right now."

"All right, Mary, you're right. It's been a lot today for someone who is new to this. My assistant will call you on Wednesday to remind you of the appointment and arrange transportation. I believe your family is waiting for you downstairs. Let's go file these bond papers and get you out of here."

She expected Donnie but Father Greg, Ellen and Vanessa waited for her in the courthouse lobby. Vanessa threw her arms around her neck. "Oh, Aunt Mary, are you okay? Was it horrible in there? Did you get the rosary beads I brought?"

She regarded her niece. "You delivered the beads? Father Greg, I thought they were from you." His brows knitted in confusion.

"No, I brought them. Aunt Emma called me. Somehow she knew you didn't have yours, and she asked me to find some. I was a little worried about going out that late to shop but a police car practically followed me the whole way. Aunt Em made sure I was safe."

Emma? She hadn't heard a peep from her since that day at the house when she found the journal. The detective hadn't mentioned Don's illegitimate son in court. That was an answered prayer. The secret was still safe. She dreaded when that information became public. Sure, she'd be shamed, and her children would be humiliated but that poor woman Isabelle, she'd have her entire life exposed once the reporters found her. She and her son were truly innocent victims in all of this. It wasn't right.

Mr. O'Hare mentioned the detective hadn't opposed her being released on bail. She was grateful for that. A thank you note might be appropriate, but Mr. O'Hare cautioned that the detective wasn't her friend. She still needed to be aware of his presence.

"What happens now, Aunt Mary?"

"Now I go home, make a hot cup of tea and soak in the tub. The detectives will continue their investigation, and I don't know what will happen next."

Father Greg touched her shoulder. "Have faith, Mary." Reassurance surged through her.

"Let's get out of here. Ellen, thanks for staying, but Father Greg can drive me home. You won't mind, will you Father? There's no sense making Ellen drive across town when you're going in my direction. I really want to go home and be alone for a while."

Ellen actually looked relieved. She bid Ellen and Vanessa

goodbye in the parking lot and slipped into Father Greg's car. "What did you think of the testimony?"

Father Greg sighed. "It certainly sounds damning. But I've read enough legal thrillers to know a good defense attorney will argue there is no proof. And Terrence O'Hare has a reputation as a pit bull on cross examination. I doubt any of this will be easy, Mary. I'll give you as much strength as I can and help you in any way you need."

For the first time in days, she smiled. "You already have, Greg, you already have."

THE POLICE DISPATCHER said Emma didn't report for duty until midnight. Mary left a message for Emma to call her. "Please make sure you write the word 'please' on the note." The more she thought about Isabelle Ganesh, the more concerned she became. She wanted to reach out to the woman. Maybe Emma could help track her down. She fell asleep with her cell phone beside her pillow.

Emma called just as she returned from church the next morning. "Are you all right? We shouldn't be talking. Detective Jones can easily dump your phone records and see this call. What's the matter?"

"Nothing's wrong. I want to reach out to the woman who had his son." She hoped never to say her husband's name again. "I—"

"That's not a good idea, Mary. In fact, it's a very bad idea. It could be used against you. Just go about your everyday business and try to live your life normally. The detectives will be watching your every move."

"Can you find her and get a message to her? I want to apologize to—"

"No, Mary, I can't do that either. I can't be involved. And

don't call me again. If you need to reach me, tell Nessie what the matter is and ask her to call me. But I can't help you. I have to go."

She scratched her head after Emma ended the call. Whose side was she on anyway?

36

E mma clocked in for her shift as if in a trance. Lunch with Jared had been a needed resuscitation of their relationship, but it didn't quiet her thoughts. Or the roller coaster of emotions she rode. She was numb that Mary still faced a murder charge. Dismayed that the judge found Jared's string of coincidences viable, despite expecting nothing less. Nauseated that even from his grave, her brother continued to wreak havoc on people's lives. Shocked that he knew about his son and ignored him and his mother for years. Years.

Don Malvado didn't deserve to live. She'd thought that seeing him sprawled on the couch that morning. She believed it now.

He deserved to die. That should be Mary's defense.

It was fortunate that the criminals took the night off so there was little more than neighborhood patrols for her to deal with. She reported a disabled vehicle and gave the car owner a ride home and helped another resident break into his home after locking himself out.

Her middle was in knots, her nerves frayed. She didn't

bother with a dinner break, just kept her eyes on the road. Good or bad, the easy night allowed time to think.

Jared was good at what he did. The best, in her opinion. Professional on the witness stand. Impressive. Every point he testified to that went to motive was not true proof of a crime. But the average juror who watches cop shows every night after dinner and sees police wrap up a case in an hour thinks they comprehend the intricacies of police procedure and the law. She'd had a couple cases where jurors inquired about forensic evidence, as if they understood the science behind it.

Terry O'Hare would point out the difference between fact and speculation. He'd invent a wild whodunnit scenario or two of his own. She'd seen him in action. But would they get it? Jurors could be fickle. Or would they believe what was a boat-load of circumstantial facts and convict Mary of murder?

She couldn't let that happen.

In conference with Terry O'Hare prior to the preliminary hearing, he confided his plans. "Today is all about listening to the state's evidence. Even before hearing it, I don't think it amounts to much, not from what my investigators have learned. I've already prepared Mary to expect the worse. You know first-hand the judges usually find for the police.

"When it's my turn in front of the jury, we're going on the offensive." He planned to point a finger at everyone in Mary's circle—her sister, her friends, even her priest.

"I'll throw shade at Father Greg and ask for forgiveness in the confessional the next Sunday," he'd joked. "I'm even going to suggest you killed him, Emma. You're certainly capable of it. And you'd know how to get away with it." Was that fact or speculation?

She wanted O'Hare's finger pointing at Donnie Jr. too. He was all about himself.

"Yes, yes, we'll find a motive for Donnie too."

Walking into the courtroom this morning, she didn't believe

it would go that far. Surely the judge would see through the thin veil of evidence. Hers wasn't the only gasp when he banged his gavel and bound the case over for trial. From the back row of the courtroom, she'd observed Mary's family and their inter-action—rather lack of interaction—with her. There was none. Mary had no one.

Beyond Mary's plight, she couldn't forget Carson White's face. He was a younger version of the brother she knew, the one she used to love, without the meanness in his eyes. Jared said it was unreasonable for her to feel responsible for them, but she did. That poor woman raised a son on her own when, had she reached out to Emma years ago, Emma would've helped, no questions asked. She sputtered a laugh at that thought. She would have asked a million questions. And confronted her brother about it. That would have been one hell of a chat.

Jared cautioned her to leave the Whites alone, to respect their wishes. She would, but that wouldn't ease the turmoil in her heart. Or her indecision about what to do next.

The bizarre letter from her brother sent to intimidate her was hidden in a fireproof box shoved to the back of the closet in her spare bedroom. Even though she read it only once, every damn word stayed in her mind's eye. His insinuation that she was a fake. "You're as phony as those fortune tellers you believed in as a little kid. How could you stand there and dishonor that uniform by accepting that award as a hero? Save a life? You took a life! You're not a hero, you're a whore. Do your bosses know your backstory? Shall I tell them?

His warning that she "better do the right thing. For once in your life, have some backbone. Admit to the drugs. Admit to the debauchery. Tell them you're a drunk, a lowlife pretending to be a good person. Tell them what an imposter you are, or I will. It's what you deserve."

And worst of all, the threats. "I'll ruin you. I'll take every-thing you have. I'll tell the newspaper the true story about

Emma Hunter, not the garbage they printed. You'll be nothing. And then I'll look at that little snit Vanessa. You turned her. She's immoral, a sham just like you. You two are exactly alike, stupid and worthless. Look over your shoulder, little sister. I'm coming for you."

Equally as vivid was the rage she felt that day, hearing his voice as she read his words. It wasn't one of his usual rampages. He was desperate and dangerous. Her wrath resurrected itself now. The motherfucker had an illegitimate son that he abandoned, and he planned to expose her for a past mistake? The piece of shit deserved to die. That was the *only* defense.

J ared's head ached the next morning as he walked to his desk. The brief time with Emma yesterday reestablished their relationship to a healthy level. There hadn't been time for sex, but after lunch they walked to an ice cream stand and ate it on a sidewalk bench. Emma held his hand and joked about the paparazzi hiding in the shrubs waiting to expose their secret. It had been a nice afternoon.

The stress was taking its toll on her, though. He supposed a sibling being murdered would result in a high stress level for anyone, no matter what the relationship. But his sense was that there was something more to Emma's anguish. She'd ordered a second drink, but reported to work forty-five minutes early. He checked.

The case was stressing out Emma and giving him a migraine. It was that feeling that the answer was right in front of him but just out of reach. Like the name of a classmate you know you know but can't recall. He fought the urge to slam his head against the wall and shake loose the information.

The message light on his desk phone blinked. It was from

Emma, speaking fast, saying that Mary Malvado had called her hoping to reach out to Isabelle White and her son.

"I told her that wasn't possible, Jared. I said I can't be involved. I instructed her not to call me again, and I pretty much hung up on her. I didn't offer to help. I'm not involved. I wanted you to know about the call."

She sounded like a child caught in a lie, frantic to talk her way out of it. He was still shaking his head when Jeff showed up with coffee and bagels.

"I thought yesterday went well. You tell a good story, Jared, but I don't think we can find a jury or a judge who will convict Mary Malvado of a misdemeanor let alone murder based on the tale you tell. We're drowning in a sea of gray. Quite frankly, I'm surprised you talked the DA into pursuing the case with our flimsy evidence, but I'm glad you did. I want to solve this murder as much as you. Where do we go from here?"

"I hear ya, partner. I convinced the DA the case would go cold unless he bought us time and got on board with charges. I told him to think of Mary Malvado as a placeholder if he wasn't convinced she pulled the trigger. Like us, he can see both sides and the judge gave us credence by holding it over for trial. The DA plans to present a plea offer just to see if Mary will bite. That might shake a confession out of her, whatever that might look like. She did it. The priest did it. The butler did it. Who knows?

"I doubt O'Hare will counsel her to accept the offer. He wrote a lot of notes while I testified, and I saw him grin. He's not stupid. He won't agree to a plea deal."

"Why would he? The only thing we can prove is that Don Malvado is dead and Mary Malvado had motive."

Hence Jared's headache. "I know. Nobody commits the perfect murder, Jeff. Certainly not someone like Mary Malvado, the queen of the meek. We missed something. Let's review."

Two hours later, his head still pounded. They sifted

through every scrap of evidence, reviewed all their notes and tossed plausible and impossible theories back and forth with no result. "What does that television cop always say? If the evidence doesn't support the premise, check the premise. We've been working on the premise that Mary Malvado killed her husband. We can't prove that. So let's agree that she didn't. Who did?"

Jeff scratched his head. "We ruled out business partners. We looked at family members and they have alibis. The priest is still a question mark. I can see him pulling the trigger, but we have the same problem with him as we do with Mary. No proof. Who else do you want to look at?"

Jared swallowed two more aspirins. His stomach still burned from the four he'd already eaten. "I don't know." He looked at his ringing cell phone. "This is Shirley. Wonder how it's going for her posing as a church member? Cross your fingers that she can provide a lead."

Shirley bypassed the etiquette of an opening conversation. "This woman has no life. She goes to church every morning and goes home until the next morning. I have no idea what she does all day in that house. Some days she doesn't walk down the driveway to the mailbox. I've politely spoken to her every morning but all I get is a weak smile or a head nod. She responds like that to everyone. It's like she lives in a private bubble. Every day is a rinse and repeat cycle. She has her groceries delivered, and she hasn't had any visitors except the priest."

Jared sat up in his chair. "The priest? He makes house calls?"

"Apparently, that's not unusual. The church ladies say he regularly visits shut-ins and congregation members who are hospitalized or ill at home. He administers communion at two nursing homes on Mondays."

"But why visit Mary Malvado when he sees her in the front row every morning?"

"Ah, the sixty-four-million-dollar question. Especially since she occasionally stays after Mass for a one-on-one in his office. I've had one personal meeting with him as a new church member. He's quite charismatic and not afraid to whip off that collar and roll up his shirtsleeves like an ordinary guy. Some of these women practically faint when he speaks to them. I've noticed he's a touchy feely minister with some of them."

Jared had already surmised that, at least where Mary Malvado was concerned.

"If Mary Malvado craved attention, I suspect the good father's consideration could be misconstrued," Shirley added.

"Or maybe not. Maybe it opens the door for a co-conspirator scenario."

"You like the priest for this?"

"I don't know, maybe."

"To be truthful, Jared, it wouldn't be a waste of resources to have a plain clothes cop follow him around for a couple of days. It won't tell us what goes on inside the Malvado house, but it will provide a clearer picture of Father Greg. Short of sneaking up the driveway and peeking in the windows, I don't know how we find that out."

MARY MALVADO DREW her sweater tighter around her. "I want to sell the properties that those businesses are on, Greg. I'm not interested in being a landlord. All 'he' ever did was complain about them. I'm in no way attached to them because they were his and neither of the kids is interested in succeeding their father. Not that he was a successful businessman. Anyway, I spoke to the tenants in both those buildings and they're willing to buy the properties once we find a will or his estate is legally transferred to me.

"I'll need help regarding the space he owns in the shopping center. Will you be able to advise me?"

"I'm not schooled in property ownership, but I'll try. Isn't Donnie Jr. directing you along those lines?"

She weighed her words, searching for the Christian way to express herself. "Donnie Jr. is only interested in an inheritance. We haven't found a will, and he doesn't believe I'm capable of an intellectual thought. Plus, he thinks I killed his father, and he's preparing to step in and declare me unfit to handle my own affairs. He knows all the financial maneuvers. My plan is to pre-empt him. I'm limited to making phone calls though. I'm stuck in this house."

"Why do you say that?"

She trembled. "I feel it every day, Greg. I'm certain someone is watching me, following me. I'm not going anywhere except Mass because of it. I check and double-check the windows and the doors day and night. I think he's haunting me."

Father Greg snickered. "Come on, Mary. There's no such thing as ghosts. You're simply nervous about your future, with a trial hanging over your head. Any normal person would be."

"It's more than that. My attorney said I might be under surveillance, and I'm sure that's what's happening. It's unnerving."

"Yes, yes, it would be. But you have nothing to hide. Staying cooped up in here doesn't look good. It casts suspicion on you. And it's not healthy for you. You'll wither. If you are under surveillance, you should make a show of acting normal. Let's go out to lunch. We can ride by the businesses and to the shopping plaza to look at the properties so you have a better sense of what they are."

"It's not a good idea for you to be seen with me, Greg, I can't risk casting you in my dark shadow."

"No, no, dear, it's my light you will walk in, God's light. You'll feel stronger, you'll see." He stood and motioned for her to take his hand. It was warm and strong, not cold and calloused the way her husband's had been. She absorbed his strength.

"All right, Father, I'll go. You've always been good at thinking for me. And I've never gone wrong listening to you."

38

Emma chewed her lip. Terry O'Hare's conference room was massive. She felt tiny tucked in an oversized black leather chair at the end of a sixteen-foot oval table. Large pieces of artwork dotted the walls, mini murals of weather scenes. A thunderstorm. A sunrise. A lone skier navigating a slope. O'Hare was a large man. He must like everything to scale.

His phone call to come in for an interview didn't surprise her. After all, she was the victim's sibling, and she'd told him on the day she retained him she'd be a character witness for Mary. He was building a defense for his client. Nevertheless, she gritted her teeth.

Attorneys didn't scare her. She drank with some of them at happy hour. The prosecutors she worked with often complimented her ability to remember facts and her poise on the witness stand. She spent time preparing for cases, rehearsing mock interrogations, and fine tuning her body language so it revealed nothing. The tips and advice the attorneys shared with her were invaluable. This meeting with O'Hare was no different. He was like a DA attempting to prove his case.

Still, her bowels rumbled.

She jumped to her feet when he burst through the door with a rollaway briefcase. The room shrank a bit.

"Sit down, sit down, Emma. I've been looking forward to this meeting. It's nice to be on the same side for a change."

She gulped.

He clasped his hands into two balls then opened them as if surprised. "The transformation from you in a police uniform to you sitting here in a dress that I must say is very becoming and high heels is remarkable. No one would guess you are a cop. This side of you is rather interesting."

Was he hitting on her? Eww. Maybe Jared was right, it was time to go public.

"I have to say I've enjoyed getting to know you outside of your police persona. I already admired you as a professional. For the life of me, I don't understand why you're not carrying a gold shield. I also want to commend you on your empathy for your sister-in-law. You—"

Enough was enough. "You understand, Terry, that I was estranged from my brother and by default Mary for a number of years, don't you? I wasn't privy to their recent lives."

"Yes, Mary has mentioned more than once that you've suddenly come out of the woodwork. Quite frankly, it surprised her, but she's grateful. I, of course, appreciate the business."

"Sure. All that said, I'm not certain how I can help you. I'm unable to tell you anything current about either of them."

For some reason, O'Hare found that funny. His belly laugh filled the room. "Let's get started, shall we? I read Detective Widows' report but tell me in your own words what you saw that morning."

Her mind went blank. "Like I said in the interview, I went into the house and saw my brother dead on the couch."

"C'mon, Emma, you're a trained observer, one of the best. Tell me everything you saw. Give me the details."

Her eyes closed, her brain set to rewind. "He was slouched backward against the sofa, blood pooling on the cushions. Obviously deceased from the massive damage to the side of his head. The windows were closed, the television off. No one else was in the house to my knowledge."

"Did you call out for your sister-in-law? Wonder where she was? Search the rest of the house in case she was injured as well?"

"No, I didn't."

"Why not? Weren't you concerned about her too?"

"I assumed she made the emergency call."

"You didn't know that for sure, though, did you?"

"Not for certain, no. But a squad car was already there. I wasn't first on the scene so it wasn't my responsibility to search the location."

He turned a page in his three-ring binder. "All right. Did you know about your brother's other son, Carson White?"

Her stomach churned. "No."

"Nothing at all?"

She felt her forehead crinkle. "No. I found out the day Mary asked me to collect her things, including the journal that the birth certificate was tucked into."

"You have no idea who anonymously mailed that to her along with the newspaper clipping?"

"None. I'd love to know, though, if you find out."

He chuckled. "I'm surprised you're not hot on the trail. What would you have done if you'd known about your nephew, your illegitimate nephew?"

She released a tense laugh. "I don't think you want to ask me that question in court, Terry. I would have killed my brother for abandoning them."

O'Hare grinned and dramatically drew a line through the middle of the page.

"When was the last time you saw your brother?"

She expelled a whoosh of air. "I can't say for sure. Years. Lots of years."

"Mary tells me that recently, he was upset about you. That he'd been ranting about an award you received that was undeserved. Did he contact you about that?"

Her mouth was dry. She swallowed air. "No, I never heard from him."

"What award did you receive?"

"It was more of a commendation from the Catholic Ministries. I saved a little girl's life. A three-year-old."

O'Hare gave her a thumb's up. "Good for you. Tell me the circumstances."

"It was pure luck that I was cruising the back street of the Catholic daycare center. A group of children were playing in the yard. Watching them play made me smile, and I stopped the car for a minute. My eyes surveyed the playground and when the slide came into my line of sight, I saw the child topple off it. I threw the car in park, scaled the fence, and rushed to her. She wasn't breathing."

"And you were in time?"

"Yes. I revived her with CPR before the EMTs arrived. She's fine and hopefully, the workers there will keep a sharper eye on their kids. None of them saw her fall. The Catholic Ministries felt the need to recognize me. I would have preferred a new pair of pants. Mine ripped going over that fence."

"As well they should. That was an incredible save. I don't remember hearing about that. Was it publicized?"

"There was a small article in the newspaper."

"And your brother saw that?"

She caught her lip between her teeth. "I don't know."

"Mary says he became irate when he read it."

She'd been taught well. He hadn't asked a question. There was no need to verbally respond. She shrugged.

"Mary says he ranted for three days about it and what he was going to do."

"My brother was known for his rampages. He ruined a lot of Christmases."

"Do you know what his plans were?"

"How would I know? I'm sure it involved some manufactured legal action. That was his go-to threat. He was always going to sue."

"Mary thinks he wrote you a letter. She says he sat at the dining room table an entire day drafting it, mumbling, swearing to get even. Get even for what, Emma?"

"I have no idea."

"Do you think he was jealous of you? Mary says he resented the fact that you were a cop."

"I don't know anything about that."

"Did you receive his letter?"

"No?"

"You didn't? Because Mary remembers the day he made a show of mailing it, declaring it would be the end of you."

Her armpits were sticky. Her deodorant was failing. It wasn't a question. She looked directly into O'Hare's eyes.

"Mary doesn't know what he wrote in the letter."

She maintained eye contact.

"What was in the letter, Emma?"

"I never received a letter from my brother."

39

What a grueling ninety minutes. She forced herself to walk slowly to her car, curious if O'Hare watched her from his second floor window. Her heart raced.

Wonder if the behavior instructors at the Academy ever envisioned their training would be used to deflect a defense attorney's personal inquiries. She was trained not to panic and she hadn't. Damn, O'Hare was good. The way he lazily perched on the edge of the table and leaned in to ask his questions was intimidating. He crowded personal space. Made her uncomfortable. But she didn't show it.

Before she knew it, his laugh bounced off the walls and he stood. "That was good, Emma, very professional. Mary doesn't know if he mailed the letter. If there was a letter and it was damaging to you or your career, you'd have motive to kill him. So would the tenants, who he had over a barrel with rents and personal insults. I don't have to prove they did it, only that they could have. I can point a finger at his son as well as his illegitimate son or his mother. There's enough people to line up for any jury to question what the state will present."

His hand extended toward hers, soft as a sofa pillow. "You won't mind if I throw you under the bus to save your sister-in-law, will you?" She'd been too stunned to speak.

"I didn't think so. We're done here. Thanks for coming in. I'll see you at the trial."

She hiked the air conditioning in her car to high and clung to the steering wheel. O'Hare was ruthless, which is what Mary needed. But at what cost? Poor Isabelle and Carson White.

Finally steady enough to drive, she headed for the highway. Of all nights, Jared wanted to meet Jeff and his wife for dinner tonight. She'd rather go home and spend her night off throwing back beers. He said the dinner would be a test run for the two of them showing up at A.J.'s wedding together. It wasn't much of a test. Jeff knew about them, even if it was unofficially. Maybe the distraction would take her mind off everything else.

SHE ARRIVED at the restaurant ten minutes later than she planned. They waited for her in the bar. Jared saw her enter and walked to greet her, placing a light kiss on her lips. This dinner was important to him. Jeff was his partner and his best friend. She didn't want to let him down.

"I'm sorry I'm late." They reached the high-top table. "Forgive me for making you wait." Jeff's wife waved off her comment and shook her hand. Emma turned to Jeff. "I'm not convinced this is a good idea." Jared's arm wrapped around her waist. "This guy is going to cost me my reputation."

Jeff raised his glass to her. "You're well respected in the station, Emma, as well as the other districts. People might question your bad taste in men, hanging around the likes of Jonesy, but it's good to finally see you two together. You'd be an asset to the detective bureau."

"Thanks for the vote of confidence. I appreciate it." Sitting beside Jared with friends did feel good. It felt right. She loved the proximity of the station to her home but, if offered the promotion, she'd volunteer to transfer to another precinct to avoid the appearance of a conflict if it concerned the administration. If they only knew how many cops slept around, they wouldn't be.

"What'd you do on your day off?" Jared grinned like a five-year old.

They'd settled this afternoon that the subject of her brother was off limits. She didn't plan to tell him about her meeting with O'Hare because she didn't want to compromise him or his investigation. Plus, she didn't want to think about it anymore. "Mundane chores. I caught up on laundry and emails."

Alicia Widows high-fived her. "No one remembers that the working woman is also the chief cook and bottle washer. Your day off is rarely a day you relax, I bet. I make Jeff wash the dishes and vacuum just to keep him grounded. He doesn't get to come home, prop his feet up and watch TV the rest of the evening."

Jeff's cheeks pinkened.

"To be honest, Jeff does more than that. I'd say the household chores are evenly divided." She winked at Emma. "Train 'em early."

Grinning, Emma eyed Jared, who raised his hands. "Hey, I'm not afraid of dishpan hands." She returned her gaze to Alicia, realizing she knew little about Jared's partner or his life.

"What do you do, Alicia?"

"I'm a personal financial advisor. I'm a certified public accountant, but I found numbers boring. I enjoy helping people plan and realize their financial dreams. Neither one of us are strictly nine-to-five, but we make it work. What about you? What made you want to become a cop?"

Emma took a deep breath. "When I was little, I wanted to

be a teacher. Then a series of events happened. My father was in a car accident. I was five, belted in the back seat and terrified. And then this man in a blue uniform reached into the car and drew me out into one of the best hugs I'd ever had, and I was safe. Shortly after that, we were awakened in the middle of the night by sirens and our neighbor's house was on fire. We all ran outside and I saw a policeman carrying the woman who lived in the house out the front door, backlighted by flames. All of us, who stood there watching, applauded. I started to think then that the men in uniforms, the police, helped people.

"But the final event, the one that Jared teases me about, happened a week later. My best friend's puppy got lost, and we were desolate. We'd looked everywhere and were sitting on her front stoop crying when up the street, here came a police-woman with the puppy trotting alongside her as proud as can be. I cried because Pogo was safe, but also because it was a woman in the blue uniform who saved him. That's when I real-ized that's what I wanted to do. As Jared says, save people and puppies."

Jared dropped a kiss on her shoulder and beamed.

Alicia's eyes misted. "It's a noble profession and from what Jeff tells me, you do the uniform proud. You followed your dreams. That's outstanding. And you paid it forward, saving that little girl." She raised her martini glass. "I hope we become friends."

She didn't have many female friends, mostly because they didn't understand her career choice. Many of her high school classmates were married and raising families. She had little in common with them. The women she met at the Academy were as busy as her. There wasn't time for socializing. If she grabbed a beer after work, it was with the partner she'd just spent a ten-hour shift with.

It might be nice to occasionally have lunch with a friend

who discussed more than crime statistics or the latest BOLO. Even a girls' weekend could be fun. She liked Alicia.

If everything went well with Mary's trial, she'd nurture this friendship.

40

Mary switched off the alarm before it rang. Every morning she woke up and stretched in the sunlight streaming through the crack between the drapes. And she smiled. It had been years since waking up thrilled her, not since the kids lived here, and she packed lunches and readied bookbags. She didn't really do anything more nowadays than when 'he' was around, but the house was happier to come home to and her step was quicker. The pantry no longer was stocked with chips, cookies, and other junk food. Vegetables filled the refrigerator drawers. If she never saw another pizza, she'd be thrilled.

Volunteering at the animal shelter had been Father Greg's idea but oh, what a difference it made in her heart. Unconditional love was foreign to her. A nurturer by nature, she finally had a purpose again. The orphaned dogs and cats were her newfound babies.

It was hard to believe a month had passed since the preliminary hearing. Her trial was scheduled to start next week. Mr. O'Hare had come to her with an offer from the district attorney —plead guilty to third degree murder in return for a reduced prison sentence of seven years, out in five years or less with good behavior. She'd been flabbergasted. She couldn't plead guilty to a crime she didn't commit. That would be a sin and she told him so.

Thankfully, the publicity about the murder died down after the first few days, but Mr. O'Hare expected reporters to be in the courtroom. He anticipated a two-day trial. She couldn't fathom two eight-hour-days to determine someone's fate. Twelve strangers deciding if she'd be allowed to continue waking up here.

After three visits to his office, all of them longer than two hours, Mr. O'Hare declared her ready to face a jury. The hours of prep work, of answering the same questions asked in different ways, of sharing personal information about her family and friends, of being reminded at every damn session that Don was dead, all rolled into one long monotonous headache.

When would she be able to move forward? Would it be in this house or behind bars?

Today, she headed to court for voir dire. Mr. O'Hare explained that was a French term meaning to speak the truth and was applicable to jury selection. A pool of one hundred people would assemble in the courtroom to complete a questionnaire about themselves, their beliefs and their personal experiences. The questions were designed to allow the attorneys to sift through the group for suitable jurors. Anyone who'd been a victim of a violent crime would not be suitable, he'd explained, nor would a newlywed or anyone with deep religious convictions. Plus, the judge had to ensure that none of the prospective jurors knew her or him or anyone from the district attorney's office. She didn't expect anyone to know her.

The initial publicity the murder had received might also complicate selecting jurors who weren't already prejudiced against her. Mr. O'Hare told her to expect a long day and to, once again, dress as if she were attending a church function. Her Sunday best, he'd called it.

She reached for the new blue flowered shirtwaist dress and cut off the tags. Little by little she replaced the old, worn clothes in her closet, the ones 'he' said were fitting for someone as small and unnoticeable as her. She hadn't wanted to shop for herself when 'he' made her feel so insignificant every day. Even her hairdresser commented on how long it had been since her last cut. The woman was kind, refraining from asking about 'his' death and instead, convincing her to color and highlight her hair. The end result was uplifting.

Today was Thursday. Mr. O'Hare expected jury selection to take a day and a half and the trial to begin on Monday. Tags hung from the other new outfits, in case they had to be returned. She might not need them by Wednesday.

ELLEN WAITED for her outside the courthouse. Moral support, she said. It was more than her children offered. Diane called her several times, but said she couldn't get away from work to be there for her. Donnie said jury selection wasn't important.

This time she entered the courtroom through the public doors. The empty room appeared larger without bodies in it. They walked to the front row. She whispered to her sister. "Mr. O'Hare said for us to wait for him here. This may take a while. You don't have to stay if you don't want to." Ellen wanted to stay.

One by one, the courtroom filled. The court stenographer, a different one from her first hearing, set up in the same corner. Two sheriff's deputies posted themselves at the front and rear doors. The young woman she recognized as the district attorney's assistant lugged a cart on wheels to the far table. Madeline, Mr. O'Hare's assistant, arrived with two rolling briefcases, pushed through the swinging door of the dividing rail, and motioned for Mary to join her at the defense table. A woman placed a pitcher of water and a tray of plastic cups on their table, the district attorney's table and at the judge's bench.

An older man in a suit chatted with the various court personnel about the grand slam in last night's baseball game, about someone recovering from rotator cuff surgery, about a new restaurant that opened. This was business as usual for them. Didn't they know the rest of her life would be decided in this room? How could they be so cavalier?

Like a bull crashing a china shop, Mr. O'Hare arrived. "You look fine, Mary, just fine." He acknowledged Ellen. "Review this list of names and tell me if you recognize anyone. Take your time. It's important."

Her hand trembled when she reached for the pages. Hopefully, the reading glasses hid the tears in her eyes. This is how it begins.

She read the list twice, the second time adding an X beside a name that sounded familiar. Madeline and Mr. O'Hare huddled at the end of the table whispering, reviewing the questionnaires. The district attorney and his assistant hunched together the same way, speaking softly and making notes. Mary sat at the table looking from side to side as if at a tennis match, her rosary beads moving slowly through her fingers. The deputies and the stenographer stared at nothing.

The older gentleman asked Ellen for identification and, after Mr. O'Hare interceded, moved her to the last row. "They want the prospective jurors to have the front row seats," he explained.

Detectives Jones and Widows arrived and sat at the DA's table. Mary looked around. Where was Emma?

"All rise."

He wasn't the same judge she saw at her preliminary hearing. This man floated to his seat, his robe whisking behind him. The nameplate read Honorable Judge Conley.

Mr. O'Hare leaned into her. "They're going to bring in the jury pool now, Mary. Most of them will sit behind us, but because of the number of them, some will sit in the jury box and look at you. It's best if you look them directly in the eye, don't stare down at the table or the floor. You want to display confidence." She couldn't show them something she didn't feel.

"I'll introduce you, ask you to stand and turn so those seated behind us can look at you. Hold your head up and stand proud. Focus on your sister back in the corner."

Dear Lord.

People filed in and filled the seats as directed by the older gentlemen. All of them wore badges with a number and the word juror. The ones in the jury box stared at her. She locked her jaw and looked straight ahead.

Judge Conley's voice was deep when he spoke, welcoming the panel and commending them for fulfilling their civic duty. "This is a murder case, ladies and gentlemen, expected to take two days, but that is not a guarantee. It will begin Monday morning at nine o'clock. The attorneys for both sides have not requested that you be sequestered, so you will be allowed to go home at night. Is there anyone who would suffer undue hardship if called to sit for this trial?"

Mr. O'Hare twisted in his seat to see who raised their hands. A woman said she was the sole caretaker of her elderly parents, and she couldn't afford to pay someone to take her place. A younger voice said he was a student with final exams next week. Another man had gallbladder surgery scheduled on Monday. Everyone, including the judge, made notes.

The district attorney stood, introduced himself, his staff and the detectives, asking if anyone recognized them. Several hands went up. "It will be my job, ladies and gentlemen, to prove to you that Mary Louise Malvado murdered her husband. She is charged with first degree murder."

Her heart stopped. Why did they always refer to her with three names?

Mr. O'Hare rose, introduced himself and Madeline. He touched her elbow to urge her to stand and introduced her. She scanned the rows, finding Ellen in the far corner and holding fast on her face. Why wasn't Emma here? No one indicated they knew her. Several admitted they'd read or seen news accounts about the murder in the newspaper and on television. When asked, they said that knowledge would not affect their ability to remain impartial. Wasn't that too risky? Would Mr. O'Hare eliminate them?

She sat down and listened while Mr. O'Hare and the district attorney singled out jurors to ask more in-depth questions. One woman was married to a cop and admitted she didn't think police made an arrest without just cause. Another woman was a news reporter for the daily paper that carried the murder stories, and friends with the metro editor who oversaw the articles.

Mr. O'Hare jotted notes beside names and one by one, the graph he'd drawn of fourteen spots in a box filled up with numbers. Twelve jurors and two alternates. After a conference with both attorneys at the bench, the judge called individual numbers, directing those people to the jury box while the elderly gentleman motioned for those already there to exchange their seats with the numbers the judge called. During the process, Mr. O'Hare and the district attorney remained standing, their hands folded in front of them. Silence prevailed between the numbers called. The whole room held its breath.

As each juror eased into the blue upholstered chair assigned to them, they leveled their gaze on her. Eight women and six men. *Take a good look, folks. I hope you like what you see because my life depends on it.* The rosary beads moved non-stop.

The judge's words came to her from far away. Her ears hummed, her heart pounded so fast she heard the blood whooshing through her veins. He told the jurors to report early on Monday. He didn't want to start the trial on Friday and then have the weekend interrupt it. He cautioned them not to discuss what little they knew about the case and to avoid any news accounts about today. She hadn't seen any reporters in the room, but then, she didn't know them all.

And then Mr. O'Hare was drawing her to her feet, tugging on her arm. The judge left and the deputies escorted the jurors from the room. The district attorney began packing up his mounds of papers, as did Mr. O'Hare, stuffing his binders into boxes. "C'mon Mary, let's go out in the hall and talk."

Ellen waited at the door with tear-rimmed eyes. Seeing her, Mary burst into tears. Her sister embraced her and walked her to the hallway where, praise Jesus, Father Greg waited. She flew into his arms. "Oh my God, Greg, you're here. Thank God, you're here. I can't do this. I can't go through with it." Her knees buckled and the priest dropped to the floor with her.

Mr. O'Hare yelped. "Mary! Mary! Get hold of yourself. Someone bring some water."

Ellen reached for her, yanking on her arms to lift her. Two deputies rushed to assist her. Father Greg's voice cut through the fog in her brain. "Mary. Come, Mary, it will be all right."

And down the hall, standing with their hands in their pockets as if they waited for the bus, Detectives Jones and Widows watched the whole episode.

41

Emma resisted sticking her head into jury selection even briefly. Jared would be angry if she did, and the attorneys for both sides would misinterpret her intentions. But damn if she wasn't curious. An attorney once told her jury selection was more a matter of weeding out the people he didn't want sitting on the panel than selecting whom he did. The jury was what was left after the process of elimination.

The judge's clerk was a friend. It cost Emma two Italian dinners with drinks but by the second phone call, she received a status report.

Empaneling the jury had proceeded faster than expected. The trial was set to begin at nine o'clock Monday morning. A balanced jury, the clerk thought. The alternates were both men, leaving eight women and four men. Of them, two women and one man were African American, and one woman and one man were Hispanic. O'Hare knew what he was doing.

"It's a good mix, Nessie," she explained to her niece on the phone. "Mary's attorney will portray Don for the bastard he was. The women should be sympathetic. Traditionally,

Hispanic and African American men are devoted to their spouses. That will play to Mary's favor when they hear what a rotten husband Don was. I haven't seen the evidence, but I don't think it's strong. Mary's attorney should have an easy time creating reasonable doubt in their minds that she did it."

"I requested two personal days off so I can attend with my mom. She received a subpoena, and she's nervous as hell. She thinks Mary did it and she's afraid she'll say something detrimental. Will you be there?"

"Mary's attorney subpoenaed me too so I'll be there, but I won't be allowed in the courtroom until after I'm called as a witness. Same with your mom, she won't be allowed inside. All of us will be together somewhere in the courthouse."

"You mean I'll be sitting by myself?"

"I would hope your cousins Diane and Donnie Jr. would be there. And Father Greg, you've met him. It's good that you're going, Mary will appreciate it. And tell your mom not to worry. Mr. O'Hare wouldn't ask her anything that would lead her to say something negative."

"Yeah, but what about the other guy?"

"Your mom can't testify to anything relating to the crime as long as Mary didn't confide in her. There shouldn't be much he can ask her beyond that. Her opinion isn't evidence."

"I'm worried, Aunt Em. My mom told me Aunt Mary collapsed at the courthouse."

Jared told her about that. He said it was "quite a show."

"I know, I heard. I think she was just overwhelmed. Hell, I'm still overcome by the courtroom setting when I first walk in there. The experience can be daunting. Try to put all this aside and enjoy your weekend. I'll see you Monday."

"Be honest, Aunt Em. Do you think she did it? Killed him?"

"No honey, I know she didn't."

∿

EMMA WAS happy she'd be on duty through the weekend. The time would pass more quickly and she wouldn't see Jared. Midnights seemed to be a cycle of go to work, come home, catch some sleep, get up and go back to work. It was difficult for her to sleep in the daytime, and there was never a window for social time. Because O'Hare subpoenaed her, her supervisor scheduled her off Monday and Tuesday.

Jared knew she was subpoenaed, so it shouldn't surprise him to see her at the courthouse. He called her twice, Friday night at dinnertime and Saturday afternoon, but she legitimately missed both calls, once while she slept and once while she was on hold with the cable company. She texted him to avoid a conversation, saying she'd call him. Friday's reports necessitated overtime on Saturday to complete the paperwork, and she was bushed when she finally made it home.

Under ordinary circumstances, she would have called him before slipping off to bed but these few days before the trial were anything but normal. Jared knew she was avoiding him. After all, he only tried to reach her twice.

MONDAY MORNING CAME TOO FAST. O'Hare didn't need her until Tuesday, but she planned to be there for the entire proceeding, even though she wasn't allowed inside to hear the testimony. She reached for a peach pencil skirt with a matching bolero jacket and a white camisole. No black today. No looking like a cop. She slipped into white leather pumps with a pointed toe and three-and-a-half-inch heel. The white designer clutch was too small for her gun, but she couldn't carry it into the courthouse anyway, since she wasn't on duty or attending in a police capacity. The hoops she'd have to jump through as a civilian to keep it with her weren't worth the effort. It would stay locked in her glove box.

The usual flock of reporters waited in front of the courthouse. She anticipated that and drove to the rear of the building, parking in the public lot. Vanessa drove in per her instructions and Emma waited for her and Ellen.

Vanessa hugged her and surprisingly, so did Ellen. Ellen trembled beneath her fingertips.

"You look great, Aunt Em. Your eye makeup is perfect. I'd love to borrow those earrings some time."

"Thanks, Nessie." She pinched her arm. "You clean up pretty good yourself." Unlike her mother, Vanessa wore a three-piece pantsuit with wedge heels. Her mother had on flats, a skirt that stopped at her ankles and a sweater over a T-shirt. Not a drop of makeup and unbrushed hair.

"Is Aunt Mary here yet?"

"Not yet. Her attorney will bring her in this door to avoid the news media out front. We can wait here for her."

"Aunt Em, will you stay with my mom? She's really nervous." No shit. Dark circles ringed Ellen's eyes and her skin was ashen. She was jittery, either from too much coffee or not enough, Emma wasn't sure.

"Don't worry, honey, she'll be fine. Here they come."

The three of them watched Mary walk toward them, sandwiched between O'Hare and Father Greg. O'Hare's assistant and another man struggled to keep up with them lugging rolling carts and briefcases. Where the hell were her kids? Mary looked younger in a printed knee-length dress belted at the waist and two-inch chunky heels. She looked confidant, her shoulders squared, her chin upright, almost vibrant. Not the collapsing femme fatale Jared described. Of course, he said he didn't buy the whole charade. She wasn't sure she did either. Vanessa threw her arms around Mary.

"I'm fine, Vanessa. You didn't have to miss work for this." Mary's voice was steady.

"I wanted to be here for you."

"Thank you, Vanessa." Mary embraced Ellen, something Emma had never seen, and turned to her. "I wondered if you'd come." O'Hare watched the exchange. So did Ellen and Vanessa. All eyes were on them.

"Good luck, Mary." Emma strode to the elevator. Jared would be waiting on the second floor with the other police officers scheduled to testify, including Sergeant Taylor, Officer Petrus and members of the evidence response team who'd searched the Malvado residence. Once the doors closed, she exhaled. What she wouldn't give to be in the courtroom the entire time. Nessie promised to relay everything that happened, but she wouldn't pick up the nuances of the jury or the overtones both prosecutors and the defense left hanging. Well, it was out of her hands.

She knocked on the conference room door. Usually she was on the other side with the LEO's before a trial, complaining about the weak coffee and cracking jokes about the witnesses. The door swung open. Had these cops, her colleagues, kidded about her?

Jared stood and came toward her, smiling. "What are you doing here? Aren't you on the other side?"

He closed the door behind him and urged her up the hallway. "You know I'm on your side, Jared. I came to wish you luck."

"Thanks, we're going to need it." He caressed her arm. "You look fantastic. Can I see you tonight? You're off until Wednesday night, right?"

"Yes, but wouldn't that be conspiring with the enemy?" She couldn't suppress a laugh.

"I'll take my chances." He looked to see if anyone was in the hall then dropped a fast kiss on her lips. "I'll call you at the end of the day and come over tonight."

"All right. Pay attention to what happens, I'll want to know everything." She rolled up on her toes to kiss him again and scurried to the elevator.

42

Mary had a moment of panic when a deputy motioned Father Greg to a waiting room. She'd prayed he'd sit directly behind her in the spectator seats and will his strength over the railing to her. His words from yesterday fortified her. "The Lord shines his light on you, Mary." They'd spent most of the day together.

He dedicated yesterday's sermon to her, rallying the congregation to pray for her and sing at the top of their lungs for her freedom. Since then, she was renewed. Inspired. Uplifted.

Gentle at her elbow, Mr. O'Hare's hand guided her to the defense table. Her heart sank seeing the number of people seated in the audience. A full house. Vanessa sat in the front row, nervously working her hands as if rinsing soap off them. Where was Donnie Jr.? Two women from church were behind her, the ever-present lace hankies bunched in their hands.

Mr. O'Hare positioned her between Madeline and himself. She discreetly wrapped her rosary beads in her hands folded in her lap. She recognized the stenographer, the deputies and other court employees. Home sweet home.

The room fell quiet. Everyone was in their place. They waited. The silence was deafening. Mary heard her heart racing, felt her stomach churning. Mr. O'Hare filled his lungs in and out, in and out. Two people at the prosecutor's table whispered over a legal pad. They waited.

An occasional cough broke the stillness. Someone shifted in their chair, causing the seat to squeak. A pocketbook snapped closed. A cell phone rang, catching the deputy's attention. He cautioned everyone to silence their devices or risk ejection.

They waited. She wanted to ask Mr. O'Hare what was taking so long, but she wasn't eager to have this trial get underway. She'd just sit silently in limbo, the border place between heaven and hell where those souls dwell who, though not condemned to punishment, are deprived of the joy of eternal existence with God in heaven. She remembered that from Bible study.

"All rise."

The judge drifted to his seat and called the room to order. Mr. O'Hare and the district attorney stood and responded yes when the judge asked each man if he was ready to proceed. He motioned to the elderly gentleman to bring in the jury and one by one, the strangers who would decide the rest of her life took their seats. She couldn't look at them. The judge welcomed them, recited preliminary instructions, cautioned the audience to remain quiet and turned the proceeding over to the district attorney.

He wore another sharp suit with shiny shoes.

Mr. O'Hare whispered, "Remember Mary, he doesn't testify. The narrative he's about to give is not evidence. Try not to react to it."

She locked her jaw.

"May it please the court, counsel, members of the jury." He

looked first at the judge, then her and Mr. O'Hare, then the panel. "Good morning, ladies and gentlemen. I'm about to tell you a story of a devout woman desperate to be free of her husband of twenty-five years. It's the defendant's story, Mary Malvado, who is charged with first-degree murder."

Her mouth went dry. He only used two names. What was that about?

"By all accounts, Donald Malvado provided well for his wife and two children and was a successful businessman. The couple lived modestly in a suburban community just outside the city and from the outside looking in, it was picture perfect.

"But behind closed doors, Mary Malvado plotted her husband's murder. We don't know for how long. It could have been weeks or months. But she wanted him dead. We'll prove that with her own handwriting, her exact words. And she had her way."

Her hand covered her mouth. "On June fourth, in the early morning hours while Donald Malvado relaxed on the sofa innocently watching one of his favorite television shows, that woman," his arm flung out toward her and she flinched, "Mary Malvado with malicious forethought and premeditation ended his life. It was a beautiful summer day, sometime between five-thirty and six-thirty, when she blew his head off, ladies and gentlemen, then, as if it were any other ordinary day, she stepped into her car and drove to church. Her husband bled to death in her living room."

Mary looked around. She was the only one sweating.

The DA continued. "It is the burden of the prosecution to prove to you beyond a reasonable doubt that Mary Malvado is guilty of murder in the first degree. This was not an easy case for us but the state trusts that you, empaneled to listen to and weigh all the evidence, will reach the same conclusion that we did. That Mary Malvado is a murderer. We are confident that the weight of the evidence we will put before you during the course of this trial will clearly establish the defendant's guilt.

"While most of you were at home that Wednesday morning making breakfast, getting your kids off to school, or dressing for work, Mary Malvado was on the second floor of her two-story home loading a shotgun." Her entire body tensed. Bile rose in her throat.

"While some of you walked your children to the bus stop or drove to your place of employment, Mary Malvado calmly walked down the carpeted stairs and into the living room of her children's home. She aimed the shotgun at her husband's head and squeezed the trigger. You'll see crime scene photos. They aren't pretty. Unlike most of the crime dramas you may watch on TV, in this case we don't have the so-called smoking gun. The murder weapon was never recovered."

A couple of the jurors leaned forward in their chairs, looking closer at her.

"The defense will argue that without the murder weapon, we can't prove Mary Malvado killed her husband. On the contrary, that only proves that Mary Malvado had a well thought out plan to cover up her actions." She gulped. She felt lightheaded.

"There's a timeline discrepancy between what Mary Malvado says she did and what the evidence will show. Missing minutes that Mary Malvado used to hide the murder weapon. It goes to premeditation, ladies and gentlemen. It proves first degree murder."

A rock in her stomach twisted and tightened. She gasped for air. She vomited on the defense table.

～

"I'm sorry." She hung over the sink in the ladies' room with a wet rag pressed to the back of her neck. Her nose leaked and tears rolled down her cheeks. "I'm sorry."

"It's all right," Madeline moistened the rag. "I saw you covering your face. I should have anticipated something like this."

The door opened and a female deputy escorted Vanessa inside.

"Aunt Mary, are you okay?" Such a sweet girl. Vanessa didn't hesitate to hug her, even though the stench of vomit clung to her like a shadow. Madeline stepped back, visibly relieved that she was off cleanup duty.

"I'm fine, Vanessa, it was all just too much. I knew I was anxious this morning. I shouldn't have eaten."

"It was hard to listen to, Aunt Mary, but I know you didn't do it. Here." She dug into her tote to retrieve a toothbrush, travel size toothpaste and breath mints. "I've only used this toothbrush a couple of times. Run it under really hot water for a few minutes and it should be fine. After all, we are related. You'll feel better once you clean your mouth and wash your face."

She did as she was told. Her eyes were bloodshot, her nose fire engine red. "What happens now?"

"The judge called a recess," Madeline said. "As soon as you're up to it, we'll resume. If you feel sick again, please give me a warning."

"I'm sorry. I don't think you have to worry, there isn't anything left to come up." Her stomach still ached. She looked at Vanessa. "Have you seen Donnie Jr.? He said he'd be here."

"I saw him arrive. He's with the other witnesses. He received a subpoena."

She grasped the sink for support. Donnie hadn't told her. "I didn't see him on Mr. O'Hare's list."

Madeline shrugged. "The prosecution must have summoned him."

"You mean he's going to testify against me?"

"Perhaps not against you so much as about his father. I wouldn't worry. If you're all right, we should return to the courtroom."

Vanessa planted a kiss on her cheek. "Don't listen to what they say about you, Aunt Mary. We know the truth."

43

The courtroom buzzed as she walked up the center aisle to the defense table. Mr. O'Hare and the district attorney watched her approach. She smiled weakly at the DA. "Please excuse me."

Mr. O'Hare drew out her chair and patted her shoulder. The table was wiped clean, his notes and papers moved to the far right, out of puke range. A wastebasket sat at her feet. Her cheeks burned with embarrassment.

The judge returned to his seat and cleared his throat. "Mrs. Malvado, are you feeling better? Are we able to proceed?"

Was she permitted to speak to him? No one had given her instructions for this. She took a deep breath to settle her nerves.

The jury returned, each one of them glaring at her. They'd had a front row seat to her meltdown. What they must think. The judge called for the district attorney to continue with his opening statement.

"Remember," Madeline murmured, "it's nothing the jury will consider when they consider the facts of the case. It's not evidence."

The DA rose and walked toward their table. "Mrs. Malvado, I hope you're fully recovered." Was she supposed to respond? He didn't give her time, instead moving to the front of the jury box.

"What you witnessed, ladies and gentlemen, is a good Catholic girl consumed by guilt."

Mr. O'Hare sprang to his feet. "Objection, Your Honor. My client—"

"Sustained. Counselor, please refrain from any editorial comment beyond the scope of your case. You may continue."

The DA buttoned his coat and continued. "As I was saying, we can't show you the murder weapon we believe Mrs. Malvado used that morning. We can show you the mound of evidence that pushed her to the point of murder. A curious relationship with her priest." The courtroom gasped. "Clear motive and opportunity. Testimony that will show Donald Malvado never had a chance to stop her, to beg for his life. At the end of this trial, you will be convinced that on June fourth, while most of us were thinking about breakfast, the defendant, Mary Malvado committed the crime of murder when she intentionally loaded a shotgun and fired one shot into the head of an unarmed victim, her husband, Donald Malvado.

"The evidence will show that in no way was the defendant justified in shooting and killing Donald Malvado. Based on this evidence, at the conclusion of this trial we will ask that you find the defendant, Mary Malvado, guilty of the crime of murder. Thank you."

The judge banged his gavel to silence the buzz. "Mr. O'Hare, do you wish to make an opening statement?"

Mr. O'Hare stood. "No, Your Honor, at this time the defense defers its opening statement."

He'd told her of his plan but after everything the district attorney said, she wanted him to deny it, to come to her defense. Wasn't that his job?

The district attorney took that as his cue. "Your Honor, the state calls its first witness. Detective Jared Jones."

DETECTIVE JONES essentially repeated what he'd said at the preliminary hearing, only with more details. The time he received the call from Sergeant Taylor, those present at the scene when he arrived, the search for the weapon, his observations of the crime scene, and his initial chat with her in the backseat. It stunned her to hear how many people he'd interviewed, church friends and relatives, neighbors whose names she didn't recognize. He disclosed details from their bank records, their outstanding debts and her current financial status, a position she was unaware of. How'd he learn all this?

The DA smoothed his tie. "Did you find a will among Mr. Malvado's files?"

Oh my God. Donnie asked about a will, but Detective Jones never said he found it.

"Yes, we did."

"Was it immediately identifiable?"

"No, we didn't discover it until after the preliminary hearing. It went initially unnoticed because it was in a sealed manila envelope marked, 'roadside mailbox specs.'"

When had Don drawn up a will?

"And what did it reveal?"

"In the event of his death, Mr. Malvado didn't provide for his wife or daughter. He willed everything to his son, Donnie Jr."

The judge gaveled the room to silence. She grabbed Mr. O'Hare's forearm. "I didn't know. I swear, I didn't know."

"Shh, Mary," he patted her hand, "shh, it's fine."

She barely heard the rest of his testimony. Donnie was so distant lately, almost belligerent. Had he known?

Mr. O'Hare approached the witness stand. "Detective Jones,

is a will or its contents proof that Mary Malvado killed her husband?"

"No."

"Is it proof of a crime?"

"No."

"Did you ask Mary Malvado if she had knowledge of a will?"

"No. Her son inquired about it, but we hadn't found it at that time."

"And why is that?"

"We thought the envelope contained information about mailbox installation. It wasn't viewed as a priority."

"In other words, the envelope was overlooked."

"Yes, at first."

"Is it possible you overlooked other evidence as well?"

"Anything is possible."

"Did you find a murder weapon?"

"Not yet."

"Are you certain, beyond a reasonable doubt, that Mary Malvado is a killer?"

"We believe she is."

"But are you certain?"

The DA jolted from his chair to object that the question was asked and answered. Detective Jones never responded.

The coroner took the stand next, and Mary closed her eyes when photos of 'him' dead on the couch displayed on a white dry erase board. The image remained fresh in her mind, she didn't need to see the pictures. The string of police officers and other experts who testified blurred from one to the next. What they said was so convincing. Maybe she did kill him.

"The state calls Donnie Malvado Jr."

She straightened in her chair to better hear his answers. He said he didn't know about the will. She didn't believe him. He'd been frantic about it.

Yes, if his father wanted him to run the businesses, he would. That was a lie.

He didn't think his parents were happily married. How would he know, he was too narcissistic to pay attention to people around him.

He didn't know why she stayed with his father. He didn't understand a sacred vow.

He was sorry his father was dead. Another lie.

"Do you think your mother killed your father?"

"I'm not sure."

"No further questions." The district attorney sat down.

Mr. O'Hare took his time standing, letting Donnie's answer sink in. His first question shocked her.

"Donnie, may I call you by your first name?" He didn't allow time for Donnie to respond. "Do you know who Carson White is?"

There it was. The scandal that would rock her world. Worse than murder. She'd reduced 'him' to ashes yet 'he' continued to make her life hell. Donnie's eyes bulged, his jaw locked. His chest rose faster. They hadn't discussed his father's illegitimate son since the day she told him about the birth certificate. Like everything else, if it didn't directly concern Donnie, she assumed he didn't care.

"I know the name." the pitch of Donnie's voice was high, squeaky.

"How do you know his name? Who is he?"

"He's a half-brother, I guess. My mother told me about him. She received a copy of his birth certificate in the mail. Someone sent it anonymously."

"Who sent it?"

"I don't know. That's what anonymous means."

Oh no, Donnie, this isn't the time to turn into a smartass. Not like your dad.

"Did you know about Carson White before that?"

"No." Did he?

"Didn't you pay for a genealogy study in January to track your ancestry? Didn't you discover then that you had a half-brother?"

Donnie stared at him, speechless.

"Did you tell your mother about the results of the family search?"

He didn't. This was news to her.

"Did your parents know that you filed for bankruptcy earlier this year?"

He what?

"Isn't it rather good timing that your father died when he did?"

The DA objected and Mr. O'Hare acted contrite.

"Did you mail that birth certificate to your mother?"

"No, I did not."

"Do you know how to handle a shotgun? Can you shoot?"

"I know my way around a firing range. I'm a pretty good shot if I do say so myself."

"Isn't it possible that you shot your father?"

Donnie jumped out of his seat. Mr. O'Hare peppered him with questions, not allowing him to respond.

"You knew your mother's schedule. You had access to the house. You asked for help in the past and your father turned you down, told you to grow up and stand on your own two feet. You needed financial help now. Your father's death would bail you out of a lot of trouble."

Donnie stomped his foot, something he'd done since he was three. "That's not true."

"Isn't it possible your mother wanted to help you, but her hands were tied? Isn't it possible that she agreed to your plan to kill her husband and let her take the blame? There is no murder weapon. No proof. Who's going to convict a sweet, Catholic woman like your mother?"

Donnie's face was as red as Communion wine. He pounded the rail in front of him. "That's not true. I have an alibi." His chest heaved.

"No further questions." And just like that, Mr. O'Hare left Donnie huffing and puffing, the jurors glaring at him.

The DA had only one rebuttal question. Did Donnie kill his father? He said no.

Did he?

44

Emma waited in the parking lot for Vanessa. "How'd it go?"

"Holy hell, Aunt Em, I don't know what to believe. Every time the district attorney questions someone, he makes it sound like Aunt Mary is guilty. And then Mr. O'Hare asks questions and turns everything around and it looks like the person on the stand did it. I'm mentally exhausted." She flipped her long, dark hair up into a ponytail and let it drop to her shoulders again.

"He made Donnie Jr. look guilty. He came off like a real buttwipe. I'm ashamed to be related to him. Mr. O'Hare made it sound like Donnie Jr. knew about the b-child."

"What?"

"Yeah, somehow he found out that Donnie Jr. paid for an ancestry search and found out. I watched Aunt Mary wipe tears from her face, and my heart broke."

"Mr. O'Hare has to make other people look suspicious, that's his job. He'll do the same to me tomorrow so be prepared. How was Jared?"

"He knocked my socks off with everything that he testified

to. If the jury listened only to him, they would convict her for sure. Mr. O'Hare kinda ripped him a new one too, but not like the others. I'm thankful I'm not sitting on that jury. I don't know what to think."

She'd be even more confused tomorrow. The state rested its case and tomorrow, Terrence O'Hare took center stage.

HE CALLED her as his first witness. Today she wore a crisp white pantsuit with red pinstripes, a red tank top, and her favorite red stilettos. Red is the color of power. She recited for the jury her credentials—four-year degree in criminology, patrolman for three years, a stint as sergeant and lieutenant's bars eight years ago.

"You have aspirations to be a detective, is that correct?"

Her shoulders straightened. "Yes sir."

"How old are you, Emma?"

"Thirty-two."

"And what was the age difference between you and your brother?"

"Twelve years."

"Is it accurate to say you weren't close?"

"Yes sir."

O'Hare established that she and her brother were estranged, which meant she had no dealings with Mary.

"What were your feelings for your brother, Miss Hunter?"

"I didn't really have any."

"Did you hate him?"

"I didn't like him. There's a difference."

"You were first in your class in marksmanship, is that correct?"

"Yes."

"And your training focused on all types of weapons, including shotguns, is that correct?"

"Of course."

"Hypothetically, Miss Hunter, if a situation existed where your brother posed a threat to you and elimination was the only resolution, hypothetically remember, based on your training couldn't you commit murder and avoid detection?"

The courtroom took a collective breath. Jared hadn't taken his eyes off her since she sat down. "There's no such thing as a perfect murder, Mr. O'Hare."

"Yes, but this is a hypothetical scenario. Based on your knowledge of crime scenes and investigations, couldn't you kill someone, hypothetically, and get away with it?"

She paused, weighing her words. "I suppose so, yes."

The judge ordered quiet.

O'Hare stood with his fingertips touching, lightly tapping each other. "Why did you sever relations with your brother?"

It was no secret to anyone who knew her. "He was toxic for me."

"Toxic enough to kill?"

"I didn't let it reach that point, sir, I cut ties with him."

"But it could have reached that boiling point?"

"It could have, yes."

O'Hare abruptly turned his back on her. "No further questions."

The district attorney stood in his place. "I have one follow-up question, Miss Hunter. Did you kill Donald Malvado?"

"Objection." O'Hare's voice boomed. "The witness is not on trial here."

She never answered the question.

Next up was Father Greg. She wanted to hear this and, since she already testified, she crammed into the back row on the prosecution side of the courtroom. Vanessa swiveled and motioned that she could make room for her in the front row, but Emma shook her head. It was better that she sit on the sidelines.

O'Hare spoke softly, almost reverently. "Good morning, Father. Can you please tell the jury what your relationship is with Mary Malvado?"

She could see his knee bouncing erratically. "She is a member of my congregation. Has been as long as I've been there, going on twelve years."

"Is she more than that, Father?"

His head dipped. "Yes, she's a dear friend."

"Did she ever confide in you about the state of her marriage?"

"Yes, she was dissatisfied."

"Did she ever confide in you that she wished her husband would die?"

"On the contrary, she prayed for his soul. She asked for strength to honor the vow of her marriage."

"Did you counsel her, Father?"

"As best I could."

"And what did you advise Mrs. Malvado to do?"

"I suggested she write her darker thoughts in her journal. I knew she kept one. I thought it might help. I'm not certain it helped. Mary was riddled with guilt over what she wrote. She poured her heart out in the confessional, which you know is privileged."

"Do you believe Mary Malvado killed her husband?"

"As God is my witness, absolutely not."

It was the final question O'Hare asked everyone. As Emma listened to each witness, a picture of her sister-in-law emerged. She must have spent a fortune on greeting cards. She never missed a birthday, anniversary, or illness. She was famous for her homemade chicken noodle soup and chocolate chip cookies. Based on what the witnesses said, she made gallons and dozens of both for the sick and invalid. She was more than a congregation member, the church was her passion. Fund raising, church projects, the welcome committee, the weekly bulletin—she had a hand in it all.

Emma formed a new respect for Mary. She didn't waste her life being married to a tyrant. She ignored her brother and dedicated herself to bringing happiness to others.

"Do you believe Mary Malvado killed her husband?"

"Do you think Mary is guilty of murder?'

"Do you believe your sister, your friend, your regular customer is a murderer?"

"No."

"No."

"No."

45

It was standing room only for closing arguments. Vanessa sat in the next to the last row beside Emma, clinging to her hand. Her mother, Donnie Jr. and Father Greg sat directly behind Mary. Despite the innuendoes, the priest held his head high when he entered the courtroom, his hand on Mary's elbow. The defense and prosecution tables were cleared of the papers, binders and reports that covered them hours earlier. The wastebasket remained within Mary's reach.

The district attorney summarized the testimony his witnesses provided. Nessie was right. When strung together, it sounded bad. But Emma knew it was all circumstantial. Would the jury understand the difference between circumstantial and proof?

Terrence O'Hare rose. If a pin dropped, everyone in the room would hear it.

"This portion of the trial is called closing arguments, ladies and gentlemen, but I'm not here to argue with you. I simply want to reiterate what you already suspect, that the state has failed to prove that Mary Malvado killed her husband. First, let me thank you for the time and attention you've given these proceedings. Jury duty is the highest act of citizenship, but it also is a disruption to your personal and professional lives. You have performed your duty admirably. None of you are professional jurors. There is no such thing. This is an on-the-job learning experience, and your job was to listen and now, it is to determine the facts. To determine the truth.

"I'd like to explain two important points of law, since none of you are lawyers. One is the presumption of innocence and the other is what proof beyond a reasonable doubt means. The defendant, in this case Mary Malvado, is presumed innocent until the state proves otherwise. She doesn't have to prove to you she's innocent. On the contrary, the burden is on the state to prove she is guilty. The state has failed to do that.

"Reasonable doubt, as defined in the dictionary, is not a doubt based upon sympathy or prejudice, and instead, is based on reason and common sense. Reasonable doubt is logically connected to the evidence or absence of evidence. What the state has presented is an absolute absence of evidence.

"It's true that someone shot and killed Donald Malvado on the morning of June fourth. Mary Malvado made that horrifying discovery and, like any good citizen, she called 911. It was the reasonable thing to do.

"It's common knowledge that the spouse is always the suspect in a case like this and, like any good citizen, she complied with Detective Jones' request to be interrogated. She willingly allowed the authorities to check her hands for gunshot residue and inspect her body for bruises. There were none. Common sense tells you that's proof she didn't fire a gun."

Emma studied the jurors. They hung on his every word. So did she.

"That, in itself, should eliminate Mary Malvado as a suspect. You can't shoot a weapon without gunpowder residue remaining on your hands. The ballistics expert told you that.

The state argues that she could have worn gloves but, not only did they never find the murder weapon, there were no gloves found. Or blood-soaked clothes. The coroner told you the manner in which Don Malvado died was not neat and clean. What does your common sense tell you about that fact?

"The state cannot provide one witness who saw Mary Malvado commit this crime, while we presented ten people who saw her at church that morning, and we could have paraded twenty or more to the stand who would've all said the same thing. She was cheerful, her usual self. Not a drop of blood on her. Do any of you think you could blow your husband's head off and then go about your normal business? Common sense tells you no. That's not reasonable.

"The state argues that Mary Malvado had motive and it points to brusque texts from her husband and financial insecurity. Show me a couple married twenty-five years who isn't short with each other on occasion and doesn't struggle with finances." A couple of jurors' heads bobbed.

"By the state's own testimony, Donald Malvado provided for his wife. How is that motive to kill him? The state argues that no one can verify Mary Malvado's actions early that morning, between five-thirty and six-thirty when the coroner says death occurred. We presented business owners, a priest and a police lieutenant who have the same issue. No one can swear to their activity in those wee hours. It doesn't prove they killed Donald Malvado.

"Lastly, the state argues that Mary Malvado's religion prevented her from exiting an unhappy marriage by seeking a divorce. On the contrary, Mary Malvado's devotion to Christ is the exact reason you should believe she didn't kill him. Thou shalt not kill. We all know that as one of the Ten Commandments. Mary Malvado exemplifies those commandments. I refer you to chapter five, verse thirty-three in Ephesians. The Bible commands wives to respect their husbands. This means revering, admiring, and honoring their husbands. I didn't know that passage before I met Mary Malvado, and I'm betting most of you didn't know it either. But Mrs. Malvado did. She's the one who educated me.

"The state presented a host of maybes and possibilities and theories but no evidence, no actual proof that Mary Malvado committed murder. They have failed to prove their case and most certainly, they have failed to show you beyond a reasonable doubt that Mary Malvado is a murderer. Look at the facts when you go into the deliberation room and ask yourselves whether you can say beyond a reasonable doubt that she is. She isn't ladies and gentlemen. You should find her not guilty."

Sweat made Emma's hands sticky. Vanessa wiped tears from her eyes. The entire room released the collective breath it held. They listened silently as the judge directed the bailiff to escort the jury out. Several spectators jumped when he slammed his gavel and adjourned the proceedings. And then the room erupted with noise.

"What happens now?" Vanessa stood with everyone else.

"Now, we wait."

46

Mary couldn't hold her head up any longer. It fell onto her folded arms of its own free will. She wanted to cry, but tears wouldn't come. She wanted to scream at the top of her lungs. But her throat was too dry.

Five hours ago, the jury began deliberating her life. They asked for dinner to be delivered. Ellen saw a second urn of coffee being wheeled down the hall. Food was spread on the table in front of Mary too. Someone ordered from a nearby Italian restaurant. Sandwiches, salads and, gag, pizza. 'He' loved pizza. It didn't matter. She had no appetite.

They waited in a conference room in the courthouse. The chairs were uncomfortable, the TV playing endless game shows. The volume was set on low, making the people jumping and gyrating look ridiculous. It would have been silly even if she could hear it. Ellen watched it intently.

In the corner, Madeline texted non-stop. Mr. O'Hare left her here to babysit them. She had no idea where he disappeared to. Father Greg and Ellen stayed with her. Vanessa was here for a while but now she wasn't. Donnie Jr. was too damn important to sit and wait for his mother's fate. He'd kissed her on the forehead and told her to call him when the jury returned. She ordered Father Greg and Ellen not too nicely to keep their phones in their pockets when the time came.

Emma must be with her cop friends. Maybe that was better.

Mary was on her last nerve. "What's taking them so long?"

Madeline looked up from her phone. "Long is good. It means they're taking their time reviewing the evidence. It could mean they can't agree on what the evidence shows. Disagreement is good for us."

Wasn't it a simple yes she did it or no, she didn't? Mary had never been called to serve on a jury. 'He' was summoned once and she'd listened to him brag for a week about how he got out of it and how stupid people were who didn't know how to work the system. She prayed her jurors weren't stupid.

Everyone jumped when the door opened and the bailiff stuck his head in. "They're back." It had taken them five hours and thirty-five minutes to agree.

EMMA SAT with Vanessa on a bench outside the room where the police congregated. Jared invited them inside, but she didn't belong in there this evening. She wasn't comfortable waiting with Mary either. Right now, she didn't belong anywhere. Not with her friends or her family. Nessie spotted her in the hall on her way back from the restroom and refused to leave her side.

"What happens if they can't reach a decision, Aunt Em?"

"The judge will meet with them to assess their impasse. He may request they continue trying to come to a consensus. Their verdict must be unanimous. If they are hopelessly deadlocked, he will declare a mistrial."

"And then what?"

She filled her lungs and exhaled slowly. That question had

been bouncing around in her head. "Well, the state could file charges again and retry Mary. Or the DA could decide to drop it, depending on how the jury was leaning."

"You mean Aunt Mary might have to go through all this again?"

"Don't worry, hon, I won't let that happen."

The door to the police waiting room opened. "They're back."

JARED DREADED the moment a jury returned. Even with the most solid of cases, you never knew what twelve strangers would do. This case was far from a slam-dunk.

"All rise."

Immediately after taking his seat, the judge summoned both attorneys to his bench. The sound system was off and their whispers were low. What was going on?

Both men looked disappointed when they returned to their seats. The judge leveled his gavel. "I'm about to bring the jury in for its decision. I caution all of you to remain calm when the verdict is read. I will not tolerate any outbursts."

Out of the corner of his eye, he watched Mary Malvado reach for the waste can. Her sister, niece and the priest sat stiff as boards behind her. Junior was missing. He peered over his left shoulder. Emma stood in the back. On Mary's side.

He'd always been told to watch the jurors' faces when they entered the box after reaching a verdict. If they averted their gazes from the defendant, they'd found him or her guilty. If they smiled and made eye contact, their verdict was not guilty.

He studied each juror as they took their seats. To a person, they all looked at the floor. What the hell did that mean?

Terrence O'Hare stood and coaxed Mrs. Malvado to do the same. The judge cleared his throat.

"The jury tells me that they are deadlocked—" the entire room gasped, "and that further deliberations would be futile."

Mary Malvado collapsed into her chair. O'Hare and his assistant drew her up to her feet and kept her upright.

"I have spoken to the panel and I am convinced more time deliberating would be a waste. I'm therefore declaring a mistrial. Charges against Mary Malvado are dismissed."

His gavel slammed and the room exploded in disruption. A handful of women clapped, Mary's sister burst into tears and Mary fell back into her chair. The priest and her niece rushed to her side.

Fuck. A mistrial. It wasn't a victory for either side. Emma had been right. There wasn't enough evidence.

He looked for her, still with her back braced by the wall. Tears rimmed her eyes. For him? Or for her sister-in-law?

The district attorney shook his hand. "I'm sorry, Jared. We knew it was a long shot going in. If you uncover any more evidence, we can re-file on her. For now, Donald Malvado's murder will remain unsolved. It was a pleasure working with you."

Jeff clapped him on the shoulder. "It was thin to begin with, partner. We're not convinced she did it."

"Well, someone did it. If not her, then who?"

Mary Malvado was making her way down the aisle, much like that day at church. Her flock followed. She paused momentarily to nod at Emma. Emma returned the gesture. No hug. No high five.

Emma waited for the courtroom to empty, for him to reach her.

"I'm sorry you lost your case, Jared, but I'm happy with the outcome. I hope you can understand that. Can I buy you a drink?"

He needed one. "That would be nice Em. Are you off tonight?"

"Yes, I have to run an errand but I can meet you at Out-Of-The-Way in about an hour. Jeff, you're welcome to join us."

Jeff declined the invite.

"I've got some paperwork to finish up, Em. I'll see you there."

47

Relief overwhelmed her. Emma locked the doors of her SUV and sat as still as a statue. Except for her hands. They shook so badly, she grabbed the steering wheel to steady them. The tears she'd controlled inside rolled freely down her face. It was over. Mary was free.

She drove home to change for her date with Jared. Nothing fancy. Jeans and a long-sleeved shirt. The evenings were starting to turn cooler.

She fished the letter from her brother out of the burn box and took it to the kitchen sink, already filled with water. Words jumped off the page at her when she opened it. Alcohol. Drugs. Abortion. Liar. One mistake when she was young. An unwanted pregnancy. She'd been stupid enough to turn to him for help. Admitted she'd been drunk and smoked marijuana. Thought her older brother was the one person she could trust.

And here he was writing to her, resentful that she'd received a commendation for saving a child, angry that she had a successful career in law enforcement, which had been his dream. Threatening to expose her past to her bosses and the news media. Threatening her life. And dragging Nessie into his perceived quest for truth and justice.

Leaning back on that sofa, a wise-ass grin on his face, challenging her, taunting her to stop him. Spitting on her was the last straw. He'd gotten justice.

She removed the barbecue lighter from the drawer and touched the flame to the corner of the letter. The ashes drifted into the water.

She slipped into her black leather ankle boots. Jared liked these shoes. The duffel bag sat on the floor behind her driver's seat. Pittsburgh was the city of bridges with more than four hundred that spanned three major rivers and countless hills and ravines. She knew the exact spot to stop. Dark and deserted. The tributary ran deep and flowed directly into the Monongahela. The dismantled shotgun dropped like pieces of rock into the muddy water.

Emma stopped in the ladies' room to wash her hands before joining Jared in their booth. She dropped a sweet kiss on his mouth.

"Sorry to keep you waiting. Are you terribly disappointed?"

The wide grin on his face said he wasn't. "I don't like to lose, you know that. But I'm not certain justice would have been served if they'd convicted your sister-in-law. She didn't act alone, and she would have taken the fall for it."

"Are you going to continue your investigation?"

Jared emptied his whiskey glass and signaled for another. "We've exhausted all our leads. Until someone comes forward with new information, it will be a cold case. But I can always hope to eventually solve it."

Emma sipped her cold beer. Tonight, it tasted delicious. "It's hard to believe, isn't it?"

"What?"

She shrugged. "Someone got away with murder."

The End

If you enjoyed **When Push Comes to Shoot,** please leave a
review on Amazon
https://amzn.to/2ZGifU4.com
It's the nicest gift you can give an author.

OTHER NOVELS BY RENA KOONTZ

Other suspense novels by Rena Koontz

Loving Gia to Death

Locked and Loaded For Justice: Saving Gia

The Devil She Knew

Love's Secret Fire

Off The Grid for Love

Broken Justice, Blind Love

Thief Of The Heart

A contemporary romance

Crystal Clear Love

A novella

Midnight Deadline

Find all of Rena Koontz's books on Amazon and Barnes & Noble

Amazon— https://www.amazon.com/Rena-Koontz/e/B0097E5PBY/

Barnes & Noble— https://www.barnesandnoble.com/s/
rena%20koontz

ALSO BY RENA KOONTZ

LOCKED AND LOADED FOR JUSTICE:
SAVING GIA

CHAPTER 1

This week's trip into hell was over.

Blake Matthews tightened the straps on his daughter's car seat, her sweet face wet with tears, her tiny chin quivering, her dark eyes downcast. How much longer was the court going to torture her like this? How much longer was he going to allow it?

The title "Family Court" was laughable. The people running this show didn't have the faintest idea what "family" meant. If they did, they wouldn't be ripping his family apart.

He dropped a kiss on top of Gia's head and slammed the door. He could use a drink right now. Just to take the edge off. His mouth watered contemplating it. First things first. Get the hell away from this place.

The hour visit with Gia's mother, his ex-wife, was excruciating. Feeling Gia tremble in his arms while Lynne tried to cajole her closer, seeing those long red fingernails come through the air at them both, sensing his daughter recoil—it was too much.

How had he ever loved that woman?

He jammed his foot to the gas pedal. The tires screeched his departure from the parking lot.

"We'll be home shortly, Peanut. Noreen is waiting for us."

He needed the woman's arms around him more than a scotch. More than Gia needed her.

No response from his little ray of sunshine. It crushed him.

These visits left his baby girl morose. Him too. He practically tasted that scotch.

"It'll be okay, sweetheart. Daddy will figure out a way to fix it."

How, he didn't know. He had the chance last year. He should have killed her mother then.

THE DOOR to Blake's truck slammed in the driveway with a bang as loud as a cannon shot.

Noreen laid her book aside, straightened her position on the chaise lounge to support her leg, and gingerly braced herself against a pillow. The burns on her back and arms had healed, but the pain remained.

Sparkly rainbow-colored sandals pounded across the kitchen tile and the hinges on the screen door squealed when Argia shoved through it, hurling herself onto Noreen's lap.

"Weenieeeee." The trembling child buried her face in her chest, and rounded fists bunched her cotton shirt into a sweaty ball. Despite the circumstances, the nickname made her smile.

Gia couldn't pronounce the r-w combination in her name at first, and instead started calling her Weenie. The pet name stuck. She wrapped her arms tight around Argia and rocked slowly from side to side.

"Shh, it's okay, honey. You're home now. It's okay."

They rode this emotional roller coaster every time Argia returned from a court-ordered visit with her mother, sobbing, shaking, and clinging to Noreen's shirt until she was cried out. There'd be a few hours of silence with Argia simply nodding yes or no or not responding at all. No amount of cajoling or bribery coaxed her out of her self-imposed muteness unless her father worked his special magic, employed his "twofer" kisses, and shared his soulful gaze with his daughter.

But these visits took their toll on Blake too. Even over Argia's sobs, chunks of ice dropping from the icemaker into his glass reverberated out to the patio. Next, he'd walk to the liquor cabinet.

She eyed the screen door while she rocked Argia, whispering comforting words to reassure her that her daddy loved her, and she loved her, and everything would be better soon. Would it?

Blake needed the same assurances but cradling him in her arms like a child wasn't the answer. She was at a loss as to how to help him. Why didn't he walk out onto the back deck? Gia needed him.

Argia's outburst subsided to sniffles, her eyes wide and staring at Noreen. The child spoke volumes through those expressive chocolate eyes. She harbored a fear no six-year-old should have to bear. A child shouldn't be so afraid of its mother.

Finally, the hinges squeaked and Blake strolled out, the alcohol in the tumbler already half consumed. He dragged a chair close to them, leaned over to drop a scotch-laced kiss on Noreen's mouth and sat, taking a hefty swallow before setting his now empty glass on the table. When he opened both hands and gestured with his fingers, Argia crawled from her lap to the security of her father's arms, settling her beloved stuffed animals against his chest and nestling her head in the crook of his arm. In seconds, her eyes closed and her breathing evened.

There was no point in asking how the visit with his ex-wife had gone. It always caused Argia to have nightmares and Blake to drink. He'd been doing that a lot more lately.

She laid her hand over his on the chair's arm. "Can I get you anything?"

His gaze at her lacked focus. Like his daughter, Blake could communicate his feelings through his gunmetal gray eyes. He was lost.

"Another drink would help. But I don't suppose that's what you meant. And you wouldn't be happy about that."

She smiled without feeling any joy. "We both know that won't help."

This was a discussion they'd exhausted over the last four weeks. Since his ex-wife's release from a psychiatric hospital to a halfway house designed to transition her back to self-sufficiency, the happy ride through daily life that she and Blake shared was jarring, like a car that suddenly gets a flat tire. They still bumped along each day making a home for Gia and nurturing a growing love for each other, but the wheels were threatening to fall off. Father and daughter dealt with the upheaval differently. Argia, they preferred the shortened Gia, went silent and reverted to sucking her thumb, a habit Blake said she'd quit two years earlier. Blake silently deflected his emotions with single-malt scotch, tamping a simmering rage.

But for how long?

Noreen squeezed his hand. "Besides, you don't drink when you have Gia on your lap, remember?"

The corners of Blake's mouth lifted. An urge to kiss him, smother his mouth with hers and absorb all his pain, washed over her right then. God, how she loved him. His biceps popped when he drew his daughter closer, protecting her from an unknown. His ex-wife was a demon all three of them still battled.

Noreen's curiosity won. "How'd it go today?"

Blake's fingers flinched ever so slightly, tightening his hold on Gia. "Remember last week I told you Lynne kept attempting physical contact and Gia resisted? She wouldn't sit on her mother's lap or hold her hand. She wouldn't even share a cookie.

"Today, Lynne *insisted* that Gia sit on her lap and that witch-doctor of a counselor supported the idea and said the intimate contact would advance Lynne's acclamation with her daughter and serve as a building block toward their reconciliation. It was pure BS. Then the counselor politely reminded me that the court orders for visitation require cooperation. Lynne smirked at that. What a coincidence that she just happened to have a copy of the judgment in front of her. I'm sure Lynne eagerly provided it. The smug look on her face said it all. She orchestrated the whole thing and there was nothing I could argue against. All the while, Lynne rocked in the rocking chair, feigning innocence."

Noreen caught her breath. "Did you make Gia do it?"

He shrugged and sipped only melted ice. "I didn't have a choice. At first, Gia flat out refused, shaking her head and covering her face with Mr. Dog and Mr. Fox." Subconsciously, Blake nudged the stuffed animals closer to his daughter.

"I finally negotiated a deal with her. Ice cream every night for a week in exchange for five minutes on her mother's lap."

He squared his shoulders. "Lynne didn't make it five seconds. I swear Gia stared at me as if to signal 'watch this.' She dropped her stuffed toys in my hands, plopped on her mother's lap and started swinging her legs back and forth, rubbing her shoes against Lynne's designer pants, and bouncing as if she played in a fun house.

"Lynne was mortified. Her shoulders jerked and she attempted to reposition Gia's legs. But my sweet girl was having none of it. Her legs swung like a pendulum."

He chuckled at the recollection.

"Finally, Lynne snapped at Gia and said something like if you can't sit still you can't sit here and Gia was like a rocket launched off her lap and back into my arms. She refused to look at her mother again. I almost laughed in her face. But Gia was shaking like a leaf. I was so angry, I was shaking too."

"What happened then?"

"Of course, Lynne blamed me for turning Gia against her. But she was careful to conceal the rage we know she is capable of. That therapy they're forcing on her must be sinking in. Either that or she remembered the security camera in the corner.

"She didn't fly off the handle like the old Lynne. No, her accusation was more calculated, especially when she suggested that monitored visits with Gia in the future should exclude me. She wondered out loud if her visits would be more successful if only the counselor was present. Predictably, the counselor was quick to validate that notion. I tell you, the whole thing was a set up."

Noreen's heart stuttered. "Blake, you can't let that happen. Gia can't go in there alone."

"I know. I'm going to call our attorney first thing in the morning. Maybe he can figure out how to convince the judge that protecting a mother's rights in this instance will destroy the child."

Gia stirred in Blake's lap, curling tighter into his embrace. "I hate to say this, Noreen, but I should've killed her when I had the chance."

Tears sprang to her eyes. "Please don't say that." She tightened her hold on his hand. "We wouldn't have been able to overcome those consequences. We'll figure out a way through this."

There was that hopeless look in his eyes again. She eased off the lounge chair and placed a soft kiss on his lips. Blake's eyes darkened with desire, sending a tingle to her thighs. They were her family now, Blake and Gia, and she'd do anything to protect them. But the only way to keep them safe was to rid their lives of Lynne Matthews.

CHAPTER 2

Noreen surveyed the occupied hospital rooms from the nurse's horseshoe desk situated in the middle of the intensive care unit. She loved her job. The children on the pediatric surgical floor exuded hope daily, despite whatever malady landed them in a hospital bed. Most of the kids welcomed her with wide smiles, oblivious to pain and focused on what truly was important to them—the cherry Jell-O or chocolate pudding she frequently surprised them with.

Blake and Gia had enlightened her about the amazing health benefits of a surprise sweet treat. She now concurred that a half-cup of ice cream worked wonders for the healing process. She'd first encountered Argia in one of these beds, suffering from a broken wrist. That night changed her life. Rather, Blake Matthews did. Ten months ago he'd stormed onto this floor challenging her authority and demanding to see his daughter.

Never in her wildest dreams would she have imagined she'd be living with the brute and loving the hell out of him and his sweet little girl. Brute hardly described the caring, sensitive, affectionate father and lover he was. She could barely stand to be apart from him, despite the joy she experienced working in this hospital.

She smiled when the elevator doors opened to reveal a flower deliveryman. Add thoughtful to that list of Blake qualities. Today marked one month that she'd returned to work full-time since the fire and the fight for her life. Blake remembered.

"Child, that man is intent on spoiling you," her co-worker Kelly chirped. She reached for the long-stem flower box. "Um, um, um, let me see what that boy is sending you now. If you weren't my best friend, I'd steal him from you."

Noreen smiled at Kelly's animated gestures, dancing in a circle with the box before setting it on the nurse station countertop, licking her fingertips and tugging on the four-inch wide black ribbon with deliberate slowness, pinkies held high. Once the ribbon untied and fell to the sides, Kelly clutched the top.

"Girl, if this is a dozen roses, you're sharing half of them with me. After all, I love that man as much as you do."

Noreen's heart trilled. That wasn't possible.

Kelly's bright smile froze, and her eyebrows knitted when the lid came off. "What in Jesus' name?" She raised bulging eyes to Noreen. "Honey, this isn't from Blake."

Noreen rose and reached for the box. Three dead roses tied with a thick black cord lay in a nest of pink tissue paper. Her hand shot backward, as if touching the brown, wilted petals might scorch her fingers. She clutched her throat.

Kelly regained her wits first. She spoke as she lifted the dead flowers and rifled through the layers of tissue. "What in God's name is this? Someone's idea of a joke? I don't see a card."

Now she lifted the box to scan the bottom. "What flower shop? No name printed anywhere. What the hell?"

Kelly threw the dead blooms back into the box and smashed the lid on top of it, then propped her hand on her hip.

"Have you told Blake about the phone calls yet? And the flat tire last week? And now this. Noreen, this isn't good. Someone has a grudge against you and they know where you work and where you live. Girlfriend, if this doesn't make you suspicious, what will? Enough is enough."

Noreen dropped into her seat, her hand pressed against her lungs, applying pressure as if it could suppress her rapid breathing. She hadn't mentioned the nuisance calls to Blake yet. If that's what they were. He had so much else on his mind. And his job as a firefighter required focus.

As for the service call to the auto club, she'd dismissed it as an inconvenience more than anything else. The mechanic hadn't found a rupture in the tire and said it simply needed air. He suggested driving into a curb with excessive force might release a substantial amount of air and inferred perhaps she'd done just that. She hadn't argued, instead questioning her past few trips. She didn't recall striking anything, not even a speed bump in the mall parking lot. She'd downplayed the entire incident when she told Blake the next day and he hadn't seemed concerned.

Of course, that was the day after a fatal fire, which hit all the men at Deep Creek Fire Station Twelve pretty hard.

She pursed her lips and regarded Kelly. "He's had so much else to worry about, I haven't bothered him about the phone calls. All of us complain about the automated calls, including you. I have no proof they are anything more than that."

"Okay, we can't prove anything about the phone calls. But these?" Kelly slapped the box. "This is a deliberate attempt to... to...I don't know what." Her hands flapped outward. "And I don't like it. Maybe we should call the police."

"And tell them what? That someone has a sick sense of humor?"

"It's one phone call. We're slow right now. Just call the police and see what they say."

"Okay, but I'm going to feel like an idiot." She retrieved her cell phone from her purse while Kelly answered another phone line. Minutes later, she disconnected the call. The sinking sensation in her stomach weighed her down. She hated feeling powerless. Kelly waited for her news.

"They won't help. I don't know who sent them and I can't tell them anything about where they came from. They wrote it off as a mean joke and told me to do the same. I'm on my own to figure it out."

The elevator door slid open again and they turned to watch Paramedic Joe Lystle stroll toward them. Seeing the flower box, he grinned. "Bet I know who those are from."

She'd prefer Joe didn't see its contents, but Kelly had other ideas. "Not Blake, no way." She lifted the lid. "This is from some sick ass person out there and we all better start paying attention to who has Noreen in their crosshairs."

Noreen slammed the lid closed. "Kelly, please. It's not a big deal."

But it was and Joe's widened eyes and slack jaw indicated he realized it too.

"Christ, Noreen, did these just come? Who delivered them?"

He scanned the halls in every direction, as if the delivery person might still be lingering in one of the corridors. He wasn't.

"Is there a card?" She might as well have not been there since Kelly answered each of his queries.

"Did you tell Blake?"

"No, she didn't and if she doesn't, that boy is gettin' a phone call from me. There's too many coincidences going on for them to be a coincidence. Do you hear what I'm saying?"

The radio on his belt pinged. "Rob's waiting for me in the ambulance. I gotta go. I just stopped to tell you Brittni will pick up Gia after school but she's taking her to our place instead of your home. We're waiting for the cable company to make a service call. The storm last night damaged our connection. Their arrival window is between three and six. Once they leave,

Brittni will take Gia to Blake's and I'm off at six so I'll be there tonight too. I'll see you tomorrow morning when you get home from work. We can talk about this then if you want."

Noreen called to him as he stepped on the elevator. "Joe don't mention this to Blake, please. I'll tell him, I promise."

He nodded and the doors closed.

Kelly leveled a mean glare at her.

"I'll tell him tomorrow as soon as he gets home. I swear."

Tell him what, she wasn't sure. That someone was trying to spook her? That she had the crazy feeling it was his ex-wife?

Then how crazy would that make him?

To continue reading Locked And Loaded For Justice: Saving Gia,
click the link:
https://amzn.to/2ZIWD9E

Thank you for your support.

Made in the USA
Coppell, TX
12 March 2023